KILLER VIEW

KILLER VIEW

ROY JOHANSEN

GRAND CENTRAL
PUBLISHING

NEW YORK   BOSTON

Copyright © 2022 by Roy Johansen

Cover design by Flag. Cover image of woman © Rekha Garton / Arcangel; city by Getty Images; car © Pickone / IStock / Getty Images. Cover copyright © 2022 by Hachette Book Group, Inc.

Grand Central Publishing
Hachette Book Group
1290 Avenue of the Americas, New York, NY 10104
grandcentralpublishing.com
twitter.com/grandcentralpub

First Edition: February 2022

Grand Central Publishing is a division of Hachette Book Group, Inc. The Grand Central Publishing name and logo is a trademark of Hachette Book Group, Inc.

The publisher is not responsible for websites (or their content) that are not owned by the publisher.

The Hachette Speakers Bureau provides a wide range of authors for speaking events. To find out more, go to www.hachettespeakersbureau.com or call (866) 376-6591.

Print book interior design by Thomas Louie.

Library of Congress Cataloging-in-Publication Data has been applied for

ISBNs: 978-1-5387-6281-3 (hardcover), 978-1-5387-1015-9 (large type), 978-1-5387-6282-0 (ebook)

Printed in the United States of America

LSC-C

Printing 1, 2021

For Tam, my sister and forever friend

Dear Readers,

I have enjoyed a long writing career—thanks to all the support from you—and one of my greatest joys was when I began writing with my son, Roy. It always amazes me when we seem to read each other's mind about a character or a plotline, and it's equally amazing when Roy surprises me with a new idea even better than my own. We've now completed nine stories together and have had an incredible time along the way.

Roy has a successful career as an author and screenwriter independent of our books together, but it still brings me great joy to be passing the baton to him for this book, Killer View. *And what a thrilling read! We're often told by readers that they couldn't put our books down, and I was happy to be able to say the same to Roy about this solo effort.*

You're about to meet—or be re-introduced to—Jessie Mercado, a P.I. who adds the suspenseful and daring action sequences that keep the pages turning. As an army vet and former bodyguard for the rich and famous, Jessie is prepared for whatever challenges the case throws her way, including plenty of car chases and shootouts.

And Roy has continued the Kendra Michaels legacy. Sometimes a character comes along who captures the imagination of readers and takes on a life of their own, and for our books written together, that character has been Kendra. She's a loyal friend who will risk anything to help Jessie with this missing persons case.

I'm happy to say that I will be joining Roy and Kendra on their next adventure, which you'll have a chance to read in early 2023. I appreciate all of my readers and never take you for granted. I want the Johansen name to always mean an edge-of-your-seat, emotionally satisfying read.

I hope you are just as riveted and entertained by Killer View *as I was.*

Iris Johansen

KILLER VIEW

CHAPTER

1

S he should have taken the million dollars.

Jessie Mercado squirmed in the back of the police car and tugged at the handcuffs clamped around her wrists. If she'd taken that lucrative job offer, she'd be in San Francisco now, probably pushing her way through a dance club and clearing a path as security director for her twenty-year-old pop-star boss.

And she'd be hating life even more than she did at this very moment. But at least she'd be a millionaire.

Jessie sniffed the air. "Hey," she called out to the uniformed officer sitting in the passenger seat. "This squad car smells like puke. Doesn't somebody hose these things out at the end of every shift?"

Officer Gataki snorted. "Union issues. Deal with it. I have to spend eight hours in this thing every day, so pardon me if I don't feel bad for you."

"Not looking for sympathy, Gataki." She glanced around. "So where's your partner?"

"Probably talking about what in the hell we'll do with you."

"You're taking me to your station, right? I'll make bail and be home in my jammies in time for Jimmy Kimmel."

"I didn't figure you for the jammies type."

"I use the term loosely. Sweatpants and a tank top."

"Okay, that I can picture."

"Please don't." Jessie leaned back against the stinky rear seat. She'd just celebrated her two-year anniversary as a private investigator, an occupation that had yielded some decent rewards along with heavy doses of frustration.

This was one for the frustration column.

It was a quarter past 9:00 P.M. in Marina del Rey, and they were parked alongside a ninety-foot yacht that belonged to basketball star Lamar Wood, L.A. Laker point guard and all-around local hero. She'd been arrested after being caught inside the apparently deserted craft. There were now half a dozen police cruisers nearby, flashers on. She suspected most of the cops were here only because Wood himself was expected on the scene at any minute.

Gataki turned back. "So what's it like in there?"

"Like it belongs to a guy halfway through a five-hundred-and-seventy-million-dollar contract. With a raft of endorsement deals to match. Nice. Really nice. You can see for yourself if you'll just search the place."

"We'd need probable cause for that."

"His kids are on that boat. I'm sure of it. He's going to leave the country with them."

"So you say."

"So his wife says."

"His soon-to-be-ex-wife."

"She's my client. Wood has been threatening to whisk those kids away for the last year, and I think it's going to happen tonight. Someone broke into the wife's house today and stole the kids' passports."

"But not *just* the passports," Gataki said. "From what I hear, they emptied the safe."

"He had to do that. Otherwise it would be too obvious."

Rap-Rap-Rap.

Gataki reacted with a start, but Jessie had already seen Lieutenant Dan Wheeler approaching in the rearview mirror. Why in the hell was he here?

"Let me in back," Wheeler shouted through the closed window.

Gataki unlocked the doors, and Wheeler climbed in next to Jessie. He looked at her and just shook his head. Wheeler was a good-looking cop, maybe forty, with chiseled features and gray-brown hair.

"Doesn't seem like your beat," Jessie said. "Did they demote you from homicide, Wheeler?"

"I was in the neighborhood."

"Ah. So you wanted a selfie with the basketball star."

"Nah. Not my game. I'm more of a Dodgers fan."

"Then what brings you here?"

"Like I said, I was in the neighborhood." Wheeler shot her a sideways glance. "And I guess I've gotten a rep as someone on the force who can work with you without wanting to slit my wrists."

"Aw, you're sweet."

"This isn't just going to go away, Jessie. Lamar Wood is practically royalty in this city, and the media is already all over it."

"Good. The whole world will know he's abducted those kids."

"His own kids. We've already been in touch with him. He says they're camping with his sister up in Yosemite."

"Out of cell phone range. Convenient."

Wheeler shook his head. "Jessie, can you even admit the possibility that you may be wrong?"

"Sure. Just not tonight."

"You always say that."

"Ask him when he gets here. See if he'll let your men search the yacht. How much you wanna bet he won't?"

A pair of headlight beams swung over the squad car's rear window. Wheeler leaned back to look. "It's a big Range Rover. Probably Wood. I'm supposed to apologize to him and do what I can to keep this from becoming a media firestorm."

"Bring on the firestorm."

"It wouldn't be good for you, Jessie."

"Only if I'm wrong."

Wheeler sighed. He climbed out of the car, slammed the door closed behind him, and walked over to the Range Rover. After a moment, Lamar Wood emerged. All seven-foot-one of him. Wood was attractive and well proportioned, without the gangly look that many men his size possessed. His aviator sunglasses were his trademark, and he wore them even now, at night and in the dim illumination of the marina streetlights.

Jessie saw Wood extend his hand as half a dozen cops converged on the basketball star. Wheeler spoke to him for a minute, gesturing a few times between Jessie and his yacht.

"He's nervous," Jessie said to herself. "He's not happy."

"You broke into his freakin' yacht," Officer Gataki said from the front seat.

"It's more than that." Jessie's eyes narrowed on Wood. "Oh, shit."

"What is it?"

Wood shook Wheeler's hand and then bounded up the short ramp to his yacht's stern. Wheeler walked back to the squad car and made the rolling-window-down motion with his hand. Gataki obliged by powering down the rear window.

"So what's going on?" Jessie said.

"He's going in to make sure everything is in order. Then he'll tell us if he wants to press charges or not."

Jessie clicked her tongue. "I guess you didn't notice the outline in his shirt pocket."

"What outline?"

"Jeez, Wheeler. I could see it from here. It looked exactly like the dimensions of a passport. Maybe two passports."

"You've got to be kidding me."

"Nope."

The yacht's engine suddenly roared to life.

Wheeler turned back toward the yacht. "No freakin' way."

Wood's boat lurched from its mooring. The cops scrambled, obviously unsure what to do.

5

"It's been untied!" one of the cops shouted. "He's taking off!"

"Shit." Wheeler pointed to an officer who had just driven up. "Call dispatch. Get Harbor Patrol on it."

Jessie leaned out of her open window. "You won't need Harbor Patrol."

Wheeler looked back at her with annoyance. "Why the hell not?"

Before she could reply, the boat's engine sputtered, and the hull echoed with the sound of grinding gears. The boat drifted lazily just a few feet from the ramp.

Wheeler half smiled. "What did you do, Jessie?"

She shrugged. "The engine might need a good flush now. That's all I'm saying."

Wheeler turned to the officers. "Get on that boat and search it top-to-bottom. There may be two kids aboard."

The officers ran down the ramp and leaped over to the yacht.

Jessie called out to Wheeler. "Hey, I can help."

"Don't push it, Jessie."

———◆———

Ten minutes later, the boat had been tied up and the cops were escorting basketball superstar Lamar Wood from the boat, along with his two children, Tricia and Alexander. Wood glared at Jessie as he was placed into the back of an LAPD squad car.

"Huh," Jessie said. "I wonder if that one smells like puke, too."

Wheeler walked back toward her car and rapped on the roof. "Okay, Gataki. Let her go."

Without a word, Gataki exited, pulled Jessie from the back, and unlocked her handcuffs.

Jessie smiled at Wheeler. "Where'd you find them?"

"Lamar had the kids hiding in the galley pantry. They thought they were playing the coolest game of hide-and-seek ever."

Jessie rubbed her wrists. "They probably were. You need anything from me?"

"Nah. The kids' mother has already been notified. She's gonna meet them at the station." He raised his left hand to show he was holding a pair of passports. "Good catch, Jessie."

"Thanks."

"It looks like he was headed to Panama if the navigation maps are any indication. From there, who knows? Those kids would've been hard to get back."

"That's what my client was afraid of."

He called over his shoulder as he walked away. "Stay out of trouble, will you?"

She replied under her breath. "Easier said than done."

A familiar female voice called out behind her. "Just another night in the life of Jessie Mercado, huh?"

Jessie turned. "Kendra?"

Kendra Michaels stepped from the shadows. Kendra was probably her best friend, a San Diego music therapist whose powers of observation made her a go-to consultant in several high-profile law-enforcement investigations. Her senses of hearing, smell, touch, and taste were honed by her first two decades as a blind person, and since gaining her sight, Kendra took nothing she saw for granted, making her a formidable investigator.

Kendra laughed. "You know, something about seeing you handcuffed in the back of that police car . . . it looked right."

Jessie smiled. "Screw you. Though I have to admit it's not the first time I've been in that situation."

"Ooh, I need to hear about that."

"Another story for another time." Jessie gave her friend a hug and drew back. "So what in the hell are you doing here?"

"A friend in the LAPD tipped me off. He said you were in police custody and might need a hand. It so happened I'm in town to present a paper at USC, so I came over to see for myself."

"Glad to give you an evening's entertainment."

"You never disappoint. I thought I might help pull a few strings, but you obviously have things under control."

"This time. But thanks for the thought," Jessie said.

"I was going to call you anyway."

"You got a craving for the El Coyote Cantina and their cheap margaritas?"

"I'm always up for that. But this time it's about a job. I may have a client for you."

Jessie nodded. "Good timing. It looks like I'm suddenly available. What's the case? Philandering husband? Sticky-fingered employee?"

"Missing person."

Jessie smiled in amusement. "Someone who wants to be missing?"

"Difficult to say. He's the business partner of a friend of mine. He disappeared two days ago."

"Sounds like a job for the police."

"They're on it, but they're not taking it seriously. At least not yet. The partner disappeared with a good-size chunk of the firm's cash reserves."

"Hmm. What kind of business?"

"I think..." She frowned. "Maybe I'd like my friend to explain that to you."

Jessie wrinkled her brow. "What's the big secret?"

"No secret. It's...an interesting firm."

Jessie looked at her for a moment longer. It wasn't like Kendra to be so coy. "Is it something illegal?"

"No." Kendra smiled. "Is that the kind of business you think I'd toss your way?"

"No, but sometimes you get drawn into some unusual situations."

"I just think he can explain it better than I could and answer any questions you might have."

"If he's your friend, why aren't *you* helping him out?"

"That's what he said. He's not really my friend. He's the father of one of my students. I told him that the best way I could help him was to refer his case to you."

Jessie raised her eyebrows. "And he was okay with that?"

"I didn't give him any choice. I'm leaving for a symposium in Vilnius tomorrow."

"Lithuania? Wow. That's some serious avoidance."

"I always told you, my music therapy research comes first."

"You have a gift, Kendra. You really shouldn't turn your back on it."

Kendra shook her head. She'd obviously heard it many times before, including from several law-enforcement agencies that had tried to recruit her over the years. But she ignored it and went her own path. So did Jessie, which was probably why they were such good friends.

"Whatever," Kendra said. "You want the job or not?"

Jessie shrugged. "I'll talk to the guy. Have him come to my office tomorrow."

"Actually... he's anxious. Frantic, even. Any way you can meet with him now?"

"Tonight?"

"He's texted me three times in the last hour, ever since I told him about you."

Jessie watched two of the police cars pull away. "Did you tell him I was being arrested?"

"I left that part out."

"It's already been a hell of a night." She thought about it. "Why not? Can he be at my office in half an hour?"

"He lives in the Palisades. I'm sure he can swing that."

"Fine."

"Thanks, Jessie." Kendra raised her phone and tapped out a text. Before she could even lower it, a reply chimed in. She looked up. "Told you he was eager. He says he'll be there. I'll follow you there and make the introduction."

She grinned. "Sounds like a plan."

———◆———

In less than twenty minutes, Jessie and Kendra parked in front of a revival movie theater on Santa Monica's Montana Avenue, in a charming block lined with boutiques and small restaurants. Kendra looked up at the theater's neon marquee, which advertised a double-feature of *Thin Man* films.

"Ever seen a movie here?"

Jessie shook her head. "No, even though I can go for free anytime I want. One of the perks of having a movie theater as a landlord. I do stop in the lobby for popcorn once in a while. It's pretty good."

They walked around the theater's vine-covered east side and headed back toward a metal security gate in the shadows, next to a small plaque that read JESSIE MERCADO INVESTIGATIONS. A silver keypad was mounted next to the door, onto which Jessie punched a six-digit number. The lock buzzed. Jessie opened the door and led Kendra up a long stairway that ended in a small reception area. The carpeted room was decorated with a desk, a sofa, and two wing-backed chairs.

"Did you ever find a new receptionist?" Kendra asked.

"Three since you've been here last. None of them lasted a week."

"You must be a tough boss."

"Why? Because I didn't like that the last one had sex with a client on that desk?"

"Eww."

"Yeah. I fired her *and* the client. And I still may have to burn the desk."

Jessie flipped on the lights, and they walked back to her main office. The room preserved the 1930s-era design of the theater downstairs with stylish light fixtures and a large mahogany desk. Matching wood accent panels and window shutters lined the corner office, and the rest of the wall was populated by framed photographs.

Kendra listened to the faint bass sounds coming from the theater under them. "I think the movies would bother me."

"I usually don't even hear them unless it's a war film or a Western. *The Wild Bunch* gave me some issues."

A buzzer sounded from Jessie's desk phone. She picked it up and heard a man's voice. "Owen Blake here for Jessie Mercado."

"You're in the right place. Come on up." She buzzed him in, and they heard his footsteps on the steep stairway. After a moment, Owen Blake appeared in the office. Owen was a handsome man with a layered haircut that probably set him back four hundred bucks every month or so, Jessie figured, probably in the same neighborhood where he picked up his expensive blue tailored suit. His shirt was open, but the creases on his collar indicated he'd been wearing a tie earlier in the day. His face was tense, jibing with Kendra's description of his anxious state of mind.

Jessie crossed behind her desk while Kendra made the introductions. "Jessie Mercado, Owen Blake. Jessie just wrapped up a case tonight—in the last hour, actually—and she's doing me a favor by opening up the office for you."

"I appreciate it," he said. "It's been a rough time."

"So Kendra tells me. Mr. Blake—"

"Owen, please."

Jessie nodded. "Owen, I usually start by telling prospective clients a little about myself."

"Not necessary."

"I appreciate the confidence, but you may want to know—"

"I've spent a good part of the day researching you, Jessie. I already know everything I need to know."

Jessie shot a glance toward Kendra. "Is that right?"

"Yes."

"It must have been a fascinating day for you," she said sarcastically.

"Oh, it was. You've lived quite a life." Owen looked at the framed photographs, which illustrated his point. "Two tours in Afghanistan, then one of the all-time champions on the *American Ninja* TV show. I watched some of your clips from that on YouTube this afternoon. Very impressive."

"Hardly," Jessie said. "But it paid some bills while I figured out what I wanted to do with my life."

"And it somehow led to you being a rock star's security director. How'd that happen?"

Jessie shrugged. "Delilah Winter saw me on that show and offered me a spot on her security detail. After a few weeks, I saw some things that could be improved, and Delilah agreed. She put me in charge."

"Simple as that?"

"Pretty much. But after a couple of years, I decided to strike out on my own and start this firm. It's worked out so far."

"Obviously, but I have one question. It's about something I read in *Rolling Stone*."

Kendra smiled. "Here we go..."

Jessie flashed a pained smile. Hardly a day passed that someone didn't ask her about that story. She'd wanted to strangle Dee for giving it to *Rolling Stone* magazine.

"Delilah Winter said she brought you a million dollars in cash to try and convince you to come back and work security for her world tour. Is that true?"

"Yep. She brought it in a knapsack and dumped it all over this desk."

"Wow."

"Excellent salesmanship on her part. Trust me, it looked damn good here. But I turned her down. This is where I belong."

He nodded approvingly. "Good. That's what I want to hear. Someone who's dedicated to her work."

"That's me." Jessie needed to change the subject. She sat and motioned toward the chairs in front of her desk. "Now I need to hear about you."

"I don't know what Kendra has told you..."

"Less than I'd like." She cast a sideways glance at her friend. "I know your partner has gone missing. But you can start by telling me about your business. What do you do?"

"We help people go to jail."

"What?"

He repeated himself, emphasizing each word. "We help people go to jail."

She crossed her arms. "Tough business model. People usually try *not* to go to jail."

"True. But if they try that and it doesn't work, then they

come to us. We're personal incarceration consultants. I'm an attorney, and my partner is from a private security background. When someone is going to prison for months or years, they need help getting their affairs in order. We work with accountants, financial planners, real estate managers, and whoever else we need. There are families who need to be taken care of, businesses and obligations that still need to be met. The world doesn't stop turning just because they're in prison. We negotiate with creditors and tax authorities, and we sometimes even help them negotiate the job market when they get out."

Jessie nodded. "A full-service operation. I take it most of your clientele has been convicted of white-collar crimes?"

"Mostly. But we do have the occasional drug lord and organized crime figure. And a couple of murderers."

"Of course," she said solemnly. "Just to shake things up."

Owen smiled. "It's never dull."

"So what happened to your partner?"

Owen paced in front of her desk. "His name is Carl Ferris. He disappeared last Friday. I saw him in the office that morning, and in the afternoon, he met with a client at the Twin Towers Correctional Facility downtown. That's the last anyone has seen or heard from him. He was supposed to be back at the office by four for a teleconference, but he missed it. That was highly unusual. He never misses meetings."

"Family?"

"An ex-wife and a kid in Texas. They've had no contact since the last child support payment went through a couple weeks ago."

15

"What about his car?"

"Also gone. LAPD hasn't been willing to do a traffic cam search for it yet, but the vehicle hasn't been hit with a parking citation."

"Anyone have a beef with him? Maybe someone from your colorful client list?"

"It's the first thing I thought of, but no. The clients love him. More than me, to tell you the truth. He's a people-person."

"I can vouch for that," Kendra said. "I've seen him in action. He makes an unpleasant experience seem a lot less terrifying for clients."

Jessie took this in. "Huh. I'd like to hear how he pulls *that* off."

"Find him," Owen said. "Then he'll tell you all about it."

"I assume the police haven't been very helpful yet."

He swore. "No."

"Let me guess. They told you he's a grown man who has every right to disappear if he chooses."

Owen gave her a surprised look. "I think I heard those very words."

"Not a shock. Adult missing persons cases usually resolve themselves after a few days. The police don't like to expend a lot of resources on cases like this, especially if there isn't a family hounding them. But those first days are crucial in any missing persons case. You need somebody on this now." She shrugged. "You need me."

"Then you'll take the case?"

Jessie thought for a long moment. It sounded a hell of a lot more interesting than tailing a movie star's son around Los Feliz to keep him from buying cocaine, which was currently her depressing, if well-paying, alternative for the week. She looked back up at Owen. "Why not? I'll see what I can do."

A broad smile lit Owen's face. "Fantastic. I can't tell you what a relief this is."

"Don't be relieved yet. I still need to find the guy. And if he doesn't want to be found, it could be difficult."

"I have faith in you. What do you need from me?"

"I have a whole questionnaire for you to fill out. All his personal information, contacts, prior residences, that kind of stuff. My rates are in there, too. I'll email you a link."

Owen gestured toward the desk. "I can fill it out here, right now."

Jessie smiled. "You *are* in a hurry. Just fill it out later tonight. It's a web form. You can do it on your phone or computer. It would also be helpful if I had a list of present and prior clients, along with any background on the cases you'd care to share. Especially the client he met with right before he disappeared."

"That I can help you with right now." He pulled a thumb drive from his shirt pocket and held it up. "You'll find several files of that type on here, including some fairly detailed information about Ferris and our clients."

"Perfect." Jessie took the drive and picked up her leather knapsack from behind the desk. She pulled out her tablet computer, inserted the thumb drive, and copied the folder labeled CARL FERRIS to her tablet. She gave the thumb drive back to Owen.

He handed her a business card. "My email is on there. Send

your questionnaire form to that address. I'll probably fill it out in my car before I even drive home."

"I get it. You're in a rush." Jessie used the tablet to email him the link.

Owen's phone chimed in his pocket, and he patted it reassuringly. "Thank you."

"I'll call you in the morning with a game plan. Nice to meet you, Owen."

Kendra signaled to Jessie that she was going to walk him out. She returned less than a minute later. "What do you think?"

"He's hiding something."

"So you noticed that."

Jessie nodded. "He's not my first client who's tried to keep something from me. It's strange he's in such a hurry. I get he's concerned about his partner, but it's a little over the top. You know the guy. What's your read?"

She shrugged. "He's more of a casual acquaintance. I liked his sincerity about helping his daughter. I asked him on the way down about why he's so frantic about this. He just said he and his partner always have each other's backs. I advised him not to withhold anything from you, and he said he wouldn't."

"I think he already is."

"If you don't want to take the case, it's no skin off my nose. If you're uneasy, forget it. Call him. Or go outside and tell him. He's probably sitting in his car, filling out your questionnaire on his phone."

Jessie looked at his embossed card. The name MAMERTINE

CONSULTANTS was printed in gold leaf, along with Owen's name and contact info. "Who's 'Mamertine'?"

"It's not a who, it's a what. Mamertine was the name of the largest prison in ancient Rome. Saint Peter was locked up there."

"Don't tell me you knew that off the top of your head."

"I didn't. When Owen named his firm, I was just as mystified as you were until he explained it to me."

"Good." Jessie pocketed the card. "But I doubt he has any saints on his client list. Just a hunch."

"I'm sure you're right. Is that where you're going to start? With his clients?"

"Probably. I'll read up on what he gives me and decide."

Kendra nodded. "Good luck. And thanks. I owe you one. I would have felt duty-bound to find someone else if you'd been too busy."

"Not at all." She was suddenly smiling. "Because if I'm still working this case when you get back in town, you're working it with me."

Kendra chuckled. "Is that the deal?"

"That's the deal. When will you be back?"

"A couple of weeks, I'm afraid. I'm collaborating on a research study after the symposium ends."

"Fine. If I'm still on the case when you get back, we're in this together. Okay?"

"Ah, you'll have this all wrapped up in a bow by then."

"Keep hoping. But I've helped you a few times on your cases. I figure you can help me on this one."

Kendra thought for a moment. "We *do* work well together."

"Damn right we do."

"It's a deal. But I should get going. Try not to get yourself arrested between now and the time I get back, okay?"

Jessie picked up her backpack and slung it over her shoulder. "No promises, Kendra. Better bring bail money."

———◆———

BROADWAY

SANTA MONICA

Owen parked his car and walked past Third Street Promenade, checking his phone for the address he had entered earlier in the evening. Up ahead, loud music blared from the open doors of a dark bar. Surely *that* couldn't be the place. No way she would have chosen that place to—

"Will she do it?"

Owen spun around.

There, from a darkened doorway behind him, Natalie Durand stepped into the light. She was a tall, dark-haired woman in her late thirties with olive-toned skin and large brown eyes. As was the case every time Owen saw her, she wore what appeared to be a tailored man's business suit with unbuttoned shirt cuffs stylishly folded back over the jacket sleeves. "Will she do it?" Natalie repeated, in her southern drawl.

Owen nodded. "Jessie Mercado is in."

"Too bad Kendra Michaels wasn't available."

"Mercado's very good. I have confidence in her."

"I hope so. We need to find Ferris before anyone else does."

"We will."

Natalie stepped closer and spoke in a fierce whisper. "If we don't, Owen . . . Ferris isn't the only one who will disappear."

Owen tried not to show how much she rattled him, but he knew he was failing miserably. He forced a smile. "I know a threat when I hear one."

"Good. Because I don't think your partner ever grasped the concept. And if Jessie Mercado does manage to find him, we need to make sure he doesn't talk to her. Or there will be yet another person who needs to disappear. I hope you understand that."

CHAPTER

2

Jessie parked in front of her house in Venice, just blocks from the beach and a short distance from the Santa Monica Pier. Her home was a single-story Craftsman with a postage-stamp-size front yard—typical for the neighborhood, which dedicated more real estate for the charming rear views of the community's famous canals. It was a breezy night, and her next-door neighbor's battery-illuminated Chinese lanterns swung from a tree with each gust, clapping against the branches.

Jessie stopped. There was another sound.

Her back gate groaned on its hinges as the wind buffeted against it.

But the gate had been closed when she left. She was sure.

She moved toward the swinging, still-creaking gate.

She'd recently had a homeless man regularly bathe himself with her backyard garden hose, but even he had been considerate enough to close the gate behind him when he left.

She stepped around to the rear of house, which was totally dark.

But she could make out a figure of a man wearing a hooded sweatshirt at her glass patio doors.

Shit! She launched herself across the yard in a tackle that brought him down. He grunted but then he moved with lightning swiftness to turn and straddle her. He swore as he blocked her karate blow to his throat. "For God's sake, Jessie. Is this how you greet all your guests?"

She froze. "Brice?" She reached up and jerked down his hoodie. Even in the darkness she could see the single white streak in that tawny hair. "Damn. I forgot about you."

"Always nice to hear." Still straddling her, he stroked her cheek. "I must say, I kind of enjoyed it. I could almost forgive you if you told me this was some kind of kinky role-playing exercise."

"Sorry, but no. I thought you were a burglar. What were you doing trying to break in my patio doors?" His touch was causing her an uncomfortable but oddly pleasant feeling. "Will you get off me now?"

"Soon." He motioned toward the wine bottle he'd dropped when she'd tackled him. "I thought I'd go inside and have a glass of wine ready for you when you walked in the door."

"So you *were* going to break in?"

He shrugged. "I learned a few tricks when I was in Paris last year playing that cat burglar. I thought I could probably manage to get in if the lock was simple enough."

She shook her head. "You could've ended up shot, in jail, or on the front page of every tabloid in the world. I installed those locks myself."

"Then I'm glad you're sure they're safe." He bent down and brushed his lips across her forehead. "And I would have been happy to suffer any consequences to test them for you."

She laughed and pushed him off her. "You're an idiot. Did you use those lines in your last movie?"

"No, and I'm insulted. I'd never use any lines on you that weren't totally original. You deserve nothing less." He sighed. "I'm afraid you're not appreciating me or this excellent wine." He stood and reached down for the wine bottle. "So can I come in?"

"You can come inside for one glass of wine. After that, you have to go. I just took on a new case, and I need to read over some files."

Once inside, Jessie stood there admiring him. It was hard not to. Brice was one of the most handsome men she'd ever seen. His broad shoulders and six-pack abs were the joy of the paparazzi when he went shirtless. Women and men also loved his chiseled yet expressive face. His blue eyes were mesmerizing, and they glittered with amusement at her now.

He was running his hand through a bowl of steel ball

bearings she kept in her living room. "You walk around with these things?"

"I grab a handful every time I leave the house. They come in handy."

"I'll take your word for it." He pulled his hand from the bowl. "I have to tell you, I'm still a bit wounded from being almost stood up."

She made a face. "Poor Jake Brice. Only the hottest actor on the planet. Between those Marvel superhero movies and that Academy Award winner last year, we all feel so sorry for you."

He opened the bottle of wine. "It isn't all it's cracked up to be."

"You like it, Brice. You may not like the fame game, but you like what you do. You like those fun adventure movies, and you like the ability to stretch yourself when you choose."

"I do." He handed her a glass of wine and took his own glass before slipping his arm around her waist and leading her toward the sofa. "And as long as I have a release valve, I can put up with the rest." He pulled her down to the couch and eased her head over to rest on his shoulder. "I can go mountain climbing or racing, help the firefighters, or try to save the tigers, and now and then Jessie sees fit to let me come and visit." He kissed the tip of her nose. "When she doesn't forget."

"It was a rough day. First of all, I got arrested."

"Seriously?"

"Yep. Handcuffs, back of a police car, the whole nine yards. I got caught right in the middle of a custody dispute."

"Did they book you?"

"It didn't go that far. Then I agreed to work for a strange company. Mamertine Consultants. Ever hear of them?"

"Mamertine? I've heard of them, but that's about it. It's not a company I'd ever need. There's no way I'd ever go to prison under any circumstances. I'd just disappear somewhere and try to convince you to come with me."

Prison. It wasn't strange that the thought had triggered that reaction in Brice. He'd been in Afghanistan and held prisoner by the Taliban for almost a year. He didn't talk about the torture he'd endured there. He'd told Jessie it was when he was released from that prison that he'd noticed the startling streak of white in his hair.

In fact, she'd first met Brice at a VA hospital when they'd both been at a benefit for PTSD patients. Somehow, they'd both ended up sitting on a back staircase, drinking coffee and talking about their war experiences. She hadn't realized how unusual that was until later. Brice was a very private person, and she'd never heard any of those stories about him from any other source. At any rate, it was a bond that was difficult to break, and when you threw in terrific, no-strings-attached sex and genuine liking, it became almost impossible.

But it was also a bond that had to be carefully managed so that neither of them came out with any harm done. They were both independent and came from different worlds. Her instincts were to enforce limits in their relationship. But she was beginning to learn how determined Brice could be under any circumstances. Determined and clever.

"You're thinking too hard," Brice said. "Not good. Would you like another glass of wine?"

She shook her head. "I should probably cut this short. I have to work tomorrow."

He thought about it. "Good idea. But I think we should go to your home gym and have a workout before you send me back to my place. It will relax all that tension."

"We already had a workout in the yard," she said dryly.

"Not enough." He pulled her to her feet. "You know, you should really let me sneak you into my gym. Much more equipment."

"My gym is fine," she said as she moved down the hall. "And I don't really need this."

"Don't you?" He opened the door to her gym and turned on the lights. "Think about it. Nothing like a good workout." He kissed her neck.

She couldn't breathe. She didn't want to breathe. She flipped off the lights and turned to face him in the darkness. "Maybe you're right. Nothing like a good workout."

———◆———

Brice didn't leave for another two hours, and after Jessie went to bed, she spent another hour or so reading through the information Owen had given her. Mamertine Consultants' client list was a who's who of wealthy convicted felons. Most seemed to be in the finance industry, but there was also ample representation from entertainment professionals and sports figures.

Oddly, a few of the client names were redacted, though Jessie was able to identify some from the descriptions of their high-profile cases. The firm seemed to have no standards regarding the types of crimes committed. Their clients went to prison for offenses ranging from embezzlement to securities fraud, from robbery to murder.

Whereas the bulk of the client list served their sentences in minimum-security prisons, the missing partner seemed to specialize in more dangerous and violent offenders, headed for San Quentin or the state prisons in Lancaster, Tehachapi, and Sacramento.

Jessie scrolled down to see his current clients, who included a trader convicted of securities fraud, a Newport Beach socialite who murdered her husband, and an armed robber. Ferris had just visited the robber at the jail in downtown L.A. before his disappearance. Jessie jotted down the prisoner's name: Colin Sackler. Sounded familiar, but she'd have to research the details of the case.

Jessie closed the file. As much as the police liked to home in on business dealings as a possible motive for crimes, it was the victims' personal relationships that were ultimately responsible for at least 90 percent of the cases she investigated.

She opened her agency cloud account where, as promised, Owen had already completed the questionnaire she'd given him. It contained the details of Ferris's previous marriage, friends, job history, clubs, and other associations. There was also some detail of his recent romantic relationships, which she was surprised to see included two well-known actresses and a local television weather anchor. But for the past year, he seemed to be exclusive with Jennifer Dayton, a UCLA law professor.

Jessie pinned the name and sent it to her personal email account. Time to go back to school.

———◆———

I-405 FREEWAY
WEST LOS ANGELES
4:40 P.M.

Jessie gunned the engine on her Harley-Davidson Sportster 883 Superlow motorcycle and wove between the bumper-to-bumper cars on the 405 freeway. She'd taken the rush-hour traffic into account when calculating the distance from her house and the UCLA campus, but the flow was even slower than its usual snail's pace.

Her phone rang in her helmet's Bluetooth earpiece. She double-tapped the helmet to answer. "You got Jessie."

"Where in the hell are you?" A man's voice. "A factory?"

"Who is this?"

"Owen Blake. Your new employer."

"You mean my *client*."

He chuckled. "Is that any way to talk to the person who's paying your exorbitant daily rate?"

"Consider yourself lucky. I could have called you my *pain-in-the-ass* client, but I resisted the temptation. And if you think my daily rate is exorbitant, wait till you see how I pad my expenses."

"I look forward to it. But I repeat my question: Where in the hell are you? I'm hearing some crazy noises there."

"That's the 405. I'm on my motorcycle. My Bluetooth helmet is supposed to filter a lot of that racket out, but maybe I need a more expensive one. Item number one for your first daily expense report?"

He chuckled again. "Forget I said anything. I just wanted to make sure all the material I gave you was clear."

"Crystal. I spent last night and most of the day poring through it all. I'm on my way to talk to Ferris's girlfriend right now."

"Jennifer Dayton?"

"Yes. She's teaching a lecture class tonight, and I'm trying to catch her before she starts. Anything I should know about her first?"

"Well, Ferris is crazy about her."

"How does she feel about him?"

"Less than captivated, I've always thought. Which may be why he's so nuts about her. He isn't used to utter indifference from the women in his life."

"Huh. He should talk to some of my exes. If he skipped town, do you think he'd tell her?"

"I called her the day after he disappeared. She said she didn't know anything, and I believed her. I'd be interested in your impressions, though."

"You'll get 'em. I'm coming up on Wilshire now. I'll check in with you later."

Jessie double-tapped her helmet to cut the connection.

She exited the freeway and rode through Westwood Village to the UCLA campus, a four-hundred-acre oasis in the city's Westside, marked by beautifully landscaped gardens, old-growth trees, and red brick buildings, many of art deco design.

She parked her motorcycle in a garage and made her way to the three-story law school building where, as was the case in every recent college visit, most of the students looked impossibly young to her. Dressed in her jeans and black leather jacket, she fit right in. And although she was a good ten years older than most of the students surrounding her, she knew she probably looked younger than most. Good genes. At least in that way.

She bounded up the stairs to the second-floor lecture auditorium and poked her head in. A woman in her midthirties was alone in the room, jotting subject headings on a whiteboard.

Jessie walked down toward her, passing row after row of desks equipped with laptop stands and power outlets. "Jennifer Dayton?"

The instructor turned. She was a slender woman with long blond hair and a tanned face. She wore capri pants, a blue shirt, and a black patterned vest. "Yes. You're not one of my students, are you?"

Jessie shook her head. "No. I'm here about Carl Ferris."

Jennifer rolled her eyes and turned back toward the whiteboard.

How touching. "Sick with worry, I see."

"Sick with something." Jennifer consulted a sheet of paper and continued writing on the whiteboard. "You don't look like a cop."

"I'm not. My name's Jessie Mercado. I'm a private investigator, and Ferris's partner hired me to look for him. He's concerned."

"Really? I've never known Owen Blake to be concerned about anyone but himself."

"I'm not getting a whole lot of concern from you, either. How are things between you and Ferris?"

"Not really your business, Ms. Mercado."

"Actually...it literally is. At least until I find him. If there's any part of you that cares about this man, do you mind answering a few questions?"

She turned from the whiteboard and sighed. "He proposed to me last week."

Jessie clicked her tongue and shook her head. "That bastard."

"He wanted to elope."

"And you wanted the big church wedding with all the frills?"

"Hell, no. I don't care about that."

"So what was the problem?"

Jennifer crossed her arms and hesitated a long moment before responding. "He wanted to keep it a secret."

"That's...different."

"You think? He asked me to drive to Vegas with him and marry him there. We'd come back the next day and carry on with our lives as if nothing had happened. He didn't want to tell anyone." For the first time, Jennifer's annoyance seemed to give way to some genuine pain. Her lips tightened. "He didn't even want us to wear rings. At least not at first."

"Why?"

"He wouldn't say. I wasn't sold on marrying him under any circumstances, but I certainly wasn't going to do it that way."

"He didn't give you a reason at all?"

"No, and of course I pushed him for one. He just said he needed me to trust him."

"There's trust, and then there's trust. If you had to guess, why would you think he'd want to secretly marry you?"

"It's insane, right? Those words sounded crazy coming out of your mouth just now. I can't think of one good reason."

"How about a bad one?"

She shrugged. "Well, he does have a reputation as something of a playboy. He enjoys seeing himself in the list of eligible bachelors in *Los Angeles Magazine*. He says he likes it because it's good for business, but I think he just likes the attention."

"Which would go away if he suddenly became an old married man."

"Right. But if that's what he was worried about, why marry me at all? It's not like it's something I wanted from him."

"He's been missing for days. You're not concerned about him?"

"He didn't take it well when I rejected his proposal. Carl Ferris is a man who's used to getting what he wants. I figured he was off licking his wounds. Maybe even in Vegas."

"His partner says he always uses a company credit card when he travels, and there's been no activity. And there's been no activity on his mobile phone."

"Shit." This was obviously news to Jennifer. Her expression was suddenly concerned.

Jessie pressed on. "Did he give you reason to believe that he might be in danger?"

"No, not at all."

"No threats against him?"

"Not that I know of." Jennifer paused for a moment. "But there is something he discussed with me."

At that moment, two students walked into the classroom. Jennifer cast a glance in their direction and then turned back to Jessie. "Come and see me in my office tonight. It's a lecture class. I'll be wrapping up around nine fifteen."

"I'll be here." Jessie pulled out a business card and handed it to her. "If Ferris gets in touch with you before then, could you let me know? There are people who are worried about him."

Jennifer looked at the card. "Yeah. I'm one of them now." She glanced up. "If you find him first...could you ask him to call me?"

"Sure."

Jessie turned and bounded down the stairs that would take her out the lecture hall's back entrance. She was almost to the parking garage when she stopped and considered pulling Jennifer Dayton out of her class immediately to talk about what Ferris had discussed with her. Then she changed her mind. Jennifer had seemed to be more open toward the end of their meeting, but she'd disturbed her once already today. Better not push it.

Jessie climbed onto her motorcycle and blasted out of the garage.

———◆———

THE ARSENAL BAR
WEST LOS ANGELES
6:30 P.M.

"Are you stalking me, Mercado?"

Jessie turned to see Detective Dan Wheeler seated at a high-top wooden table in the packed restaurant. She had just entered Arsenal moments earlier and was about to leave when Wheeler had called out to her. She sat down across from him and grimaced at his enormous burger, oozing with grilled onions and mushrooms. "That's kind of disgusting, you know."

"Of course I know." He took a massive bite. "You didn't answer my question. Are you stalking me?"

"Actually, yes. You're not answering your phone. This is the third West L.A. cop bar I've been to in the last half hour. I was starting to lose hope."

"I turn it off when I'm at dinner. And why do you think I only eat at cop bars?"

"The free or heavily discounted menu items for our boys in blue."

"You think I'm cheap?"

"Hey, if I knew I could walk into a restaurant where the waiters would give me free food, I'd go there, too. I'd never eat anyplace else." Jessie took one of his french fries.

"Help yourself. So what do you need?"

"I'm working a new case. Missing person."

"Minor or adult?"

"Adult. His name is Carl Ferris. He's a personal incarceration consultant."

"Mamertine?"

Jessie rolled her eyes. "Jeez, was I the only one in this city who hadn't heard of them?"

"Be glad. It's only because you associate with a higher class of people."

"I wouldn't say that."

"I guess it could also be a lower class of people."

"That's probably more like it."

"So how long has this guy been missing?"

"Three days."

"That's nothing. He could just be nursing a bottle of tequila on the Baja peninsula."

"Well, his girlfriend did just reject his marriage proposal."

"Then it's settled. That's where I'd be."

"This doesn't feel that way."

Wheeler took another bite of his burger. "Has anyone filed a missing persons report?"

"Yes." Jessie slapped the canary-yellow report copy on the table in front of him. "Filed by his business partner. LAPD isn't taking this as seriously as we'd like."

He glanced at it and then shrugged. "This really isn't my thing, Mercado. I solve murders, remember?"

"That didn't stop you from wading into a basketball star's custody dispute last night."

"That's because you were involved. My captain thought I might have a chance of talking some sense into you."

Jessie took another french fry. "I'm involved in this. If you want to try and talk some sense into me, have at it. But only after you get some A/V guys checking traffic cams to see where he went after he left Twin Towers last Friday. He was driving a red Lamborghini. Shouldn't be too hard to track."

Wheeler glanced over the report for a moment longer. "Can I take this?"

"Sure, it's a copy the client gave me. I have the file saved in my tablet."

He folded the report and jammed it into his jacket's inside breast pocket. "I'll talk to the officer working your case, see what I can do. Are you working any leads of your own?"

"Still early stages. I'm running something down with his girlfriend."

"Good." He pushed his plate away. "I'm done here. You can have the rest."

She made a face. "No, thanks. You've ruined it now."

"How's that?"

"Before, we were sharing your dinner. Now I'd just be a pathetic scavenger swiping food off dirty dishes."

He smiled. "You're an odd duck, Mercado."

"I've been called worse. Called worse by you, as a matter of fact. I must be winning you over." She stood. "Thanks, Wheeler. I'll be in touch."

Her phone rang as she was walking toward the parking garage.

"Having a good day?" Brice asked when she picked up. "Can you break for dinner with me?"

"It's been fairly productive, but not really good. It would be good if I'd actually found the guy. And since I just had french fries at a restaurant with a LAPD cop, I guess that would constitute dinner since I haven't eaten anything else."

"I can do better than that. Pick the restaurant."

"And then have your fans or paparazzi move in on us? That's not better and you know it."

"Carryout? We can bring it to my place."

"Same answer. You're surrounded, and it's not my situation of choice."

"I thought that might be your answer. It's difficult, but we can find a solution." He paused. "Because last night was extraordinary."

She wasn't going to deny it. Those hours might have been among the most passionate she had ever experienced. He was a fantastic lover, but it didn't matter. Afterward she had told herself that it wasn't a relationship that she should continue. As he had said, it was damn difficult.

"The french fries were fine. And we both have problems enough without searching for more."

"Only I'm finding it a problem *not* to search for a solution. I can never see why there shouldn't be one when I want something this badly. So why don't you meet me, and we'll discuss it?" His voice was coaxing. "I can be very persuasive, and you're not unreasonable. Otherwise I might be tempted to just keep on trying."

And she might be tempted to listen. "I don't have time to discuss anything today. I have work to do."

"Later tonight?"

"I have a meeting with a teacher at the university after nine tonight. I won't put it off."

"Then I'll be at your place at midnight. No seduction. Only discussion and a glass of wine. Agreed?"

It wasn't as if she couldn't trust him to keep his word. And this might be the last time she saw him, she thought regretfully. "Agreed."

"Then I'll let you get back to work. See you tonight." He ended the call.

It was the right thing to do, Jessie told herself. One glass of wine and then she'd be able to say a goodbye to Brice with no hard feelings. That's how she'd want to end it, because she genuinely liked and respected him.

———◆———

PARKING GARAGE B
UCLA
9:00 P.M.

Jessie checked her phone. Almost time to meet up with Jennifer Dayton. She'd spent her evening researching Ferris's client list, and most were fairly innocuous. She was sadly not surprised how quickly many of his white-collar clients were already free after serving only short stints in prison. Stick up a convenience store, go away for a decade. Destroy the livelihoods and retirement nest eggs for dozens of hardworking people, and eighteen months was about par for the course.

Two clients seemed like worthy subjects of further investigation, and she was surprised Owen Blake didn't single them out. She'd have to discuss it with him later.

Jessie swung her leg over her motorcycle and walked through the parking garage. There were more cars than she might have expected, probably due to some parking spillover from a jazz concert at Royce Hall. Music wafted in from a party somewhere, and she could hear students talking as they made their way across campus.

Jessie entered the law building and bounded up the same stairs she'd taken that morning. This time she took an additional two flights to the faculty offices, which lined one side of the floor across from the building's two largest lecture auditoriums.

Jessie pulled out her phone to double-check the office number Jennifer Dayton had given her. She followed the numbers down the deserted hallway until she reached 406.

Jessie knocked on the door. No answer.

She tried the knob. Locked.

Jessie stepped back and looked at the crack beneath the door. No light.

She was almost twenty minutes early, so there was no reason to expect—

"Ms. Mercado."

Jessie turned to see Jennifer walking down the hall toward her.

"Thank you for meeting with me, Ms. Dayton, especially this late. I know it's been a long day for you."

"I wanted to talk someplace more private. It's about Carl's work. It may be of some help to you."

"Of course."

CLICK-CLACK!

It was the sound of a door lock. Jennifer's office door.

In the next instant, the door swung inward, and a figure barreled out of the office!

BLAM-BLAM!

Two shots were fired from a gun in the figure's left hand. It was a large man, dressed entirely in black and wearing a face mask.

Jennifer staggered backward. Jessie instinctively leaped toward the shooter, grabbed his wrist, and struck his hand against the doorframe. As they struggled, her fingernail sliced twice into his wrist, forming a bloody, jagged *X*.

BLAM! BLAM! Two more wild shots ricocheted down the hallway.

She struck his wrist twice more, and his gun flew from his hand and slid across the floor. She punched him in his chest, stomach, and throat. He doubled over and groaned in pain. Just when she thought she had him on the ropes, the assailant barreled toward her and threw her against the wall.

Wham! She felt the pain in her back, legs, and neck. Damn, that hurt. Had something broken?

No time to check. He was going for the gun.

Jessie scrambled across the floor and got there first. She grabbed the gun and whirled around.

The man spoke. "Don't do it, Mercado," he hissed. "I'll kill you and everyone close to you. You don't know who you're dealing with."

Her grip tightened on the gun. "Enlighten me."

The assailant whirled and sprinted down the hall. She raised her gun to aim, but he'd disappeared around the corner.

Shit.

Jessie glanced down to see what she could do for Jennifer Dayton.

Nothing. She was dead. She'd caught both his bullets, one in her chest, the other in her forehead.

Can't let this thug get away with it. Jessie ran after him. She bolted to the stairs, where she could hear his footsteps pounding on the floor below.

Jessie half ran, half flew down the stairs and pushed open the building's main doors. Dammit. No sign of the guy. She didn't know if he'd gone to a parking garage, or maybe—

She spotted him! He was in the shadows, sprinting past the Dodd Hall classroom building.

Jesse jammed the gun into her jacket pocket and leaped over a row of shrubbery lining the sidewalk. She darted across the narrow courtyard and ran around to the building's far side. With any luck, she'd cut him off and—

Crap.

The concert had let out, and hundreds of people were spilling out of Royce Hall.

Jessie scanned the crowd. Lots of smiling, chattering

people, meandering down the sidewalks toward the parking garages.

But on the plaza's far side, a lone figure walked in a totally different rhythm. With speed, with purpose. And he was walking toward the auditorium, not away.

It was him!

Jessie ran across the plaza and entered the theater lobby just twenty seconds behind the man.

She stopped. There were a few people lingering there, hunched over their phones, waiting for their companions in the bathrooms.

She ran through a set of double doors into the large auditorium. The wide-aisled seating area was illuminated by art deco lighting fixtures and bordered by a U-shaped upper level. She saw only a few student volunteers picking up trash and discarded programs.

But the tall stage curtain ruffled for a moment, and she caught a glimpse of the black-clad man slipping behind it. Jessie ran down the long aisle and leaped onto the stage. She ran into the right wing and stopped, letting her eyes adjust to the darkness.

She listened.

Footsteps, slow and deliberate.

And coming right for her.

Jessie reached into her pocket and quietly pulled out a handful of ball bearings. She took one and tossed it toward the rear of the stage right wing. It bounced and rolled on the wooden floor.

The footsteps stopped.

She didn't breathe. *Take the bait, asshole...*

The footsteps moved away.

Good man...

She tossed another ball bearing. It hit the floor and rolled. The footsteps changed course.

It was working. She had a shot at cornering him.

Jessie moved quietly, working her way along the black curtain runners.

The footsteps stopped.

She froze. Silence.

He was listening, waiting for her to make a move.

She crouched in the darkness. Where in the hell was he?

The remaining ball bearings clicked in her hand. Shit. Jessie went still. Maybe if she tossed one more into the—

A plastic bag snapped over her head!

She tried to turn, but hundreds of pounds of force struck between her shoulders and knocked her down. Ball bearings spilled from her fingers and rolled across the floor. Before she could recover, her arms were pulled behind her, and a zip tie closed over her wrists. After a quick frisk, the gun was pulled from her jacket pocket.

Gasping for air, she rolled on her back and faced her attacker. The black-clad figure still wore the face mask. He hefted the gun as if trying to decide whether to use it on her.

She felt pressure against her throat, and only then did she realize that the plastic bag was probably sealed by another zip tie. The bag pulled taut over her nose and mouth as she inhaled the last of the trapped air.

She writhed on the floor, eyes bulging and watering.

Getting light-headed. Vision fogging.

"Die now." Her attacker pocketed the gun and moved away.

He figured her for as good as dead. Which she would be if she didn't do something fast.

She rolled onto her side and rubbed her head against the stage floor, trying to get some traction on the mask.

It wasn't happening.

She sucked in with every bit of lung capacity she had left, trying to pull the plastic back past her lips.

She closed her mouth. Not quite there.

She inhaled again. This time she almost passed out. Still not enough.

One more time. If she lost consciousness, it was all over.

One . . . Two . . . Three . . .

She narrowed her lips into a tight O and sucked in with everything she had left. The bag's surface pulled past her lips and brushed across her front teeth. She bit down and caught the edge.

Contact! She could do this . . .

She thrashed her head up and down, side to side. The plastic wasn't giving way.

Shit.

And her teeth were losing their grip . . .

She bit harder and threw her head back.

Whoosh.

Success. Cool, fresh air rushed through the hole she'd made in the bag.

She took a deep breath. Damn, that felt good.

"Ma'am, are you all right?"

Jessie squinted through the moist, foggy bag. A pimply-faced student volunteer was leaning over her.

"Can I help you?"

Jessie took another long breath. "Yeah. Start by pulling this bag off my head. Then we'll work on the hands. Sound like a plan?"

CHAPTER

3

Forty-five minutes later, Jessie sat on a bench facing the law building's main entrance, which was now covered with yellow police tape and guarded by several uniformed police officers. The red flashers from half a dozen squad cars strobed against the building as detectives and the forensics team members moved in and out of the main doors.

One of the cops was Detective Wheeler. He walked up and plopped down on the bench next to her. "You know, you don't look so good. That wound on your neck looks pretty raw. They have a world-class hospital right here on campus. How about we let 'em take a look at you?"

"I don't need a doctor." Jessie pulled the cotton-polyester blanket from her shoulders. "I don't even need this blanket. One of your uniformed officers gave it to me. Why do cops always think women need a blanket after every traumatic experience?"

"You mean you don't?"

"Not really."

"I'd feel better if you saw a doctor."

"I'm not here to make you feel better, Wheeler."

"Your neck is cut, and it's starting to bruise."

"That's what I get for sporting a zip tie as a choker. I appreciate your concern, but I'll be fine."

"Okay." Wheeler leaned back on the bench. "So tell me why Jennifer Dayton is dead."

"A big asshole shot her. At the same time he tried to shoot me."

"But why?"

"No idea. She wanted to tell me something about Ferris, something that someone obviously didn't want me to know."

"And you have no idea what that is?"

"No. I told you she rejected Carl Ferris's marriage proposal. What I didn't tell you is that, for some reason, he wanted their marriage to be a secret. At least for a while."

"She didn't tell you why?"

"She didn't know. But it certainly didn't make his proposal more appealing to her."

"I wouldn't think so."

"And she gave me no reason why anyone would want her dead."

Wheeler shrugged. "Ferris wouldn't be the first spurned lover to take it out on his ex."

"Ferris? But why would he kill me? This guy definitely wanted me dead."

"I guess you just have that effect on people, Mercado."

"I haven't had time to make any enemies in this case yet."

"Come on, give yourself a little credit."

"I'm not buying that it's Ferris," Jessie said.

"I'm really not, either. Just a possibility to explore. The plastic bag the killer tried to snuff you with is already on its way to the lab. They'll check it for prints and DNA."

"Good. Your crime scene tech has already swabbed my fingernails."

"Did you get a piece of the guy?"

"I scratched the hell out of his right wrist when we were fighting over his gun. Two deep cuts that crossed each other."

"Well done."

"Did you make any progress on getting a traffic cam search for Ferris's car?"

"Not yet, but it'll definitely happen. It's a murder case now, and finding Ferris will be a priority."

Jessie watched as the medical examiner's stretcher arrived, carried through the front door by two attendants. "It's my priority, too. I hope you're open to sharing what you come up with."

"Within reason, but it's a two-way street. Promise to play nice with us?"

"Don't I always?"

"I'll let that go. Are you sure I can't talk you into going over to the hospital for a quick checkup?"

"There's nothing quick about a hospital emergency room."

"There is if you're escorted by a dashing police detective who's willing to flash his badge around and demand some special treatment."

"That really works?"

"Every time. Come watch me."

"As entertaining as that might be, I'll pass." She turned and walked back toward the parking garage. "Later, Wheeler."

Jessie walked past the law building and made her way back to the parking garage. She cast a quick glance around. She sincerely doubted that the son of a bitch would still be lurking around with all the cops and media flooding the area, but it still creeped her out to be alone in the parking structure.

And her throat was throbbing. Maybe it was a little worse than she'd told Wheeler. She ducked into a restroom and took a look in the mirror. The bruising was nasty looking, but she'd be able to take care of it when she got home.

When she got home.

Brice!

It was almost the time that they'd agreed to meet.

There was no way she was going to let him see her like this. If Wheeler had been concerned, she could imagine how Brice would feel. She felt her pocket. Dammit. She'd dropped her phone in the hallway outside Jennifer Dayton's office. The area was still an active crime scene, and she knew she was still hours away from getting her phone back. She'd take it up with Wheeler in the morning.

A tousled-haired teenager was coming out of one of the stalls, and Jessie grabbed her. "Can I borrow your phone? I lost mine, and I won't be a minute."

"Sure." She was looking at Jessie's throat and frowning. "You okay?"

"Fine." She turned away and dialed Brice. "Hi, I just wanted to call and cancel. I'm too tired to talk tonight. Suppose we do it tomorrow or the next day?"

Silence. "No problem. Everything fine?"

"Just tired. It's been quite a day. See you."

"Absolutely." He ended the call.

Jessie handed the phone back to the teenager. "Thanks. I appreciate it."

"You're welcome." She was still frowning. "You ought to be careful who you hang out with. No one should treat you like that."

"You're absolutely right. I won't let it happen again."

Jessie ran out of the restroom. A few minutes later she'd reached her motorcycle, mounted it, and started it up. She flinched as the vibration hurt the bruised muscles of her back. A hot shower was definitely in order.

———◆———

Thirty minutes later, she was putting her motorcycle away and then walking into the house. First the hot shower, and then she'd—

The kitchen lights were suddenly blazing, and Brice stood up from the chair where he'd been sitting. "Hello, Jessie. I didn't mean to startle you, but I promised a young woman named Kim I'd take care of you."

Jessie froze. "What are you doing here? I told you I was canceling."

"Yes, but you didn't tell me the truth about why." He walked toward her. "I know how strong you are. You wouldn't have canceled just because you'd had a rough day. You wouldn't have let it beat you. You don't break dates once they're made."

"Maybe I was avoiding you." She was shaking off the surprise. "And how did you get inside?"

"You were wrong. My cat burglar training did come in handy to open those patio doors. Of course, I did watch you when you entered your code into the alarm panel last night. That might have had something to do with it." He grimaced. "I wasn't sure you'd let me in, and I wasn't going to take a chance." He reached out and touched her bruised throat. "Though you might not have been in shape to keep me out tonight. Are you going to tell me how this happened?"

"No, I just want you to go away so that I can shower and get to bed. None of this is your business."

"You lied to me."

"Because I knew you'd probably act like this. It doesn't take a psychic to see that you're instinctively protective. Hell, you got a couple of medals for it in Afghanistan. I can take care of myself, Brice. That's why we were going to have that discussion."

"I thought it was because my career got in your way." He

waved a hand. "But we're not going to talk about either one right now. I'm only interested in seeing that you're okay, like I told Kim."

"Kim?" She frowned. "Who the hell is Kim?"

"The Kim Clarkson you borrowed the phone from in that bathroom. In fact, she was the first one to tell me you'd lied. Before that, it was guesswork."

"But why would she—" Then it all came together. "You noticed the number wasn't mine, and you called it back."

"I was uneasy. As I said, it wasn't like you." He was still touching her bruised throat. "Kim was concerned. She said she told you to stay away from anyone who would do that to you. She said you promised her you would." His lips tightened. "But you won't, will you? Who beat you up, Jessie?"

"I have no idea. He was wearing a mask," she said curtly. "I'll worry about that tomorrow." She wearily rubbed her temple. "Go away, Brice. I want to go to bed."

"I'll leave after I see that you're as all right as you can be." He was nudging her toward her bedroom. "Did anyone check you over? Did you go to the hospital?"

"I didn't need to go. It's not as if I haven't been hurt worse than this before. I'll be fine after a good night's sleep."

"And you didn't report this assault to the police?"

"Of course I did. I had to do it. There was the body . . ."

"Body," he repeated grimly. "Yes, I believe I'm going to have to hear more." They were in the bathroom, and he was turning on the shower. He helped her strip off her clothes and then closed the shower door. "Stay in there as long as you think you need it. After you're done, I'll help you dry off and put some salve on that throat. Then you'll be able to get rid of me."

"You can leave now," she said.

"Not yet. After all, I promised Kim. Besides, I want the details on why you were going to stand me up again. *Complete details.*"

She didn't answer. She could argue with him later. The hot water was running over her and felt wonderful. She arched her neck and moved her head from side to side, stretching the muscles. This was what she'd needed.

She stayed in the shower for over thirty minutes and enjoyed every second of it. Then she turned off the faucet and opened the door.

She was immediately enveloped in one of her huge Turkish body towels as Brice whisked her out of the shower. "Stand still." He dried her off briskly and thoroughly and then wrapped her wet hair in a smaller towel as he helped her on with her terry-cloth robe. "That should do it."

"Are we through?" she asked. "You do know I regard this as an imposition?"

"Goes with the territory." He was leading her out of the bathroom toward the living room and settling her on the couch. "I knew I'd have to come here the minute Kim told me about those bruises."

"You should have left me alone."

He shook his head. "Not possible." He handed her a glass of wine that was on the end table. "Drink this while I'm putting salve on your throat." He took a tube out of his pocket. "It's a very good salve. I use it a lot while I'm on location and end up with nasty bruises myself. Though most of them are not deliberately inflicted...I hope."

"I have my own salves."

"And I'm sure they're excellent," he deadpanned. "They'd have to be. But try mine. It was concocted by a stuntman who'd been in the business for three decades. That should give you a sense of confidence. You told me you've done some stunt work yourself." He was rubbing the salve gently on her throat. "And while I'm doing it, you can start telling me how the hell this happened so that you can get rid of me as soon as possible."

"Or I can just say nothing."

"But then you might have a very long massage. Get it over with. I can be very determined." He met her eyes. "I need to know this, Jessie."

"No, you don't. You're just curious." She shrugged in frustration. Oh, well. "If it will get you out of here." She quickly and as succinctly as possible filled him in on what had happened over the past few hours. Then she drained her glass of wine and looked at him defiantly. "Satisfied?"

"No." He refilled her glass. "But I don't believe I'm going to get any other information unless I dig a little deeper. You were alone tonight? Do you always work alone?"

"Not always. Frequently. Sometimes I work with Kendra and Lynch."

"Not with the police?"

She raised her brows as she shook her head. "That's why they call us private investigators."

"You'd have been safer if there had been someone with you." He was frowning. "You almost died because you were there alone. I think you should work with someone. You need a buddy system."

"You've got to be joking. Usually, I have no problem." She stared at him. "I had no problem tonight. I got away from him, didn't I?"

"But you almost didn't. Next time it might be different." He was thoughtful. "And he wanted to kill you. He told you that he did. He wanted you to be there. Why?"

She shrugged. "Any number of reasons. He might have thought I was dangerous to him. Or sometimes a killer decides to target a person because they want to punish someone close to them. Or else they want to warn someone to back off when they're getting too close." She paused. "This man was... different. There was an ugly viciousness from the minute he came out of that door. He thought he had us trapped, and he was terribly angry that I went after him there at the end. He wanted to strike out at me any way he could. He said he'd kill me and everyone close to me. I think he meant it."

Brice was studying her expression. "Everyone close to you," he repeated. "That bothered you. Everyone has friends. But what about your relatives? Do you have anyone close in this area?"

"Not really. Only my father in the high desert. No one would want to take him on." She frowned. "But why am I thinking about myself? I know that bastard was definitely also aiming for Jennifer. Maybe he killed her as a warning to Carl

Ferris to cooperate. Or she might have died because she was talking to me."

"I'm sure you could go on and on," he said, "but I'd prefer you didn't. It only convinces me you should get a buddy to cover your back. When is your friend Kendra supposed to return from that conference?"

"A couple weeks. But I can't count on her. This is my profession, Brice."

"I understand. I just wish you could wrap up this case and go on to something less lethal."

"That's none of your concern."

"It might be." He asked suddenly, "Why don't I fill in with buddy duty for a few days until Kendra comes back?"

Jessie's mouth dropped open. "That has to be the most terrible suggestion of the century. The reason you were coming tonight was to end this disastrous relationship."

"No, it wasn't. We weren't in agreement on that subject. And I don't want you to get killed before I find out if I'm right and you're wrong."

"I already know that I'm right," Jessie said. "Go home, Brice." She got to her feet. "I'm going to bed. Thank you for your help...which I didn't need." She headed for her bedroom. "If you want to be helpful, lock yourself out."

"I'll do that." He was suddenly smiling. "And it's not a bad idea, Jessie. In fact, it's growing on me. We can work this out."

She said firmly, "Goodbye, Brice."

He smiled as he headed for the front door. "Good night, Jessie."

She crawled into bed only a few minutes later and turned off the bedside light. She was exhausted, and she thought she'd go right to sleep but evidently it wasn't going to happen. Her mind was brimming with the events of the evening. The death, the violence, the threat that had so disturbed her. And, of course, Brice with his absurdly dramatic entrance into the evening. *Don't think about him.* There was probably no doubt that he'd try to get his way if he thought he was right, but she had other things to consider.

Brice had been correct: The killer's warning was hanging over her. Because that murderer had walked away thinking he had killed her, but it wouldn't be long until he found out that he'd failed.

And then he'd come after her again.

Or maybe strike first at the person who might hurt her the most. That's what he'd said. She didn't know how soon it would be before he decided who.

Her father was tough; he wouldn't appreciate her interference in his life.

I'll kill you and everyone close to you.

———◆———

CACTUSVILLE, CALIFORNIA
12:15 P.M.

"I'm five miles from town, Dad," Jessie said. "Where do I find you? The workshop or the bar?"

"It better be the bar. You're probably pretty thirsty after that ride from the city. We're almost finished here anyway." He shouted to someone in the background. "Are you an idiot? I told you to use the torque wrench."

"Or not?" Jessie chuckled. "It's okay. I can come to the workshop. I'll grab a water from your fridge."

"The bar," her father said firmly. "The hired help has to know who's in charge here." He ended the call.

Jessie was still smiling as she made the turn into the desert town of Cactusville. Her father had never gotten over the military training and discipline of his long army career even after he'd retired to this small town. He'd opened a motorcycle repair shop that was now known statewide and had a waiting list that was impressive. But he'd insisted on hiring only locals and training them to his specifications, which could sometimes be a bit traumatic to all concerned. Whether it was a high school kid out to make a little extra money or a drifter who thought he was just passing through, by the time her father had finished with them, they were experts...whether they liked it or not. She'd gone through that tyranny herself and had a moment of sympathy for the idiot who had picked up the wrong tool.

The small bar was straight ahead, and she could hear the sound of the music from the jukebox blaring inside. She pulled up beside an ancient tan Toyota and turned off her bike. She was already taking off her helmet when she entered the bar. The cool dimness felt wonderful.

"I ordered you a beer," her father called from a booth in the back. "But what kind of fool would ride her Harley here at this time of day? It's pushing a hundred."

"I started early. It felt good then." She leaned over and kissed his cheek. "And I'm glad to see you, too." She sat down and took a long drink of her beer. "This tastes wonderful. Thank you."

"Because I'm right," he said sourly. "You should have melted into the tarmac."

"Of course you're right. I don't know how I made it through Afghanistan without you. It was a little hot there, too."

"I don't know either," he said gruffly as he reached out and took her hand. "I guess you were just lucky."

"That must be it." She leaned back, studying his face. "You look great. How do you feel?" It was the truth, she realized with relief. He appeared as strong and vigorous as usual, far younger than his fifty-nine years. An old war wound left him with a slight limp, but his brown eyes were clear and alert.

"How should I feel? I have everything I want here." He suddenly grinned. "They're even considering making me mayor of the town. They think, if I could run an army, I should be able to keep this little burg functioning."

"Are you going to do it?"

"Probably not. I'm too lazy. And I might not have time to go fishing with you when you come visiting." He took a swallow of his beer. "Is that why you're here, Jessie?"

His tone was definitely mocking, and she tilted her head. She knew that tone, and her dad almost always had an agenda when he used it. "I think you know it isn't... General. But I'm curious about what you believe I'm doing here."

"I'm not sure. You have to remember I'm just an old

soldier who's a little out of touch. You wouldn't be trying to manipulate me, would you?"

She snorted. "Machiavelli couldn't manipulate you."

"I hope not. He had no scruples." He smiled. "That's something you have in spades, Jessie. But you've always been competitive and intelligent and ready to take the initiative if you see the need. I've always been aware that I might someday become the object of that initiative. You care about me. I can remember when your mother was dying, and you were going to every specialist on the planet trying to save her. You were only a teenager, but you wouldn't give up." He paused. "You couldn't save her, though, and neither could I. And I don't need you to save me. But I'm wondering why you might think it necessary."

"I wouldn't insult you by thinking you can't take care of yourself." She hesitated. "I just wanted to make sure every-thing was good with you. I'm working a new case, and the killer didn't directly attack the logical victim but someone they cared about."

"And it triggered an alarm?" He smiled wryly. "Of course it would. Well, now you've warned me. I'll be on the alert for any bad guy that drifts by. I like my life, and I've no intention of bowing out prematurely. Besides, it's not many parents who have a daughter as interesting as you. I have to see what you'll come up with next." His smile faded. "But the question is, are you also the logical victim?"

"No, of course not," she said quickly.

He gazed at her. "Then why do I have Jake Brice working on that motorcycle in my shop? He could ruin it."

She froze. "Jake Brice? What do you mean?"

He shrugged. "You said you started early. He started earlier. He pulled into my driveway at six fifteen this morning."

"On a motorcycle?" she asked blankly.

"No, in that piece of Toyota junk outside. He must have gone to a lot of trouble to find a car that old and decrepit. I can see why he might want to be incognito, but I told him he could have struck a middle note."

"You know who he is?"

"Doesn't everybody? I liked that last superhero movie he made." He grinned. "He reminded me of me in my prime."

"I didn't send him," she said. "I wouldn't do that, Dad."

"He didn't say you did. He just said he'd heard about me and wanted to meet me." His smile widened. "Who wouldn't? Other than that, he said that he'd been a little worried about you on that motorcycle and thought he'd offer you a lift if you had trouble."

"And that's why you said I shouldn't ride the Harley in this heat?"

"It occurred to me he could be right."

"He wasn't. And it wasn't any of his business."

"He thought it was." He shrugged. "Look, he didn't speak about you at any time after telling me why he was here. We talked about a hell of a lot of other things, but I did most of the talking. I like the bastard. We got along fine. He even knows a little about motorcycles." He made a face. "Not a lot. But he was interested in learning."

"He was the one you called an idiot?"

"Yes, he didn't care. He laughed about it. I told him I'd have to be really hard up to ever hire him for the shop."

Yet Brice had managed to establish a connection as he always did, she realized. "Is he still at the shop?"

Her father shook his head. "He's at Lou's Diner. He said he was going to get something to drink so we could have the time alone together."

"How considerate."

"Actually, it was. He knew I'd mention him, and he didn't want to get in our way. He thought you'd be angry." Her dad leaned back in his chair. "So why don't you go to Lou's and have it out with him? I'll tune up your Harley, and after work we can throw some steaks on the grill."

"Sorry, Dad. I can't stay. I'm working a case."

"Is everything okay?"

"Fine." She started to leave and then swung back. "I don't want you to worry. I just felt uneasy and wanted to see you." She nibbled at her lower lip. "But if you decide you ever want to come and visit, I have a spare bedroom."

Her father threw back his head and laughed. "Is that where this was going? You want to protect me in spite of yourself?"

"Maybe. I know it was dumb. I can't help it."

"I know you can't," he said gently. "But I can, and I will. I taught you that a long time ago, but every now and then you slip back. We're both tough cookies, Jessie. We'd both be uncomfortable any other way. Next time just phone me. Okay?"

Ten minutes later, Jessie walked into Lou's Diner.

Brice was sitting at a booth with a tall iced tea on the table before him. He held up his hands. "Busted?"

"Yes, you are." She sat down across from him. "In spades." Her gaze raked him from head to toe. He was wearing boots, jeans, and a worn chambray work shirt open at the throat. He had a black baseball cap pulled over his hair with CACTUSVILLE TIGERS emblazoned on it in red. "What the hell are you doing here? What game are you playing?"

"No game at all." His gaze was on the black-and-white silk scarf around her neck. "Nice touch. I always liked polka dots. Salve work?"

"Yes. I repeat, what game are—"

He was motioning to the waitress. "Donna, could you bring another pitcher of iced tea? Jessie's had a long trip."

"I saw her roar into town," Donna said as she brought over a cup of ice. "Good to see you again, Jessie. Kind of hot day, isn't it?"

Was everyone going to mention that? "I didn't notice. Nice to see you, Donna. How's your daughter?"

"Being a teenager." She turned and went up front as two customers came in the door.

Jessie immediately turned back to Brice. "Making yourself at home? Or researching a movie?"

"You know better than that," he said quietly. "Though if I have to pick, I'd choose option one. Your father's got quite a setup here. This town's almost a throwback to the 'fifties, in the best sense." He smiled. "Though James Mercado is no *Leave It to Beaver* dad. Tough as rawhide. But I bet everyone respects him when they're not intimidated."

"Of course they do," she said curtly. "They respect and understand him. He's built that trust. The last thing he wanted was to settle in a place where he'd have to pretend to be something he wasn't. He'd spent his life in the military barking orders and getting things done. He wasn't going to change after he retired."

Brice nodded. "I got that impression. But he also coaches a high school football team. How did they do this year?"

"They didn't win the regional. But they will next year." She looked at his Cactusville Tigers hat. "Don't tell me he gave you that hat?"

"With scorn and disapproval." He grinned. "He said that stupid streak in my hair was a dead giveaway, and I should cover it with something. So he threw the hat at me. He was already pretty disgusted with my choice of that beat-up Toyota, so I didn't dare refuse. Besides, I decided I like it."

"I'm surprised he didn't try to convince you to get rid of the streak."

"He did, but I told him it just grows back." He shrugged "And he said that he once had a POW in his command who had that problem. By the time he finished telling me the story, he'd forgotten about that stupid streak. Because that led to another story. He's had one hell of a life, Jessie."

"Tell me about it," she said dryly. "I followed him from post to post." She suddenly realized that she was being distracted from his main offense. "He told me that he'd been doing most of the talking. Evidently that was the truth. But you're very good at getting people to tell you things. I'm no chatterbox, but I've noticed you managed to get me to open up when I had no intention to." She paused. "What did you talk about?"

"Everything. Nothing. You?" He shook his head. "I won't deny that I probably know much more about you than I did before I came. But I was careful not to be the one to bring you up in the conversation. I knew that would make you angry. Still, your father loves you and is proud of you, so you kept dropping into his dialogue. I admit I didn't try to discourage him."

"Which would be the same thing."

"Perhaps. But I still claim the high ground."

"How can you claim any such thing? This was an intrusion, Brice."

He nodded. "Yes, but it was done in the most diplomatic way possible. And it's not as if I was spying on you. I wasn't even sure that you'd be coming here today. I just had a hunch. I could see how upset you were about him last night. I was just sort of tagging along in case you needed a hand."

"With my father?" she asked incredulously.

"Well, that was a plus. But since you were concerned about him, I felt I should know something about him. In case I figured a way to help."

"My father won't even consider letting me help. You think he'd let you interfere?"

He shook his head. "I'm still thinking about it." He added quietly, "I meant what I said when I told you that it wouldn't hurt to have a buddy system to help out on this case. The more I thought about it, the more I was worried. I don't like the idea of you working without Kendra and Lynch as your usual backup. I'm not working right now. I've decided you could use me."

"I told you that's the worst idea I've heard in the last decade."

"I think you said century last night. I must be making progress. You'll get used to it." He smiled cheerfully. "I'll audition for you. I'm great at auditions."

She had a sudden memory of Brice a few nights ago in her exercise room.

Brice must have been reading her expression, because his smile was now purely mischievous. He shook his head. "I'm good at auditioning," he said softly. "But I'm better at performance."

She jumped to her feet. "Whatever it was, it's history." She turned toward the door. "I'm going to try to get over being pissed off at you, Brice. Because I believe you had good intentions. But this is my job, my case, and I'll handle it myself. From now on, stay away from my father, and stay away from me."

"I don't know if I can do that, but I'll consider it. I really am worried, Jessie." He leaned back in the booth and sighed. "I guess that means I'm not supposed to show up at the barbecue tonight?"

Of course her father had invited him, she thought resignedly. "Be my guest. I've already told him I won't be there."

"Why not?"

"I have a job." She headed for the door. "Right now, I need to go talk to my client. But enjoy your steak."

CHAPTER

4

Jessie rang the doorbell and then banged on the front door of the stately one-story house in the upscale Pacific Palisades community where Owen Blake lived. Darkness had just fallen on the neighborhood, which was eerily still compared with the hustle-bustle almost everywhere else in the surrounding area.

She heard footsteps, and Jessie stepped back so that the occupant could get a good look at her through the peephole. The door finally opened to reveal Owen Blake, wearing sweatpants and a T-shirt.

"I've been trying to get hold of you all day," he said. "You were supposed to report back to me after you talked to Jennifer Dayton. Next thing I hear, she's dead."

"I know. I was there when it happened."

His annoyed expression morphed into something at least close to concerned. "Are you all right?"

"Fine, but I've been busy. There were things I had to take care of. Nothing went well last night."

A look of dread crossed his face. "Did you find out something about Carl?"

"No. Nothing about your partner."

"Jessie, do you want to come in?"

"No."

Owen stepped out of his house and pulled the door closed behind him. "What happened?"

Jessie gave him an abbreviated version of the evening's events. As the words tumbled out, it felt as unreal as it had when she'd told the police the night before. She was glad she hadn't told her dad.

After she finished, Owen shook his head. "Wow. I'd say you earned your padded expenses for the day."

"Yeah. Funny thing is, I told only one person I was going to visit her. That was you."

"Me?" Owen laughed.

Jessie didn't laugh. "Yeah. I didn't tell anyone else."

"You think I killed her?" His smile faded. "Is that why you came here?"

"I came here because it's easier to see if I'm being lied to."

Owen stared at her in disbelief. "Now you're calling me a liar."

"Hey, it's better than a killer. I know you didn't pull the trigger. The guy had abs you could only dream about. But you could have sent someone. Or told someone, even quite innocently."

"I told no one."

"You were extremely interested in what I was doing yesterday. Why?"

"Why not? I'm a hands-on kind of guy. Ask anyone I work with. Isn't it the same with your other clients?"

"No. Almost none. They want results. They don't breathe down my neck unless they have a reason."

"I gave you my reason. I like to be kept in the loop." He shook his head. "I can't believe this. When I hired you, I didn't expect to be accused of murder."

"I didn't expect to see one, much less almost be one. Who did you tell about our conversation yesterday afternoon?"

"No one."

"Are you sure?"

"Positive. I was in my car. It was one of half a dozen calls I made on my way home from the office. I honestly didn't give it much thought after we spoke."

Jessie looked at him for a moment longer. She didn't think he was lying, but that still didn't mean she totally trusted him. "I almost died last night. Is there something else about this case I should know? Something you haven't told me?"

"Like what?"

"You tell me. I need to know what I'm up against."

"If I knew the answer to that, I wouldn't have hired you. I just want to find out what happened to my partner." He paused. "But you just said something that rang a bell for me. About how he wouldn't want anyone to know if he and Jennifer were married."

"I figured he's a player."

"That's true. But it's more than that. He was a secretive guy. He doesn't want me talking to a lot of his clients."

"Why not?"

"I'm not sure. In the beginning, we would both work with everyone. We each had our specialties, so it made sense for us to work together for each client and divide up our duties. It's still that way, for the most part. But in the past few years, there have been some clients he hasn't wanted me to have any direct contact with. We had some arguments about it."

"Did he tell you why?"

"Not really. It's not unusual for partners in a firm to be possessive over top clients, but there's been no rhyme or reason to the clients Carl chose to corner for himself. But the work got done, so I never made a big fuss about it."

"I'd like a list of those particular clients."

"No problem. They're in the client list I gave you, but I'll point out the ones he was secretive about. You've probably already looked at one of them."

"Which one?"

"Colin Sackler. He's the guy Carl visited right before he disappeared."

Jessie raised her eyebrows in interest. "The armed robber?"

"He was caught trying to hold up a financial services firm in West L.A. Anyway, he was one of Carl's special clients, all his own."

"Sackler's at Twin Towers?"

"Just for a few more days. He's about to be transferred to Tehachapi to serve his sentence. I've been familiarizing myself with his file. Since Carl is gone, I'll have to go see him in the next couple of days."

"Don't do it before I go."

Owen looked at her for a long moment. "When will that be?"

"Tomorrow morning. Make a call to grease the wheels for me, will you? Say I'm doing it on behalf of your firm."

"I'll call and put in for a visitor pass right away."

"Thanks."

"I won't ask what you think you're going to find out from him."

"Good, because I don't really know." Jessie turned and headed toward her parked motorcycle.

"Shit," he whispered.

She turned back. "What's the problem?"

He jiggled the doorknob. "I locked myself out."

"Stand back." She quickly walked back toward the door.

He held up his hands. "You're not going to kick it in. I spent a lot of money on this door. It was imported from Spain."

"Relax. This seems to be my week for locks." She pulled a thin leatherette case from her inside jacket pocket and slid out two rigid wire lockpicks. She went to work on the knob and opened his door in under ten seconds.

He gave her an impressed nod. "Wow. This lock's supposed to be pick-proof."

"There's no such thing." She pocketed the leatherette case. "But this is a good lock."

"It couldn't stop you."

"No." She smiled. "I guess that must mean I'm just that good. I'll be in touch, Owen."

———◆———

JESSIE'S HOME
12:35 A.M.

By the time Jessie arrived home and put away her motorcycle, her email inbox contained a message with a list of Ferris's "special" clients, most of which she'd already researched. She spent over an hour looking for any similarities among them. Other than the fact that they were mostly sentenced to medium- and high-security prisons, there was no obvious common ground.

Jessie's phone rang. She'd downloaded her cell phone's backup files from the cloud and was now making do with her sluggish older device. She recognized the number on her screen and answered it. "Hello, Brice."

"Hello. Your father grills a mean porterhouse."

"You actually stayed?"

"Of course. I didn't want to be rude, unlike some people I know. I just got home."

She shook her head. Unbelievable. "What did you talk about?"

"Lots of things. Motorcycles. Music. The headstrong woman in our lives. How's your case going?"

"I meant what I said. Stay out of my business. I'm beginning to feel stalked. You went out of bounds today."

"I probably did. But I had a reason," he said soberly. "I don't have that many people that I'm close to, and I'm scared shitless when there's a chance I might lose one. I've lost too many already. I've never been able to step back because the rules say that I shouldn't offend someone's tender feelings. As long as things are great, I can be cool. But things aren't great, and you were shutting me out."

"And I'll continue to do it. I take care of my own business."

"And so does your dad, but you got on your Harley and rode down there to make sure he was okay and would stay that way." He paused. "The two of you have this independent stuff going on, but I bet you weren't happy when you left him tonight."

"He has a right to his own opinion and free will."

"Absolutely. But I have a right not to have to worry about you, or the way you're feeling about him, if there's anything I can do about it. So I told you that I'd think about solutions, and I did."

"Yes?" she said warily.

"When I was making *Sun Comet* in Russia two years ago, the insurance companies were going nuts because I'd had threats. They wanted to load me down with security. And I was too arrogant to want them trailing after me when I could take care of myself. So we came to a compromise. They hired John Brenner. He was an expert with assholes like me. A complete chameleon who could fade into the background with no trouble, but who also had been trained by the CIA and would be able to spot a shady character from miles away. He worked as a cameraman when I was on location in Moscow.

No one believed he was anything else. But before the shoot was over, he'd managed to arrest a felon who was planning to kidnap me."

"And what does that have to do with me?"

"I called John when I got back today and hired him to act as bodyguard for your father."

"Are you crazy? Cactusville is a small town. There's no way that he won't stick out like a sore thumb."

"Wrong. I told you, he's a chameleon."

"I won't be involved in this insanity," she said flatly.

"You don't have to be. If we get caught, blame it on me." He paused. "But we won't get caught, and your father will be safer, and you'll be better able to sleep at night."

"It's not going to change anything."

"I believe it will, eventually. You're a reasonable woman. We're very good together. And I'm very patient."

"Not," she said definitively. "I don't want to be your buddy just because you're worried I can't handle my job. The entire idea is ridiculous."

"I believe you handle your job beautifully. I'm the one who's having trouble. I admit I'd much rather we spent the entire time hanging out in the gym, but I don't think I could convince you of that."

"You wouldn't. I'm going to hang up now."

"Wait. What are you going to be doing tomorrow?"

"What I should have been doing today. Following up with my job and trying to get a lead on my missing person. Good night!"

"That doesn't sound too dangerous. Good night. I'll be

keeping an eye out just to make sure that you're safe, but you won't hear from me as long as everything appears to be going well. But if you have a problem, just give me a call, and I'll be there for you."

"I won't call. You haven't been listening."

"I've been listening. But when you go to bed, think about your father and how easy it was to get rid of the problem with no anguished soul-searching about robbing him of his independence. He'll be safe, John will never let him know he's there, and you had nothing to do with it. There's nothing wrong with protecting the people you care about. On the contrary, it's very right."

Brice ended the call.

Jessie stuffed her phone in her pocket and headed for her bedroom. Brice was an idiot and a busybody, and her father was bound to find out who this John Brenner was and be angry with her and everyone involved.

Except Jake Brice. He'd probably be able to talk himself out of the whole mess. He'd had no trouble so far with her father. Well, who *did* he have trouble with? He was the golden boy.

Yet that golden boy had been imprisoned and tortured and seen many of his friends killed around him. Was it any wonder he was ruthless about keeping anyone he cared about safe?

She was making excuses for him. He had no right to interfere in her life. She'd been absolutely correct to call a halt to seeing him.

But when she went to bed, Brice's words were still echoing in her mind.

Your father will be safe. John will never let him know. There's nothing wrong about protecting the people you care about. It's very right.

———◆———

TWIN TOWERS CORRECTIONAL FACILITY
DOWNTOWN LOS ANGELES

Jessie felt her pockets as she walked from the parking lot toward the massive Twin Towers jail. She knew she was only allowed to bring her ID and a key into the facility's visiting area, and she didn't want to fool with a rental locker. She'd deposited her phone, money clip, and ball bearings into her motorcycle's storage compartment, so she was covered. She was wearing her "prison bra," free of any of the wire support structures that might set off metal detectors and that were disallowed in every setting that put her in direct contact with inmates. She didn't think she'd forgotten anything.

She looked up at the complex as she approached. The Twin Towers Correctional Facility, at 1.5 million square feet, was one of the world's largest jails. The six-story white towers were bridged by an almost-equal-size medical building that provided hospital and mental care for L.A. County's inmates.

Jessie walked through the glass doors that would take her to the visitor center, and after a surprisingly fast check-in process, she was escorted to the conference room where inmates normally met with legal counsel. Owen definitely knew which strings to pull for her. It was a simple room, eight by twelve feet, centered by a small table and four plastic chairs.

Jessie sat and waited just long enough to wonder how she'd ever survived in the days before smartphones filled every idle minute. Then the door opened to reveal a guard and an inmate whom she assumed to be Colin Sackler. The handcuffed prisoner was dressed in an orange jumpsuit.

The guard guided Sackler to the other side of the table and threaded a second pair of handcuffs through a thick iron hoop protruding from the tabletop. The guard fastened the cuffs to Sackler's wrists and then left the room.

Sackler stared at Jessie and smiled. He looked more like a blue-collar tradesman than an armed robber, Jessie thought. Sackler appeared to be about fifty, shorter-than-average height, with bushy eyebrows that matched his silver hair. His hands wore calluses and dark fingernail stains that looked like they belonged to an auto mechanic.

"You're not Carl Ferris," he said.

"Were you expecting him?"

"I saw an unfamiliar name from Mamertine. I thought maybe he came and brought an associate." He raised his cuffed hands in an attempt at a wave. "I'm Colin Sackler."

"Jessie Mercado. I'm a private investigator hired by Mamertine. Are you aware that Mr. Ferris has gone missing?"

This instantly got Sackler's attention. He sat up in his chair. "No. I just saw him a few days ago."

"I know. He disappeared right after he left you. No one has seen him since."

"That's too bad." He held up his cuffed hands. "Afraid you can't pin that one on me."

"Wouldn't dream of it."

"Uh-huh. The last time I heard that, I ended up in here."

"Trust me, I'm not looking to jam you up. I just want to find the guy. I'm hoping you can help."

"How?"

"I want to know everything you can tell me about your last conversation with him."

Sackler leaned back and thought about this for a moment. "Maybe we can make a deal. Knock some time off my sentence in exchange for my cooperation?"

"I'm not a cop, Sackler. I can't cut a deal for you. I thought you might want to help Ferris out."

"I barely know the guy."

"Well, you hired him."

"Actually . . . I didn't."

Jessie gave him a curious look. "You're his client, aren't you? He's been making arrangements for you ever since you were sentenced."

"That's correct."

"Then how can you say—?"

"I didn't hire him. I don't know who did. Mr. Ferris just turned up here the day after my sentence came down. He said that an anonymous friend was paying his firm to take care of me. Mr. Ferris told me what his firm did, and he explained that he was going to do everything in his power to make life easier for me, starting now. He arranged for movers to pack up my home, and a paint-and-finishing crew was going to come in and freshen the place up. A property management firm would keep it rented, so that the mortgage, property tax, and insurance would be covered until I get out. Their financial managers would keep all my bills current. And he said his firm has an in-house attorney who would keep my appeals on track. All fees would be taken care of. Sounded like a good deal to me."

"A great deal. That's what Mamertine does. But who do you think this 'anonymous friend' is?"

"No idea."

Jessie leaned forward and half smiled. "Come on. You can't have that many friends who would step up for you like this."

"To tell you the truth, I didn't think I had any."

"So you didn't think that was strange?"

"Somebody giving me something for nothing? Of course it was strange. I asked who it was, but he wouldn't say. I let it go."

"Just like that?" Jessie smiled and flipped back her hair. She saw Sackler's eyes light up. Of course. Guys in jail tended to register excitement with even the slightest bit of feminine attention. Something to keep in mind.

"Just like that," Sackler replied. "You know, I'm not exactly in a position to look a gift horse in the mouth."

"If it was me, I'd be doing everything I could to find out who would do this on my behalf. You weren't curious?"

"Yes. My first instinct was to tell him to go to hell. I didn't want to be in the position of owing anybody, you know?"

"You know what it looks like, don't you? Like someone is trying to make things as comfortable as possible for you so you don't rat them out. Like maybe whoever hired you for the job that put you here?"

Sackler's tone became frosty. "No one hired me. The only other person who was in on the job is now dead. Did you even bother to read up on my case?"

"Sure I did. But there's the story that comes out in a trial, and then there's the real story. I want the real story. Who else was in on it?"

"Nobody."

"Throw me a bone, Sackler. A man's life may depend on this."

"I'm telling you, there was nobody pulling my strings. This was entirely between me and Gordon Laney."

"The dead guy."

"Yes."

"Okay. Let's go back. You guys decided to stage an armed holdup of a brokerage firm of all places. Not a bank, not a casino, not anyplace where there's actually a lot of cash. Whose bright idea was it to hold up that place?"

"It was Gordy's. He got a tip that there was a foreign investor who placed big cash deposits with the firm every Tuesday morning like clockwork. It seemed like an easy score. Their security isn't set up to protect against armed robberies. A place like that, it's all checks and wire transfers. But according to Gordy's sources, this investor would bring in three or four hundred thousand cash money every week. Crazy, huh?"

Jessie thought about the million dollars she'd once seen scattered across her desk. "Yeah, crazy."

"We did our homework. We found out where the safe was,

and we mapped out our exits. So we barged into the place with assault rifles and Kevlar armor, and we made the firm's president open the safe for us. But it was empty."

"Your friend got a bum tip?"

Sackler shook his head. "I don't know. Gordy was pretty upset. He made the president give him his car keys. I'm still not sure why. I guess he figured if he wasn't going to get away with the money, maybe he'd get a car out of the deal. Anyway, a second later he got his head blown off by a security guy we didn't know about. He was dressed in a suit like everyone else there. I managed to get away, but the cops got me before the end of the day. They got an ID on Gordy pretty quickly, and I came up on his record as a known associate. Ain't that a bitch?"

Jessie thought about this for a long moment. "Where did Gordon get his tip about the money?"

"No idea."

Jessie shot him a doubtful look.

"I'm serious. But he said he trusted his source, whoever it was."

"Okay, Sackler. Let's get back to the last conversation you had with Carl Ferris. As far as we can tell, you were the last person to see him. What did you talk about?"

"He was just giving me an update. After my conviction, they decided my new permanent home will be the state prison in Tehachapi. They're finishing up some renovation work, so I'll be here for another few days. Mr. Ferris said my car had been sold, and we got a good price. I have a house in the valley, and he said they're almost finished cleaning it up and getting it on the rental market. If all goes well, it'll be pretty much paid off by the time I get out."

"Lucky you. How long will that be?"

"With good behavior, seven to ten years. I pled it out."

"Not bad. They usually try to charge you for the death of accomplices."

"Hence the plea."

"Did Ferris talk at all about what he was going to do after he left you that day?"

"I don't think so." Sackler thought about it. "He bitched about it being rush hour. I offered to change places with him, and he apologized for the lack of sensitivity." Sackler chuckled. "He's a nice guy. I hope you find him."

"Me too." She leaned close to him. "Do something for me, Sackler. Think some more about that last time you saw him. He may have said or did something that's not occurring to you right now. Something that could be helpful to me. I'll be back in a couple of days."

His face lit up again. "Yeah?"

"Yes. And in the meantime, I'm guessing that Ferris's partner will be taking over your arrangements."

"Fair enough. Just as long as he goes the extra mile for me like Ferris did."

"What do you mean?"

Sackler shrugged. "I was getting harassed by another inmate here, a guy named Davis. Major abuse. I mentioned it to Ferris, and the very next day Davis turned up with two black eyes, a busted nose, and a swollen jaw."

"Ferris made that happen?"

"I hear one of the guards worked him over. And Davis never messed with me again." Sackler chuckled. "He won't come within ten feet of me."

"Do you know which guard?"

"Winston. Shane Winston. Big, burly guy, I sure as hell wouldn't want to go up against him. However it happened, I'm glad Mamertine has my back."

She got to her feet. "Evidently just part of the service. Have a good day, Sackler."

———◆———

Jessie left the jail and rode her motorcycle to the West L.A. neighborhood of Century City. It was an area that had once been part of the massive Twentieth Century Fox studio backlot before being cleaved off and sold to the developers of upscale condos and office buildings. Mamertine Consultants was on the thirtieth floor of a high-rise across the street from Fox Plaza, better known around the world as "the *Die Hard* building."

After checking in with the receptionist, Jessie glanced around the beautifully appointed lobby with its Italian tile, custom wood panels, and dramatic lighting. Business was obviously good.

Owen Blake appeared. "Any news?"

"No. I just spoke to Sackler at Twin Towers. Who's paying his tab?"

"I can't tell you that."

"Sure you can."

"No, I mean I have no idea. Since Ferris disappeared, I've been trying to find that out. It's not in any of his records."

"Try pulling up a check image from the bank."

"There is none."

"Why is that?"

"Cash transaction."

Jessie shook her head incredulously. "Is that how your clients usually pay?"

"Almost never. Well, except for the drug dealers. They're extremely fond of cash."

"Aren't we all." She looked up and around. "I'm sure you have cameras everywhere, right? Can we cross-index his schedule with your security camera footage? Maybe at least get a visual on whoever paid for Sackler's services?"

Owen nodded. "I think we can do that. I'll check with security and get back to you."

"Good. Another question. Did your company ever pay any of the guards at the jail to run forcible interference between your clients and any other prisoners harassing them?"

He shook his head. "That would be illegal. The farthest we'd go would be to offer a protest to the prison authorities on his behalf. Why?"

"Sackler was very grateful to Mamertine for hiring a guard named Shane Winston to use force to get an abusive prisoner off his back."

"I don't know anything about that."

"Ferris obviously did."

He shrugged. "Like I said, we often didn't communicate. But it wasn't in our client agreement."

"That doesn't mean he might not do it. It appears to go along with the philosophy of making prison easier for your clients. I'd like to know more about him."

"I'll help any way I can, but like I said, he can be a secretive man."

"I have some contacts in the administration office at the jail. I'll give them a call when I leave here and see what I can find out. But there is one thing you can do for me: Give me the key to your partner's house."

"You want me to give you . . . ?"

" . . . the key to your partner's house. I assume your office manager has the keys to your houses and cars. Otherwise, how could you abuse your overworked assistants and interns with performing your menial tasks and personal errands?"

"Just so you know, those errands free us up to be more productive and keep the lights on here."

"Right. Key, please. I want to check out his place and see if there's something there that can help me."

"Sorry. It so happens we don't have his key. It's in the custody of an LAPD police detective. He was here just a little while ago, asking me all kinds of questions. He's investigating Jennifer Dayton's murder."

"Detective Wheeler?"

"You know him?"

"Sadly, yes. Our paths have been crossing a lot lately."

"He said that he was going to check out the Ferris house around noon tomorrow, and he needed access."

"Damn."

Owen smiled slyly. "But why do you need a key? You

showed me this morning how skilled you are with locks. You could always bypass the detective and go there today?"

And it was obvious the bastard didn't care how much trouble that might get her into with the LAPD as long as he got his answers ASAP. "I try to work with law enforcement when I can. I'd like to keep my license. I can wait until tomorrow to join him there." She turned to go. "Believe me, I've no desire to take advantage of your services, Owen."

"Just a suggestion." Owen shrugged. "I didn't mean to offend you."

"You didn't." But her dislike for him was increasing, and it was difficult not to show it. "I just wanted to make sure that everything was clear. I'll just settle for a tour of his office. Can you take me back there?"

He hesitated. "I have a client here right now, but sure. This way."

Owen motioned for her to follow him past the reception area and down a long corridor. As they walked, he pointed out the offices along the way. "Our real estate brokers work out of these offices up front. It's a big part of what we do, so most of the traffic is concentrated here."

"Makes sense."

Owen pointed to a pair of offices ahead. "Those are our financial managers' offices, and just beyond that, we have a paralegal and our office manager."

They turned the corner, and the hallway widened to accommodate eight cubicles. "Assistants, bookkeeping, and payroll are here. My office is on the left, Ferris's office is on the right."

Owen's office door was open wide enough for Jessie to see that a middle-aged couple was seated on a sectional sofa. The woman was crying, and the man appeared to be trying to comfort her.

"My newest client," Owen whispered. "He's going away for embezzlement, and his wife can't accept the fact that her life is about to change. I need to get back to them now, but Ferris's assistant can help you." He leaned toward a young woman working at a cubicle. "Sienna, could you come here for a moment?"

The woman stood and joined them. She was a blonde in her early twenties, and she wore her hair in a pixie cut. "Yes?"

Owen gestured to Jessie. "This is Jessie Mercado. She's the investigator we've hired to look for Mr. Ferris. Please show her his office and answer any questions she may have."

"Of course."

Owen grabbed a box of tissues from Sienna's desk and walked to his office. He closed his door behind him.

Jessie turned to Sienna. "I guess emotions can run high in a business like this."

"Understatement of the year." Sienna smiled. "The criers are the easy ones. It's the yellers who scare me. I suggested installing a metal detector in the reception area, but the partners thought it might give off the wrong vibe."

"They might've had a point."

"Maybe." Sienna opened the office door and flipped on the lights. "Here it is, just the way it was when Mr. Ferris walked out the other morning."

Jessie stepped inside. It was a large corner office with

spectacular views of West L.A. and Santa Monica, all the way to the ocean. The desk was larger than any human could possibly need, with a high-backed leather chair and two smaller seats in front of it.

On the other side of the room, a leather sectional sofa set matched the one she'd spotted in Owen's office, offering an informal alternative to the more businesslike desk and chairs.

Jessie turned toward Sienna. "In my experience, it's the assistants who really know what happens in an office. What do you think happened to Ferris?"

"I wish I knew." Sienna walked to his desk, which was populated by a variety of fidget spinner toys. "I do know he was stressed to the max, and I'm not sure why. Things have actually been going well here. He might have been having trouble at home."

"Trouble with Jennifer Dayton?"

"Not that I know of. I always thought she was the kind of woman he should be with. Not like those actresses he liked to date."

"Could he have angered one of those women?"

"Sure. He can be a jerk. I would never date him."

Jessie smiled at the young woman's forthright attitude. "Don't mince words or anything."

Sienna shrugged. "I tell him that all the time. He appreciates straight talk. It's one of his best qualities."

"Good. I appreciate it, too. So how is he a jerk?"

"He can be incredibly self-absorbed. You know the type. And he thinks his time is more valuable than anyone else's. In every area of his life except work, he keeps people waiting, and he almost never apologizes. That's gotten him dumped more than once."

"I can understand that."

"Totally. But he's totally mystified that anyone would ever take offense."

Jessie looked at the freestanding bulletin boards lining one entire wall of the office. The boards were covered with black vinyl. She pulled away one of the vinyl covers and peeked underneath.

"What's this?"

"Info on our clients that we're taking care of while they're away."

"In prison," Jessie said.

"Yes." Sienna smiled. "We're told not to say the *p* word around here, especially when we're with our clients. Apparently, that word makes them uncomfortable."

"Huh."

"Yeah, it doesn't make much sense to me, either. Call a spade a spade, right?"

Jessie flung the vinyl cover back, revealing photos and documentation for Mamertine clients. "I recognize these."

"You probably have most of them on the computer files you were given. I helped Mr. Blake pull them together for you." She flipped back the vinyl cover on another board. "Mr. Ferris likes putting everything up here so he can walk around with his telephone headset on and see all the info with just a quick look. Clients like to think their stuff is always top of mind."

Jessie looked over the boards. "Did he have reason to be afraid of any of these people?"

"I don't think so. Not even from the yellers. There have been some tense phone calls when they can't get a good price on their rental or their cars aren't selling fast enough, but nothing that's had us watching over our shoulders."

Jessie took one last look around the office. As unique as Mamertine's services and clientele were, she was impressed how well-run and *normal* the firm seemed, probably not unlike dozens of other professional businesses in the building.

"Thanks, Sienna. I'll show myself out."

JESSIE'S HOME
9:20 P.M.

Jessie's phone was ringing, and she glanced at the ID.

DELILAH WINTER.

She quickly picked up the call. "Dee? I thought you were on tour. Are you okay?"

"Fine." Then she asked, "Are you at home?"

"Yes."

"Stay there. I'll be right over." She ended the call.

Jessie shook her head. It was an unusual call, but then Dee was always unusual. It didn't necessarily mean anything was wrong. She was one of the world's biggest pop stars and had been since she was a kid of fourteen. At twenty, she was more disciplined than most other artists, and Jessie had always found her totally endearing, even when she'd caused her boundless headaches.

But she was always as good as her word, and she'd said she'd be right there. Jessie hurriedly took off her tank top and grabbed a loose turtleneck that would hide the bruises on her throat.

Ten minutes later, her doorbell rang, followed immediately by a pounding on the door.

When she opened it, Dee rushed into her arms and swung her around in a circle. "You should really give me a key to that front door. How are you? I've missed you. What have you been doing?"

"I've missed you, too." She gave her a hug. Delilah Winter in person was as beautiful as she appeared on concert stages and television appearances, with her milky-white complexion, red hair, and electric gray-green eyes. Even dressed in jeans and a colorful Bohunk T-shirt, she had star power. "What have I been doing? Working. Isn't that what you're supposed to be doing? Why aren't you in San Francisco?"

Dee shrugged. "I finished the North American leg of my tour there last night. I was going to stay a couple of days, but I decided it would be nice to sleep in my own bed." She smiled. "Or I could bunk here with you."

"What?"

"Why not? We haven't been able to hang out together for a long time. I was in Europe and then on tour. I missed you."

"You said that." Jessie smiled. "I missed you, too. But you have a beautiful house in Beverly Hills you could be sleeping in. My place is too small for you. You'd be bored here."

"No, I wouldn't. You do all kinds of interesting things. So where have you been lately? A stakeout?"

"Nah. Just getting Lamar Wood arrested for trying to abduct his own kids."

Dee clutched her chest. "Damn, Jessie. If you make him miss the start of the season, there will be a few thousand Lakers fans coming here to drown you in your canal. I should come here and protect you."

"They'll have to get in line. I don't make many friends in this business."

"Obviously not." She was looking around the living room. "Hey, maybe you can make me some coffee with that Van der Westen Speedster I gave you."

"The what?"

"The coffeemaker. The Van der Westen Speedster."

"I didn't realize that's what it was called."

"Yeah. It sells for twenty thousand dollars, you know."

"*What?* No, I didn't know. I would have made you take it back."

"I didn't pay for it. The company gave it to me for letting *Vanity Fair* include it in a kitchen photo spread I did. Is the coffee any good?"

"Honestly, I haven't had time to work through that huge manual. It looks good on my counter, though. I've still been using my old Keurig."

"Works for me. Let's go get some."

Five minutes later, Dee was holding her hazelnut cream coffee and pacing restlessly around the living room and kitchen of Jessie's house. Dee stopped and looked at the living room wall, which was adorned by what appeared to be a hodgepodge of random objects that included a watchband, a baseball, a cuff link, a coffee mug, and over two dozen other items.

"This wall has grown," Dee said. "So each of these things played a part in solving one of your cases?"

"Yep. Some of the best stuff is still sitting in police evidence rooms, but almost all of my cases are represented here."

"I still don't know why you'd want to bring your work home with you like this."

"I do a lot of my best thinking at home. And these things remind me that a break in the case could come from anything that might catch my eye."

Dee stepped closer to inspect the items. "I recognize some of these things." She suddenly frowned in disappointment. "But what about *my* kidnapping? Didn't that make your wall?"

Jessie smiled as she took a sip from her mug. Dee now spoke so casually about what had been a horrible and traumatic experience, her mid-concert abduction from the Hollywood Bowl just a few months earlier. "I thought I might give you more time to heal before I started putting reminders up for you to see."

"I've healed enough. Put it up, whatever it is. I don't want all the good spots to get taken."

Jessie opened a drawer and produced a brightly colored disposable mobile phone. She tossed it to Dee.

"This? This is the clue that broke my kidnapping case?" Dee looked disappointed.

"This belonged to a member of your stage crew. Adrian Nash."

Dee's eyes widened. "The guy who helped the kidnappers."

"Yep. Kendra Michaels and I had to root through a big barrel of trash in a 7-Eleven parking lot to find the packaging for this phone. We used it to track him down to his RV out in the desert."

"He's dead, isn't he?"

Jessie nodded. "He took a bullet to the brain in the backseat of my SUV. Kendra and I almost died with him. But before that, we got just enough information from him to help find you. You might owe your life to that phone."

"How'd you end up with it?"

"My car was in the shop for weeks, all shot to hell. Over a hundred and sixty rounds. The repairmen found this phone under one of the seats. I figured I could use it for my wall." Jessie unpeeled a Command picture-hanging strip and affixed it to the back of the phone in Dee's hand. She stepped back and motioned toward her wall. "Have at it."

"Really?"

"Yes. Anyplace you want."

Dee walked back and forth, cocking her head as she inspected the wall. She finally placed it slightly right of center.

Jessie nodded her approval. "Good."

"Now maybe you can tell me why some of these other things are here. Like the frozen yogurt container. Or that tube of lipstick."

"Another time."

"Aw, come on . . ."

"I need to review the records of some people involved in a new case I've just taken on."

Dee's eyes lit with excitement. "Tell me about it."

"No."

"Why not?"

"Ever hear of client confidentiality?"

"It's me you're talking to here. I'm practically an employee."

"You're not. You're the head of your own multimedia empire."

"Your job is more fun."

"Fun? Did you hear the part about a hundred and sixty bullets being fired into my car . . . while I was driving it?"

Dee smiled. "Awww. For me, you know you'd do it all over again."

"Maybe. That's beside the point."

Dee looked down at the open front pocket of Jesse's knapsack, where Owen's business card protruded. She pulled it out. "You're working for Mamertine?"

"They're one of my clients." Jessie snatched the card back. "You know them?"

"Of course."

"I'm almost afraid to ask how."

"I've never needed them, but all the celebs use Mamertine when they have to do serious prison time. Remember when the rapper Filler K shot up her boyfriend's house and cut off a couple of his toes with an ax?"

"Who could forget?"

"She went to prison for eight months. Mamertine made all the arrangements for her. Then, when said boyfriend got revenge by burning down Filler K's mother's house, he got sentenced to fourteen months."

"Another Mamertine client?"

"You know it. By the way, Filler K and the boyfriend are getting along great now. I had them over to the house right before I left on tour. They're trying to have a baby."

"Such a sweet story."

"Love conquers all. You can hardly even notice the boyfriend's limp."

Jessie smiled as she pocketed the card. "I obviously need to bone up more on Mamertine and their clients. Which is why you need to go home."

"Okay, okay. I'm tired anyway. But I'll be around for the next few weeks in case you need backup."

Jessie laughed at the waif-like teenager standing in front of her. "Backup? How exactly would that work?"

"Don't be so scornful. I've got about a dozen badass three-hundred-pound security guys on my payroll for the duration of my tour. Until we leave for the next leg, they're pretty much doing nothing but eating, working out in my home gym, and playing video games. If you need 'em, they're all yours. *That's* how that works."

Jessie nodded. "Wow. I'm impressed. Generous offer. I'll keep that in mind. Thanks, Dee."

"See! I didn't even say that you had to take me with them. But that might come later. I've been pretty bored lately." Dee pulled out her phone. "I'll text my driver to come pick me up. He's just down the street."

"Okay."

After Dee finished her text, she turned toward the framed photos lining the small foyer. These were more personal than the ones in Jessie's office, mostly featuring friends and family members. A few featured Dee herself, but several included Jessie with a handsome, bespectacled man.

Dee pointed to the man. "Are you finally going to tell me who this guy is?"

"No. Your driver is waiting."

"I pay him to wait. That's what he does. Who's the guy?"

"Nobody special. I've been meaning to get rid of these pictures as soon as I find some others that fit these frames."

"Bullshit. You give prime placement to all his pictures, and your ceiling spotlights are aimed right at him. It's a good thing I have a strong sense of self, because all my pics are in the shadows."

Jessie reached forward and swapped one of Dee's pictures with one that featured the bespectacled man. "There. Happy now?"

"That isn't the point. The point is, who is this guy?"

"Let it go, Dee."

"Why? Is he dead?"

Jessie laughed at the bluntness of her question. "What if he was? You'd feel pretty bad about badgering me about him."

"Not really."

"He isn't dead. Sometimes I might wish he was, but no, he's not. At least I don't think he is."

"Now we're getting somewhere. Well, since you won't tell me about him, who else is in your life lately? You never talk about anyone. It gets very frustrating when I'm an open book."

"A fascinating book, which is why you're on magazine covers every week. My life isn't worth talking about."

"I think it is." She was suddenly no longer smiling. Her expression was dead serious. "Murder. Death threats, Jessie?"

And that was the reason for Dee's sudden visit, Jessie realized. She grimaced. "Shit, I was hoping you hadn't heard about that nonsense. How did you learn about it?"

"Pauley, one of my bodyguards, is an ex–LAPD cop. He still has buddies on the force. He thought I'd be interested."

"He shouldn't have told you. I'm perfectly safe."

"How do I know that?" Dee asked. "How can anyone know? I think I was right to try to get you to let me stay here. That's what we should be doing." She added soberly, "All the time I've known you, I've thought you were a combination of Wonder Woman and Electra. When you'd let me go to those movie stunt jobs of yours, you dazzled me. But maybe even Wonder Woman could use a hand occasionally. I want to be here for you."

Jessie was touched, even as she felt frustrated. It was getting pretty bad when even Dee thought she had to protect her. She forced a smile. "So that I'd have to worry about you getting kidnapped again? I appreciate the thought, but I'm in no danger. And you're much safer at your place." Jessie opened the front door for her. "The only thing we should be doing is getting you into your car and back to your mansion and your three-hundred-pound security guys."

Dee raised her hands in surrender. "Fine. But this isn't over."

"It definitely is."

Dee stepped outside. She lingered for a moment before turning back around. "I've missed you, Jessie. It's good to see you, even if you're not being reasonable." She stepped back inside and hugged her.

Jessie squeezed her tight. Dee was adored the world over and partied with movie stars, pop icons, and royalty, yet there was always an undercurrent of loneliness there. "We'll get together again soon, I promise."

"We better. It hasn't been the same since you walked out on me."

"I'm always here for you, Dee."

"Yeah, I know." Dee made a face. "I just want it all. One of these days..." Dee nodded and turned and walked toward the street, where an SUV was waiting for her. But she stopped on the corner and called back, "But it *really* isn't over, Jessie."

And it might not be, Jessie thought as Dee got into the car. Dee could be very determined, and she was no longer the immature teenager she'd been when Jessie had first taken the job with her.

She could only hope that Dee got so busy with her frenetic lifestyle that she forgot about anything else.

Not likely.

Her phone was ringing. Brice. Another check-in call. Suddenly the frustration she was feeling about Dee erupted and boiled over. "I'm fine," she said curtly when she took the call. "I might not be Wonder Woman, but I'm fully capable of taking care of myself and my career. And I don't need you or anyone else to give me aid or assistance."

Brice gave a low whistle. "Bad day? Wonder Woman? You must tell me about it sometime, but this obviously isn't the moment. Since it sounds more like exasperation, rather than threat, if you need someone to talk to, give me a call." He cut the connection.

He hadn't given her the opportunity for more than that brief explosion, and he hadn't said anything to increase her sense of frustration with him and the situation. He had actually been sympathetic. Somehow that signaled a triumph for him. She shouldn't have taken the call.

Because he'd probably call again tomorrow.

CHAPTER

5

A s promised, Carl Ferris's house was less than ten minutes' drive from Owen's office. It was a beautifully landscaped two-story home with plantation shutters and a white picket fence that, upon closer inspection, was made of solid iron.

Only in L.A.

The driveway gate was open, and Jessie could see Detective Dan Wheeler's car parked near the house's side entrance. Jessie parked her Harley behind it and ran to the double-door main entrance. She pressed the doorbell button and heard chimes play the song "Jailhouse Rock" inside.

Cute.

After a moment, she rapped on the door.

No answer.

She tried it, and it was open. She stepped inside. "Wheeler?" she called out. "It's Jessie Mercado."

Wheeler stepped into a doorway, holding his service revolver. He cursed and holstered the gun.

"Really?" Jessie stared at him in disbelief. "Expecting a ground assault, Wheeler?"

He looked a little sheepish. "It's a murder case, after all. I wasn't expecting you."

"Why not? Just one more item on the missing persons checklist. I assume that's why you're here?"

"You assume correctly."

"Find anything?"

"Like a yellow legal pad with detailed handwritten plans about where he's going and what he's doing while the rest of the world thinks he's missing?"

"Yeah."

"No, I didn't find anything like that."

"Maybe you didn't look hard enough."

He gestured toward the house behind him. "Be my guest."

Jessie walked past him and toured the two-story house, which, like many upscale houses she'd visited, seemed more like a showplace than a comfortable, lived-in home. Imported tile or high-density wool carpeting in every room, along with wallpaper and patterned ceilings that were custom all the way. The kitchen was breathtaking, centered by sixteen burners spread across two massive Wolf cooking ranges, replete in all their chrome, black, and red-knobbed splendor.

Wheeler shook his head. "I bet that those things cost more than my car."

"Probably. But try cooking dinner for two hundred with

106

your SUV." Jessie started opening the cabinet doors, peering inside, and closing them before moving on to the next.

"What are you looking for?"

"This." Jessie reached into a cabinet, pulled out a waste can, and turned it upside down. Nothing dropped out. "Empty."

"Too bad," Wheeler said. "I hear you do some of your best work in garbage cans."

"Hey, whatever it takes. This place is clean. Really clean."

"Maid service comes every morning. We're bringing them in for a statement today or tomorrow."

"Good." She put the can back into its cabinet. "So what's the backyard like?"

"I'll show you. It isn't exactly understated."

He led her through an atrium that opened out to a large rock-lined pool with fountains firing twenty feet into the air.

She turned from the fountains. "Unless there's blood on the pavers, I've seen enough."

"No blood on the pavers."

They walked back into the house.

"Okay, so this was a bust," Wheeler said. "Owen Blake told me you went to Twin Towers yesterday to talk to their client. I don't suppose he had any idea where Ferris went."

"No." Jessie stared at a small, carpeted reading nook just off the atrium. It had been freshly vacuumed, like every other carpet in the house. "Let's go back into the study."

"Why?"

"Maybe nothing."

They retraced their steps to the ground-floor study, a room covered by a handwoven Chinese carpet. The rest of the décor picked up the Asian influence, even to the stately desk with its inlaid panels.

"Interesting," she said.

"Is it?"

Jessie knelt to get a closer look at the rug. "Every other room has been swept by what looks like a big industrial vacuum cleaner. Always in a grid pattern, left to right and back again. That isn't the case here. It's much more haphazard, like the way I vacuum."

"Me too."

"For some reason, someone else vacuumed this rug. And they used a smaller machine than was used everywhere else."

"There's a vacuum cleaner in the utility closet next to the laundry room."

Jessie nodded. "I know. And it seems like it might be the right size. Would you mind getting it for me?"

"Sure."

"And Wheeler... You probably shouldn't touch the handle in case there are some prints on it."

He held up his gloved hands. "Give me some credit, Mercado." He left the room and was back in under a minute with the Hoover upright vacuum cleaner Jessie had seen in the closet.

He placed it next to the carpet, and it lined up perfectly with the vacuum impressions there.

Jessie carefully opened the vacuum cleaner's vertical compartment and removed the dirt bag. She pulled the knife from her pocket, opened it, and sliced open the bag. It was filled almost entirely with dust, but scattered throughout the bag was a thick, red sparkly material.

"What is that?" Wheeler said.

"Beats the hell out of me." Jessie raised the bag to look closer.

Wheeler reached into his jacket's inside pocket and produced a plastic evidence bag. "I'll take this in and have the lab give it a look."

Jessie put the bag down and pulled out her phone. She photographed the strange red material from different angles and focal lengths. "Okay."

Wheeler scooped it up and placed it inside the plastic evidence bag. He smiled. "Jessie, you managed to have us wallowing in the dirt after all."

Jessie winked. "Just stick with me, Wheeler. Always an experience."

———————

Jessie left Ferris's house with Wheeler a short time later and waved to him as she pulled on her helmet and hopped on her motorcycle. She raised her phone and took one more look at the photos she'd taken. What in the hell was this stuff?

She trusted Wheeler to check it out, but she also knew that the LAPD crime lab could easily get backed up for weeks or even months. She'd been involved in more than one case in which the forensics report landed long after the perps were in custody. She needed to think of someone who could look at her pics and give her a quick answer.

Jessie started her motorcycle and roared out of Ferris's neighborhood. She headed west on Pico Boulevard while she cycled through her mental Rolodex of possible consultants. She knew people at USC and Cal Tech, but she wasn't sure if a photo would be enough. She cursed herself for not snatching a sample from the vacuum cleaner bag. Damn.

The traffic sounds around her suddenly grew louder, as if someone had turned up the world's volume. The colors were more intense. What in the hell?

She checked her rearview. It appeared as if all the cars were lining up behind her, synchronized in pursuit.

What was happening?

Her motorcycle's roar was deafening. The vibration felt as if it would shatter every tooth in her mouth.

Her stomach churned. Her nostrils burned.

But she had to get away from all those cars that were chasing her.

Wait. Was one of the cars actually flying?

She gunned her engine and wove between the lanes of traffic. Shit. All the cars up ahead were now swelling two or three times their normal size, making them impossible to pass.

What in the holy hell?

Suddenly she couldn't hear anything but her heart pounding in her ears. Her motorcycle had left the road, she realized. But she wasn't flying, which meant—

Wham! Darkness.

Sky. Clear blue sky.

"Ma'am? Stay with me, ma'am." She was vaguely aware of a pair of chubby fingers snapping over her face. "Ma'am?"

With no apparent break in time, she was suddenly in an ambulance, and two EMTs were working... Working on her, she realized. She tried to speak, and only then was she aware she had an oxygen mask over her nose and mouth.

Lights. Fluorescent lights, one row after another, passing overhead. She was on a gurney, being wheeled through a hospital. Couldn't mistake that awful smell.

The fog rolled back over her until she could see and hear no more.

Jessie opened her eyes.

She was still in the hospital, but everything was now quiet except for the occasional beeping of the monitor next to her. She had a splitting headache, but aside from that she felt surprisingly good.

She tried to sit up, but a strong hand pushed down on her shoulder. "Don't even."

She looked up blearily. It was Wheeler. "What happened to me?"

"Just relax."

"What happened to me?" she repeated.

"You've been through a lot."

"And you're starting to piss me off."

He smiled. "Now I know you're going to be okay."

"I need answers, Wheeler."

"You were exposed to a powerful narcotic. A hallucinogen. You cracked up on your bike."

"Wow." She looked at him. "That red stuff we found!"

"I thought the same thing, but no."

"Then what could it be?"

"We found it in your helmet. Someone smeared it right below the nose guard. It's odorless, so there's no way you could have known."

"My helmet?" Jessie thought about this. "I left it on my bike in Ferris's driveway."

"I know. We're going to do a door-to-door to see if any of the neighbors saw something."

"Good luck with that," she said sarcastically.

"I know, I know. But everybody has exterior security cameras these days, so we have a shot of catching it on video."

She nodded. "I gotta tell you, that's some freaky stuff. I thought cars were actually flying."

"Flying? Maybe I should try some of that."

"Trust me, you don't want anything to do with it." She patted her arms and legs. "But I feel surprisingly good for having just put my bike down."

"You don't know?"

"Know what?"

He hesitated. "According to witnesses on the scene, you were going about three miles an hour when you had your accident."

She stared at him. "Three miles an hour?"

"You crossed two lanes of traffic and put your bike down in front of a pickup truck. It ran over your back wheel."

"Three miles an hour? I thought I was flying."

"I'm sure you did," he said dryly.

"That's kind of embarrassing."

"Not at all. You'd been drugged. We figured that's when you finally lost consciousness."

"Unbelievable. Why would anyone bother doing that to me? A bullet would have been a lot more effective."

"Maybe they wanted it to look like an accident. If you'd been killed, that's probably what we would all still think." He paused. "That's the second time, Jessie. You said that being with you was always an experience, but this is over the top. Do you know something you're not sharing with me?"

She shook her head. "This is all crazy. I need to get the hell out of here."

"Tomorrow at the earliest."

"Oh, come on. I feel fine."

"They want to hold you for observation."

"Observation? I haven't seen a nurse or doctor since I woke up."

"They're steps away. This is the best place for you right now."

"I disagree." She pulled her covers off before she realized that she was wearing only a gown that had been hiked up almost to her waist.

Wheeler held up both hands as if he'd been struck by a blinding light. "Whoa, whoa!"

She pulled the covers back over her. "Calm down. Where are my clothes?"

"Still down in the ER?"

"That's not how it works. They're either in that cabinet over there or in a tray under this bed. Will you help me?"

"At least let a doctor see you before you bolt."

"Then get one in here fast."

Wheeler walked to the door and turned back toward her. He held up his hand. "Stay, Mercado."

"I'm not a dog, Wheeler. Ten minutes."

He vanished. The minute he was out the door she got up and was heading for the cabinet. It was a good guess. She pulled out her clothes, carried them back over to the bed, and started to change into them. After she was dressed, she turned in a slow circle to see how steady she was. No problem. No dizziness, though she still had the headache. But even that was beginning to fade now. No perceivable damage from the drug, though its after-effects on that crowded freeway might have been fatal. It was clear somebody out there didn't like her...or what they thought she might find out.

Tough. She was definitely beginning to get pissed off. She was tired of being a target because of Carl Ferris.

———◆———

JESSIE'S HOME
8:05 P.M.

Jessie had just opened her refrigerator to see what she could find to eat for dinner when her phone rang.

She glanced at the ID and inwardly groaned. Dear God, it was Dee. Not a good omen after the day she'd had.

"Are you all right?" Dee demanded. "I knew I shouldn't have listened to you."

"I'm absolutely fine," Jessie said. "Who told you?" She was searching for a name. "Pauley with the LAPD? Well, his contacts should have told him that the hospital released me right away. I'm home and had a shower to wash off that hospital smell, and now I'm going to have a bite to eat and then get back to work." She added, "And you have to stop worrying, and give Pauley another assignment that doesn't involve his old pals with the LAPD."

"I wouldn't have known except for Pauley. You wouldn't have told me."

"Exactly. Because there was nothing to tell." She drew a deep breath. "Dee, you and I both have our jobs to do, and we shouldn't mix the two. I wouldn't get up on the stage at the Hollywood Bowl and start belting out rock tunes."

"I might pay to get in, if you did," Dee said. "And that has nothing to do with this. This is about friendship and taking care of each other. I don't want to hear about anything like this happening again. Just be kind to them." She ended the call.

Be kind to them? She frowned in total confusion until she heard the doorbell.

Panic shot through her. Oh, shit, Dee wouldn't have done it, would she?

Jessie threw open the front door.

Four men stood on her doorstep. Dee hadn't exaggerated:

They were all giants on the scale of The Rock, and they each could well have been nearly three hundred pounds. They were dressed in sweatpants and T-shirts and were looking at her with cheerful grins.

One man with a blond crew cut and bright blue eyes took a step forward. "I'm George Keller, Miss Mercado." He jerked his thumb at the other men. "Bob Kosack, Bill Lewis, Zach Dacksano. Miss Delilah said this was going to be a surprise to you, but we want you to know that we'll keep you safe. You won't have to worry about a thing." He patted a holstered firearm at his side. "I'm a two-time Olympian. Men's twenty-five-meter rapid-fire pistol. I've never medaled, but there's always next time."

Another man stepped forward. "Bill Lewis. Mixed martial arts. I don't need a gun to protect my clients or myself."

A bald man with even bigger muscles stepped forward. "Bob Kosack. I'm a former professional wrestler, ma'am. Nebraska state champion three years in a row."

The last of the men waved. "Zach Dacksano. No specialty, except that I'm ten years older and twice as strong as any of these doofuses. You'll be safe with me."

George held up a large sack. "And we brought you dinner. Miss Delilah said you liked Pink's." He looked at the other guys. "So do we. But we don't want to be in the way. We'll take our sandwiches out on your patio."

"How...nice." She shook her head to clear it. "But there seems to be a mistake. I don't need you. So you should go back to your boss and tell her thank you, but no thanks." She gestured around the house. "And you can see I don't

116

have room for you, either. Delilah can make you much more comfortable."

"That's not important. We brought sleeping bags. We'll camp out if you don't have room for us." The other men were nodding eagerly. "We promised Miss Delilah we'd keep you safe. She's been real good to us. We'll keep that promise." George added, "You don't have to worry about a thing. Where you go, we go. Anything you want, we'll do."

"I want you to go back to Delilah."

"Except that," he said. "She said that you might not want to accept the favor. But you can see we have to do what she wants."

She could see they were all Dee's devoted employees and probably would lay down their lives for her. Not to mention facing arrest if Jessie called the police to throw them off the property.

And how was she going to do that anyway when these polite bodyguards were gazing at her with those cheerful grins and those Pink's Hot Dogs bags in their hands? Besides the fact that though it wouldn't matter to Dee, the story would be on every channel on tonight's news.

George was gazing at her earnestly. "Everything's going to be all right. Is it okay if we go eat on the patio?"

She threw up her hands. "Sure. Or the dining room. There are sodas and beer in the refrigerator. But don't get too comfortable." She went into the living room and punched in Dee's number. No answer. Straight to voicemail. She left a message. "I may strangle you. I'll give you five minutes to call me back and get these gentle giants out of my house. After that, I'll handle it myself."

Five minutes passed, no return call.

What could she do?

Be kind to them, Dee had said.

And Dee had known that Jessie would blame her and not those bodyguards she'd sent to do her bidding. So she thought she'd virtually tied Jessie's hands and left her with a fait accompli.

No way!

She drew a deep breath and then swiftly punched in the number.

Brice picked up the call on the second ring. "Jessie?"

"You said if I needed you, you'd come. I need you."

"Where are you?"

"Home." She paused. "Be careful. Maybe avoid the patio."

⬥

Jessie had the lights out and the door unlocked when Brice slipped into the living room an hour later. He lit his phone and saw her sitting on the couch across the room. "I thought you might be curled up in here after I searched the grounds and saw your guests outside." He sat down beside her. "Would you like to tell me why you have four gigantic men playing cards on your patio?"

"Because they didn't want to offend me by coming inside. They even have their own sleeping bags." She added between set teeth, "But I want them gone before it comes to that."

"I would think so. They don't appear to be attractive lawn ornaments. Would you care to tell me who they are?"

"My bodyguards."

"I beg your pardon?"

"It's a long story."

"I think I should hear it, don't you?"

"I have a friend who was worried about me and sent her security crew to guard me. It became . . . complicated."

"I already approve of her, but maybe not the complications. I think you'd better elaborate."

But long before the elaborations were completed, Brice was leaning back on the couch laughing, and she wanted to hit him. "It's not funny. I'm furious with Dee. I want to shake her."

"But not enough to hurt her feelings or focus a barrage of publicity on her or her career." He was still grinning. "I've never met your friend Dee, but she must have done something to earn that affection."

"She can be wonderful. When she's not a pain in the ass. She always means well." She shook her head in frustration. "She even asked me to be kind to those guys who have set up a poker night on my patio. She doesn't want me to hurt their feelings. She didn't even think twice about the fact that they're going to be a pain in the ass, too. What am I supposed to do with them?" He was starting to laugh again, and she glared at him. "I didn't bring you here to amuse you. You can leave now."

"I'll stop. It was the idea of you being trailed by that quartet like a puppy with four tails . . ." He was still grinning. "Okay,

119

why am I here?" He added in a guttural, gangster tone, "Am I supposed to break you out of this joint? Do I take those guys on all at once? Or one at a time?"

"Don't be ridiculous. You haven't been paying any attention to me. I'm aiming for subtlety and brains, not brawn. I want to get rid of her crew permanently... and happily."

"And my part in this project?"

"How the hell do I know?" She waved a vague hand. "You're this beloved superstar who works with casts of thousands. You must deal with security crews like this all the time. You even had that chameleon character John Brenner you sent to my dad on speed dial."

"How did that work out?"

"I have no idea. I haven't heard anything about him from Dad."

"Then it went very well?"

"I guess." She returned to the main subject. "I've dealt with security teams myself, but you have to have more experience."

"So I'm elected."

"If you choose to accept. Otherwise I'll find another way."

"I choose to accept." He added thoughtfully, "But it's going to be a challenge..." His face was suddenly lit with humor. "And maybe a hell of a lot of fun."

"I'll settle for the challenge." She was gazing at him warily. "You have an idea?"

"Maybe. But I'll have to see if it grows on me. I believe the first thing will be for you to take me out to the patio and introduce me." He was looking around the dark room. "But I'm not impressed by your bodyguards at the moment. They let me sneak in here while they were out on the patio playing cards."

"I've been going back and forth to the kitchen and letting them see me until you got here. They know nothing has happened to me."

"And you're defending them?"

"What can I say?" She shrugged. "They brought me hot dogs from Pink's."

When Jessie opened the patio door with Brice in tow, there was a sudden silence. Then there was a low whistle. "Shit, it's Comet Man!" Suddenly they were on their feet and surrounding Brice. Jessie only had time to rattle off their names and say, "Jake Brice. He's a friend who wanted to meet you. He said it was important you got to know each other." But they were ignoring her and crowding around Brice with the enthusiasm of kids at a circus.

Then she took a step back and watched Brice take over the show. He was laughing and talking, just one of the guys, answering questions, telling stories. Listening to their stories. Then suddenly he was sitting down on the patio playing cards with them. He glanced at Jessie as he started to deal. "Want to sit in?"

"No, thanks. You go ahead. I have some work to do." She supposed she should be grateful she'd been included, she thought with amusement. Actually, she was enjoying watching Brice weave his spell. There was no question he was enjoying himself, but there was also no doubt that every one of those guys was going to think that Brice was one of his best pals before he was through. She didn't know where this was going, but she imagined Brice had an idea now. She went back inside and got them all beers before she went to her room to wait.

It was over two hours later that she heard them moving through the house. Laughter. Footsteps. It was clear they were trying to be quiet, but they weren't succeeding. Too many beers?

And they were heading for the gym.

She was too curious not to go see what they were up to.

Three of the guys were sitting on the floor, lounging against the wall.

Brice had stripped off his shirt and was on the mat wrestling with George. As she watched, Brice rolled over and clamped his legs over George's neck.

Shouts. Whistles. "*Comet. Comet. Comet,*" the bystanders were chanting.

Then George was down!

And Brice was laughing as he got to his feet. He saw Jessie leaning against the doorjamb. "Just having a little fun," he said. "We got tired of the usual bets. I'm taking them on one at a time, their choice of martial arts. Anyone who puts me down gets to be in my next movie." He turned to Bob, who had just gotten to his feet and was strolling toward him. "Let's see . . . karate?"

Bob nodded. "I'm black belt." He grinned as he started to circle. "I'll try not to hurt you."

"Want to put money down, Jessie?" Brice asked.

"Nope." She smiled. "I read somewhere that you never had stunt doubles. But I wouldn't want to bet against these guys." She turned to leave. "Let me know when you're finished. I think I'll go out and get some fresh air. The testosterone is pretty heavy in here. Good luck, everyone."

She left the room and went through the house to the patio.

She sat down in a garden chair and waited.

Brice came out an hour later. He was pulling on his sweatshirt. "Mission accomplished. The guys are getting in their truck now." He dropped down in a garden chair next to her. "They said to tell you goodbye, and they might see you later. Nice guys."

"Yes, they are." She suddenly noticed his lower lip was bleeding a little. "You're hurt. How did that happen?"

"Karate. I can't always be perfect. It's fine."

"How did you manage to get rid of them?"

"With subtlety and brains. Just like you said." He shrugged. "But it wasn't easy. They had to be sure you'd be well taken care of since they'd promised your friend Dee."

"That's what all the fighting in the gym was about?"

"Of course. I had to show them that I could keep up with them."

"Well, you didn't keep up with the guy who gave you the bloody lip."

"Or maybe I had to show them that I wasn't *that* much better than they were. We all have egos. But I accomplished my objective."

She was studying his face with narrowed eyes. "What objective?"

"I told them that I'd take over." He smiled. "Since we were such great buddies anyway."

She swore beneath her breath. "No, Brice."

"Yes. Think about it. It had to be fate. I had nothing to do with Dee, and yet there was suddenly a reason why we were on exactly the same wavelength. The only way I was going to get those guys to leave you alone was if they were sure that I was good enough to do their job. Dee would only be happy if she thought you were safe."

"Fate? That's bullshit."

"It's only the one job. Stop making a big thing of it." He smiled. "You can't afford me for more than that."

"This isn't what I wanted, Brice."

"Well, this is what you got. You called me, and I ran to you. If you send me away now, you'll just have to work it out for yourself." He tilted his head. "And while I was bullshitting with the guys, they told me what happened today that caused Dee to press the panic button. You forgot to mention that. That's two close calls in a few days." His lips tightened. "You can use some backup right now, and I'm here to take the job. Let's give it a try."

"Did you come in here with a bloody lip so that I'd feel sorry for you?"

"You'll have to decide for yourself." He looked her in the eye. "What time do you want me here tomorrow?"

She didn't answer at first. Surely, she could manage to make this work for the next few days. Yet she had the idea that she might be making a mistake. Then she said slowly, "Eight."

"Great." He smiled as he jumped to his feet. "I'll be here. Now I'd better go tuck in your guys."

"Tuck . . . what do you mean?"

"I told them to check in at my place for a while. I've got plenty of room, and I said that they should hang around in case I needed some extra muscle. It made them feel better." He was heading for the backyard gate. "I locked the front door. Be sure you lock this one . . ."

7:50 A.M.

"What? No motorcycle?" Brice was standing on the sidewalk outside Jessie's house when she backed her SUV out of the garage the next morning. "I'm disappointed. I was looking forward to the authentic Jessie experience."

She looked in her rearview mirror and saw him smiling mischievously at her. He was wearing the Cactusville cap her father had given him, black jeans, and a T-shirt and couldn't have looked more the charismatic movie star if he'd worn it tattooed on his chest.

"This *is* the Jessie experience. It's not as if I'm chained to my motorcycle. Get in the car. I don't want anyone to recognize you. I would have thought you'd know that."

"I did." He jumped in the passenger seat. "But I thought I'd let you set the pace and the depth of disguise you wanted.

We'll work on it together. Sometimes just being me can be useful as a distraction. I did wear the hat." He buckled his seat belt. "Why no motorcycle?"

"It's in the shop. When I got drugged, I put it down on Pico Boulevard. The back wheel got run over by a pickup."

"Better the wheel than you." He was silent a moment, and then he smiled. "I was looking forward to riding tandem with you on that bike. But this could be cozy, too."

"No it can't. Anyone looking in the windows would recognize you. They aren't darkened, and one glance would be enough. We'll have to do something about you."

"Now?"

"No, not now. I'll deal with it later. I want to get downtown to the jail and catch Shane Winston at the Twin Towers auxiliary parking lot before he goes on duty. Just pull your cap down and stop smiling. Everybody knows that damn smile."

"Cap down, no damn smile. Got you. Would you like to tell me why we want to catch Winston?"

"He's a guard who beats up prisoners who harass Mamertine clients."

"We're going to be the good guys who turn him over to his boss to get his just punishment?"

"What? No, you're still stuck in those superhero movies. I need to talk to him and find out if Carl Ferris hired him to do that recently, and if he has any idea where I can find him."

"Actually, I like that even better. The role has more texture and depth."

She could feel her lips twitching. "You're impossible."

"That's been brought to my attention." His smile faded.

"A little humor doesn't hurt, but I'm not going to make this difficult, Jessie. I know I have to let you call the shots. I want this to work."

"No, a little humor doesn't hurt." She pulled into the parking lot, parked, and looked at a photograph of Winston on her phone. Her gaze was searching the lot. "Heavyset...in his forties...bald..."

"Uniformed dude coming out from between those two cop cars," Brice said, his gaze narrowed. "And he definitely looks like someone who would take money to beat guys up. We've got him."

"*I've* got him," she said as she got out of the car. "You wait here."

She ran across the lot. "Mr. Winston! Could I have a word with you?" She stopped in front of him and smiled. "You're a difficult man to reach."

He looked at her doubtfully. "Yeah?"

She nodded. "I tried to phone you last night. I just want to ask you a couple of questions about Carl Ferris. Can you spare a moment?"

"No." He pushed by her and walked toward the building. "I have nothing to say to you."

"His partner is concerned about him. I know you wouldn't want him to—"

Winston whirled and gave her a shove that slammed her against the front of a parked Tesla.

Screw him, she'd tried to play nice. She allowed herself to slide down to the concrete, slipping her boots between his feet. She gave a jerk that made him lose his balance and fall to the ground beside her. "So sorry." She jumped to her feet and held out her hand. "Let me help you up. You wouldn't want anyone to think that I'd done this to you. What an embarrassment."

Winston's face flushed. "You did it on purpose."

"How can you say that? It was clearly an accident." She dropped her hand. "After you pushed me. Anyone could see it. But I wouldn't want to cause you any trouble. All I want is for you to answer a couple of questions."

"The hell I will." He was scrambling to his feet.

"Jessie. Are you all right?" It was Brice running toward her. He wasn't supposed to be out of the car, she thought. Great. And he'd taken his cap off and that white streak was shining in the sunlight. "I saw you hit the ground." He turned to Winston. "Are you okay, Officer? Is there anything I can do?"

Shane Winston's jaw dropped as he looked at Brice. "Comet?"

Brice made a face. "It must make you sick to see me playing one of those roles when it's really you officers who are the heroes."

"No, I love your movies."

Of course he did, Jessie thought. Even this brute had a soft spot for *Comet Man*.

"Thanks. You're very generous," Brice said. "Well, if you're sure you're all right, I'll get my assistant out of your way. I'm sorry if she gave you any trouble. She was just doing some research for a movie I'm thinking of making. Mamertine gave me the idea."

128

"She should have told me it was for you," Winston said. "I wouldn't have given her any trouble." He looked at Jessie. "I thought she tripped me on purpose."

"Jessie?" Brice shook his head. "She wouldn't do that. Not on purpose, anyway. If you'll forgive her for causing all this disturbance, I'd appreciate it if you'd answer those questions."

Winston smiled back at him. "Sure. Just so you don't make me look bad on the big screen."

She thought she was going to throw up.

"No, it's just background stuff," Brice said. "We thought we'd start with a real-life company and build on that." He gestured to Jessie. "You're on, Jessie."

She forced a smile. "Thanks, Mr. Brice, sir. I'll be just a few minutes. You can wait in the car. We wouldn't want Officer Winston to be bothered by paparazzi, would we?"

"Whatever you want," Brice murmured. "Nice to meet you, Officer. Take good care of her." He strode quickly across the parking lot.

She turned to Winston. "Are we ready?"

"Sure." He was still looking after Brice. "You think maybe I can get a selfie with him?"

She gritted her teeth. "First question . . ."

———◆———

When Jessie got back to the SUV, Brice had put his Cactusville cap back on and was scrunched down in the seat.

"What were you thinking?" she said as she slammed her

car door. "You said you were going to try and make this work."

"I wasn't thinking. I was just reacting when I saw him push you into that car. You have a right to be pissed off."

"And I am. Trust me, I could have handled the asshole."

"But perhaps not before he hurt you," he said quietly. "I couldn't sit here and see that. That's what the buddy system is, as far as I'm concerned. I don't give a damn about solving this case. That's up to you. I'll just hang around and do what you tell me. The only thing I'll ask is that I'm there with you in case the going gets rough. You don't keep me stashed in the car."

"You're freakin' Comet Man!"

Bryce tilted his head. "It didn't go too badly. I told you sometimes being me can be a distraction. It depends on what I'm up against. It just happened Winston thought of himself as a superhero, too. That made us temporary brothers."

"It could have gone another way. He's a bully, and he might have decided to take you down."

Brice nodded. "But it didn't, and I could always have relied on my buddy to jump in and help. I could tell that you were ready to go after him. It was very neat the way you brought him down." He changed the subject. "Did you get the information you needed?"

"For what it was." She started the car and drove off the lot. "I was right about Winston being hired by Ferris to protect his clients' backs while they were in the jail. It's been going on for years. Every time there's a problem that requires him to step in and save a client's ass, Ferris pays him a thousand dollars. He usually receives his payment later at a downtown diner as a cash drop-off. He didn't receive the last scheduled payment from Ferris."

"Not a good sign."

Jessie nodded. "I didn't think so, either. But it's another piece in the puzzle. Winston didn't think that Owen knew about the deal."

"And you thought he might?"

"I didn't know. Like I said, another piece of the puzzle."

"So what do we do now?"

"Now we go back to my house. You're going to shed Comet Man and become someone more normal that I can deal with."

He grinned. "Then I haven't blown it?"

"I've no objection to having you hang around, as long as you don't get in my way as you did just now. And I agreed to this buddy thing, so it's partly my fault. I should have laid down stricter guidelines." She glanced at him. "But now you have them. Don't disappoint me, Brice."

He leaned back in his seat. "I wouldn't think of it. You'll keep me in line. I can see it's going to be a wonderful relationship."

CHAPTER

6

When they arrived at her house, Jessie drove into the garage. The streets were now busy, and she didn't want any of her neighbors to see Brice. "Why don't you go inside?" She jumped out of the car. "I've got to phone Owen and then maybe Dee. Doing your makeover might not be as easy as I thought."

"Your wish is my command." He opened the kitchen door.

She started dialing as she sat down at the kitchen table. Dee first. She didn't know how long it would take to get through to her. She hadn't returned Jessie's calls last night.

And Dee didn't answer her call this morning, either. She left a voicemail. "Stop hiding out. You wanted to help me? Well, I've got something for you to do that has nothing to do with furnishing me with guys that resemble something from a Hercules movie. But I need you right away, or not at all."

She paused. "And you might not be able to help after all if you don't have that makeup artist, Sheree, still living with you." She hung up and took a sip of the coffee Brice had set before her. "That should make her curious enough to bring her around. She's probably feeling guilty anyway and will need just a little shove."

"You know her very well." Brice sat down across from her. "You said since she was fourteen? But she knows you, too, if she managed to pull those shenanigans on you."

"She meant well. She's got a good heart. She was worried about me." Her lips thinned. "But she can't do anything like this again. I'll have a talk with her. Still, I might as well take advantage of any guilty feelings she's going through now." Her phone was ringing. "And here she is." She picked up the call. "Hello, Dee. I was very angry with you. But you might be able to get off easy if you help me solve this little problem I'm having."

"I did the right thing," Dee said in a rush. "You know I did. You wouldn't let me help you."

"I disagree. But we'll discuss it later. Right now, I'm only interested in payback."

"Payback?" she repeated. "What did you do to my guys? They haven't called me. It was all my fault. I told you to be kind to them. You didn't call the cops, did you?"

Jessie looked at Brice with raised brows.

He made a zipping motion across his lips.

"No, they were just told not to call you."

"Are you sure? I told them I wanted to know how things went."

"But you gave them to me. They weren't your business after that."

Silence. "They would have called me. Something has to be wrong."

"Or something could be very right with them. They might have found something interesting to occupy them." She changed the subject. "Do you want to help me, or not?"

"Of course I do. What do you want me to do?" Dee paused. "You mentioned Sheree. Why?"

"I need a makeup job, and she's the best in the business. Can you send her over right away?"

"Why? Are you doing a TV show or something?"

"Something. Is she still with you? Can you send her?"

"Naturally. You're the only one who ever ran out on me, Jessie."

"Is that supposed to make me feel guilty?"

"Yes." She was silent. "But it never works. I'll send her. What kind of equipment?"

"Everything. It's a major job."

"Really?" Dee was suddenly interested. "Then it must not be you. No one could call you a major job."

"Sure they could. Just send her right away. I have things to do today."

"What things?"

"Goodbye, Dee." Jessie ended the call. Then she leaned back in her chair and gazed at Brice. "Done. Sheree Lu's fairly fantastic, and she should be able to make you look very different from either Comet Man or your real identity.

You're experienced with makeup magic. You know what it can do."

He nodded. "But I was looking forward to playing with you. It would have been fun." He paused. "How much time do you think we have before she's at the door?"

"Thirty, forty minutes." Her eyes were narrowed. "Why?"

"Just wondered if we'd have time for a workout."

"No." She looked him in the eye. "That's not why you're here, is it? We're already having problems with the arrangement."

"Not unless I can convince you it's needed therapy for us. I'm told I can be very convincing."

"Yes, you can be. But that's all the more reason why I shouldn't give in to you. That's not the direction I want to go, Brice."

"Then we'll play it your way," he replied, rising to his feet. "Because I'm not going to have you sending me away because I broke the buddy rule. Of course, we could just fill the time by discussing those photos in your foyer."

"What photos?"

"That disgustingly good-looking man wearing the glasses. He's in three different pictures. You know how many pictures of me are there?"

"Mmm, zero?"

"Yes, but who's counting?"

"You obviously are."

"Who is he?"

She smiled. "You can ask Dee about him when she comes."

"Does she know?"

"No, but she's just as curious about him as you are. It would give you something to talk about."

"I'll snap a picture and have it run through facial recognition software. I know people."

"I know seventh graders who can do that for you. And no matter who does it, it still wouldn't work."

He wrinkled his brow. "How are you so sure?"

"I'm sure. Want some toast and jam?"

He chuckled. "Fine. We might not have time to grab a bite after your Sheree gets here."

She picked up her phone. "First I have to call Owen and see if he has time to see me today. I want to tell him about my meeting with Winston."

"You can't just tell him about it on the phone?"

She shook her head. "I want to see his face."

"You're not trusting him?"

"I'm not sure." She shrugged as she punched in his number. "There have been a couple of things that have bothered me. I'd rather be face-to-face." She got the receptionist. "Jessie Mercado. I need to see Owen today."

"I'm sorry, Ms. Mercado. He's at a meeting this morning, and from there he'll go straight to a benefit luncheon at the Hotel Bel-Air. Perhaps you can call him later?"

"I'll give it a try. Thank you." Jessie ended the call. "Well, it seems I won't be able to see Owen this morning. Maybe this afternoon."

"Then you can oversee my transformation." He placed toast and jam in front of her. "You can protect me. Some of those makeup gurus can be dictators."

"I imagine you survive them fairly well," she said dryly. "They must get a huge kick out of turning you into Comet Man." She nibbled on the toast. "Besides, Dee can protect you. Sheree does everything Dee tells her to do."

"Dee is coming? I didn't hear that."

"Neither did I. But I'll bet she'll be here. She was entirely too curious."

"You didn't try to stop her."

"No, I thought you might as well meet her. You have custody of her guys, and she's worried about them." The doorbell rang, and Jessie got to her feet. "And there she is. She was obviously in a big hurry." She headed for the door. "Relax. I'll let them in and take the edge off her first questions."

She threw open the door and saw Sheree Lu and Dee on the step. "Hi, Sheree." She smiled at the beautiful woman. "Thanks for coming to the rescue."

"I had no choice," Sheree replied with a shrug. "Dee pulled me out of the house without even my coffee."

"Jessie has coffee. She'll give you a cup," Dee said impatiently. "Though she's never used my coffeemaker." She confronted Jessie. "I wanted to see what you were up to. What did you do with my guys?"

"They're safe. Though I don't know what they're doing at the moment." She moved to one side to allow them to enter. "Come in, and we'll ask." She went ahead of them into the kitchen. "Brice, do you know what the guys were planning on doing today?"

"They said something about video games," he said as he got

to his feet. He smiled at Dee, who had stopped short in the doorway. "I could call and ask."

"Holy *shit*." Dee's eyes were wide with shock. "Jake Brice?"

He sighed and nodded. "And that's the root of our problem. Even you know who I am." He turned to Sheree. "I hear you're quite wonderful. Maybe you can help me? Jessie was very upset with me this morning."

"We wouldn't want that," Sheree murmured. She looked a little dazed. "I'll do whatever I can."

Dee walked toward Brice and held out her hand. "I'm Dee. What the hell are you doing here?"

"Doing whatever is best for Jessie." He shook her hand, his smile gentle. "The same thing you're doing. I'm very glad to meet you, Dee. Jessie's told me a lot about you. And the team you sent to help Jessie has told me even more. I want you to know we're on the same page."

"Are we? I didn't even know you knew her." She whirled on Jessie. "Why didn't I know?"

"Why would you? I don't know everyone in your orbit, Dee."

"That's different. *He's* different. You were laughing the other day and saying I wouldn't be interested in your ho-hum affairs. Jake Brice isn't ho-hum, Jessie."

"Thank you, Dee," Brice said. He made a clicking sound. "Ho-hum, Jessie? I believe I'm hurt."

"Be quiet," Dee said without looking at him. "I'm your friend, Jessie. You should have told me. Why didn't you?"

"Because he's who he is. It's complicated."

"Well, is he living with you?"

"No, at present he's living with the four giants you foisted on me."

"Hey," Brice interrupted, "I have an idea. Why don't you take Sheree into the living room and discuss my metamorphosis. Let's go out on the patio, Dee, and I'll try to clear things up." And with that, he whisked Dee out the patio door.

Just as well, Jessie thought. She turned to Sheree. "Coffee?"

Sheree nodded. "I definitely need it." Her gaze followed Brice. "I didn't know I'd be working on Jake Brice."

Jessie handed Sheree the cup of coffee. "He's insisting he wants to stick around and help me, but I won't be able to function efficiently if I have to contend with his effect on everyone around him."

"So you don't want him to look like himself?"

"You don't have to make him into a monster. Just completely . . . different."

Sheree nodded. "Get rid of the golden warmth and superhero ambience and maybe go for tall, dark, and dangerous. I've seen him act. He could pull it off."

"Definitely. Can you do it right now?"

"Sure." Sheree finished her coffee and set the cup on the end table. "Let me get my kit out of the car. I'll have to take over your bedroom and bathroom. How much time do I have?"

"Two, three hours max."

"It will be a push." She headed for the front door. "But I'm up to the challenge."

Dee and Brice came in from the patio ten minutes later. Dee made a face at Jessie as she came across the room. "I've decided to forgive you. Brice explained everything, and you seem to have treated my team okay. At least, he did. But you could have let me know what you were doing."

"Hard to do. You weren't answering my calls."

"Because I knew you'd be difficult." She smiled at Brice over her shoulder. "But it all worked out for the best. I got what I wanted, and so did Brice."

"And that only leaves me," Jessie said flatly. "But I'm glad you're both satisfied." She met Brice's eyes. "Sheree won't be satisfied if you don't get into the bedroom and let her start to work on you. I gave her a strict time schedule. I want to try to make that luncheon that Owen is attending."

He grinned. "I'm on my way. Who am I supposed to resemble? Elvis Presley? Hugh Jackman?"

"It's a surprise. Sheree is looking on you as a challenge."

"May I go watch?" Dee asked. "After all, she was my gift to you."

"No, neither one of us is going to get in her way. We'll just be on call if Sheree shouts that she needs something." She motioned to Brice to go. "See you in a couple hours."

Dee watched him leave. "I really like him. He's special. How did you manage to get hold of him?"

Jessie shrugged. "It was just one of those relationships that you sort of fall into without thinking. He probably won't be around long."

"Pity. You ought to do something about that." Then she

turned to face her. "I really am sorry, Jessie. But I didn't know what else to do. I was scared."

"I know you were. Next time, why don't you talk with me instead."

"I'll try. But sometimes you seem to brush me off. Then it seems easier to just reach out and make things happen."

And she was probably right, Jessie realized. Though she always meant to spend more time with Dee. "Then maybe we should both reach out and make an extra effort." She slid her arm around Dee's waist. "Come on. Let's go sit on the patio and talk and wait for the great unveiling."

———◆———

Sheree came out on the patio two hours later. "I'm a genius. Come and admire me. No one is going to recognize him."

"That's hard to believe," Jessie said as she followed Dee back to her bedroom. "But I'm hoping for the best."

"You got the best. You got me." Sheree stood aside as she reached the door. "Drumroll, please."

Brice was leaning against the wall with his arms crossed over his chest. "I'll give her one. She did a damn good job." He smiled at Sheree. "Though it wasn't painless."

"I had to hurry. But you took it well."

"Holy shit." Dee stared at Brice in shock. "You look like Zorro or something."

"That was Antonio Banderas," Brice said. "I'm much taller, but I think she stole a few other features from him."

142

Jessie circled Brice. "From the other side, you look more like Cary Grant."

He smiled. "I can live with that."

Tall, dark, and dangerous. It was what Sheree had envisioned, and what she'd delivered. His hair was now gleaming black, and she'd cut and fashioned it with her usual artistry. She'd even managed sideburns. His skin was tanned with subtle highlights to accent his high cheekbones. His nose was . . . different. It was more aquiline in shape and changed the entire look of his face when paired with his dark-brown contacts. He was wearing tight black jeans and a white shirt that Sheree had sent her assistant out to pick up along with a waist-length black jacket and boots that increased the slightly dramatic look she was striving to create. "Sheree did a great job. I wouldn't recognize you at first glance." She gazed at him objectively. "I'd have to study you, and not many people would bother to do that."

"I don't know about that," Sheree murmured. "I made him quite visually appealing. I couldn't take something that good away without replacing it with something of equal value."

"Thank you." Brice grinned. "But I'm happy with being totally incognito. My only question is, are you sure this spray tan will stay on after a shower? I don't want to have to re-apply it all over my body all the time. It took you almost an hour."

Her eyes were suddenly twinkling. "Well, maybe I was being extra careful. It will last for at least three days. After that, give me a call, and I'll come running."

Dee chuckled. "I bet you will."

Brice turned back to Jessie. "So am I presentable enough to escort you to that luncheon today?"

She nodded. "If you'll all get out of my bedroom so that I can change? Owen might not be eager to talk to me if I show up at the Hotel Bel-Air in my usual garb. I want at least ten minutes of his time."

"You always look wonderful." He was heading for the door. "Though maybe not as interesting as Sheree made me look."

"Give me ten minutes." She slammed the door behind them.

———◆———

TROPICAL GARDENS
HOTEL BEL-AIR

"There he is." Jessie nodded at a table across the garden. "He has a few people with him."

"And one of them is the L.A. chief of police," Brice said. "What kind of benefit did you say this was?"

"I didn't say. The receptionist never told me." She looked at the welcome sign on the buffet table. "Cops for Kids. Why?"

"Because it's one of my charities. I take kids out to my place in the mountains once a month. I received an invitation for this. I probably know most of the police, politicians, and donors here." He made a face. "And they know me. This might be a challenge."

"One I didn't want to face. I was counting on you being

able to fool relative strangers, not a room where everyone is familiar with you. How well do you know them?"

"Well, I got drunk with that police chief. He's a nice guy."

"And he's probably very observant. He might recognize your voice even if your face fooled him." She sighed. "We can't risk it. Go to the bar and get a drink and don't chat with anyone. I'll go talk to Owen and pick you up on my way out."

"My first attempt, and I'm already a failure. Too bad. I wanted to meet Owen."

"Why?"

"You're not sure he's one of the good guys. I wanted to see what I thought of him." He shrugged. "Between that prison in Afghanistan and all the grifters I've run into here in L.A., I've known a good many bad guys in my time. I'm fairly good at spotting them." He gave her a little nudge. "But you're right. I'll get a drink." He turned and headed for the bar. "By the way, you look fantastic in that white dress. I really like you in your black leather jacket, but a change is nice, too."

"Gee, thanks for giving me your approval." She turned and headed for Owen's table.

Owen smiled and got to his feet when he saw her making her way through the tables toward him. "Jessie, how good to see you. You look wonderful today." He turned to the police officer. "Rand Korbin, this is my associate, Jessie Mercado. Rand is the police chief of our fine city."

Korbin tilted his head. "Jessie Mercado. I know that name. Do you work with the city?"

She smiled. "No, but I do get around. You might know someone who knows me." She turned to Owen. "I don't want to disturb you, but could you give me five minutes?"

"Certainly." He smiled at her, then winked at the police chief. "Can you blame me, Rand? She's such a charmer. I'll be right back."

He strolled toward the swan pool. "What is it, Jessie? Couldn't this have waited?"

"You're the one who demanded daily reports. That goes both ways. When I hear something, I sometimes need clarification. Understand?" She didn't wait for a reply. "I had a talk with Winston this morning, and he told me that he was on Ferris's regular payroll to watch your clients' backs in jail. A thousand bucks per incident. So it wasn't just Sackler. It's an ongoing service for several of your clients. Are you still telling me that you didn't know?"

"Of course. Do you think I'd lie to you?" He paused. "What did Winston tell you?"

"He said, as far as he knew, you didn't know." She was watching his expression. "I was surprised you'd let a partner have that amount of freedom. You weren't interested in what he was doing on behalf of your firm?"

"I told you, he was always secretive, but he made us a hell of a lot of money. Why would I want to rock the boat?"

"I can understand that. But I need to know more about what he was doing."

He sighed. "Join the club. I'm having to deal with a few of his personal clients right now, and it's been impossible for me to make contact with some of them. I can't even see what Ferris has been doing for them."

She stopped and stared him in the eye. "Maybe we should find that out."

"*I'll* find out, but there's nothing to indicate that these clients have anything to do with his disappearance."

"But we can't rule it out. You've got to know more than you're telling me. Think. Give me details."

"I've given you what I have." He shook his head. "I'm sorry, Jessie. I promise that I'll pass along whatever I find out, okay?"

"You do that, but in the meantime, I'm not going to keep beating my head against dead ends. I'm going to find the answers. That should make both of us happy." She paused. "And I think that I'll start by digging into those accounts you're having such trouble with. I need to find out what else Ferris was doing."

"Fine."

"But he kept a lot of secrets from you. You should know that what I find might not be good for Mamertine."

"That almost sounds like a threat." He pursed his lips. "But of course it isn't. You know I want to find Ferris. That's all that's important."

Her gaze was searching his face. "Yes, that's all that's important. I'll get your answers, Owen." She smiled. "And now I'll let you get back to your police chief. You'd better hope he doesn't remember where he heard my name. I'm not known in the better circles the two of you inhabit. You might have to make explanations." She turned and headed for the bar.

Brice turned toward her as she approached. "Well? What's the word?"

"He's lying," she said. "Let's get out of here."

———◆———

As Owen watched Jessie walk around the hotel's events pavilion toward the driveway, Natalie Durand moved out of the surrounding guests toward him. She was wearing her usual tailored suit with flipped-up shirtsleeves, which she somehow was able to make appear faultlessly elegant. "That was Jessie Mercado, wasn't it?"

"Yes."

"She's even more attractive than in her photos." Natalie sipped from her champagne. "Any news about our friend?"

"No." Owen stepped away from the crowd, and she followed. He lowered his voice. "She's been asking questions down at Twin Towers. She knows about the business arrangements we have with some of the staff there."

Natalie nodded. "It was inevitable that she would find out about your special services. The question is, how much noise will she make about it?"

"It'll be fine. Her focus is on finding my partner."

"I hope so."

Owen lowered his voice even more. "Those 'special services' were never my specialty. It was always Ferris's department."

"Too bad." She shrugged. "Seems like that would be the most interesting part of your business."

Owen looked at her as she smiled and waved to a group

of business leaders. As in every social situation where he'd seen Natalie Durand, she was perfectly at ease. In the past few minutes, he'd seen her talking and laughing with the police chief, a pair of city councilmen, a movie studio head, and the mayor of Los Angeles. She glided effortlessly from one group to the next, expertly tailoring her banter for each audience.

Almost everyone there knew Natalie's story, he was sure, which certainly helped grease the social wheels. She'd been born to a poverty-stricken family in rural Mississippi, one of three children to a single mother. It had been a fairly uneventful childhood until she reached the age of eleven, when she shot and killed a man who had broken into their house and was sexually assaulting her mother.

She became something of a hero in the gun-rights community, speaking at rallies and conventions during her high school years, still managing to sidestep criticism as to why a child should have such easy access to a gun in the first place. A prominent gun-rights lobbying group awarded her a full scholarship to Princeton, and after graduation she joined Gauntlet, a multinational armored car company based in Los Angeles. As she rose through the ranks, Natalie expanded the company portfolio to include several other services in the security industry, and she became Gauntlet Industries' president and CEO within seven years. The company was a generous contributor to political candidates and their causes, making Natalie a popular fixture at events such as this one.

Owen nodded toward the mayor and his aides. "You had them eating out of your hands."

She made a face. "They'd better be, as much as I've contributed to his political action committee."

"I thought they were just charmed by that Southern accent of yours."

She laughed. "That doesn't hurt. But my accent doesn't charm men as much as it makes me less threatening to them."

"A lot of men like strong women, Natalie."

"Secure men do. Regrettably, most of the men at this party do not fall into that category."

"Including me?"

She looked at him appraisingly as she finished her champagne. "The jury's still out on you, Owen. It all depends."

"Depends on what?"

"If you can do what needs to be done when the time comes."

He nodded. "You know, there are moments when that Southern accent makes you sound infinitely more threatening, not less."

"Good." A sudden smile lit her face with charm. "Because I need to know I can count on you, Owen."

"You can. And right now, all that needs to be done is that we find my partner."

"It's frustrating." She shook her head. "I could have an army of investigators on the case, but I can't risk having anyone connected with me looking into it."

"I have every confidence in Jessie Mercado."

"Even if she continues to poke her nose into some uncomfortable corners of your company's business?"

"Even if."

"I do appreciate a man who has trust in his own judgment. It makes me feel so safe." Natalie nodded toward the mayor, who had stepped toward a lectern to make a few opening remarks. "Let's go listen to the mayor, shall we? Be sure to laugh at his jokes, especially the bad ones. He likes that."

———◆———

Jessie's phone vibrated while she and Brice were still waiting for the parking valet to bring her car around. She checked the screen and answered it. "Wheeler, I was just talking to your boss's boss. Are you here?"

"I have no idea what you're talking about, Mercado."

"I'm at the Hotel Bel-Air, where the LAPD upper ranks are stuffing their faces with crab cakes and ridiculously expensive champagne. I was sure you wouldn't pass up the chance for more free food."

"Uh, I think that event is a little above my pay grade. But I'm glad you're enjoying yourself. I've been busy trying to solve a murder."

"Any progress?"

"Well, the A/V team has pulled all the downtown traffic cam footage from the afternoon of Carl Ferris's disappearance."

Jessie's breath left her for a moment. "Tell me they got something."

"Well, they did, and they didn't."

"What does *that* mean?"

"The cameras got him leaving the parking structure at Twin Towers, and they tracked him heading south through about two miles of surface streets, all the way past Olympic Boulevard. There are no cameras for a few blocks after that, and Ferris's car never comes out the other side. Or any other side, as far as we can see."

"Have you been down there?"

"Not yet. I'm talking to some of Jennifer Dayton's colleagues in a few minutes, and her sister is flying in from Boston this afternoon. Since Carl Ferris is your focus, I thought I'd clue you in."

"Thanks, Wheeler. Appreciate it. I'll head down there now. Text me that traffic cam dead zone, will you?"

"Will do." He sighed. "Hope you enjoyed your crab cakes."

Wheeler cut the connection.

Brice turned toward Jessie as her car rolled up the driveway. "Anything from this Wheeler?"

"Maybe. We're going downtown."

"Have you known Wheeler a long time?" Brice asked as he climbed into the passenger seat. "You sounded...friendly. Have you worked cases together before?"

"You might say that. Though *together* isn't really the word. Most police prefer to keep private detectives like me at a distance. They think we get in the way. Sometimes they're right. And sometimes I think that they don't go far enough." She shrugged. "So we have slight disagreements depending on how stubborn I get. That's one of the reasons I ended up in handcuffs on the way to jail when I trespassed on Lamar

Wood's yacht the other night. Wheeler was on the scene. I was lucky he listened to me and searched the boat."

Brice's face registered his surprise. "Lamar Wood? What were you doing on his yacht?"

She shot him a glance. "Don't tell me. He's another friend you get drunk with? Or are you just another basketball fan who believes it's okay for him to do anything he wants to do? Do you know everyone in L.A.?"

"No, but I don't live in a bubble. I'd really hate what I do if I didn't interact with people. I don't get drunk with him. He doesn't drink, and he's a health nut. Completely self-disciplined. But I do know him. I've done a couple of benefits with him. He's a good guy. What were you doing on his yacht?"

"He was trying to kidnap his two kids and take them out of the country. His wife hired me to keep an eye on him. She was right, they were on the cruiser."

He was shaking his head. "He's crazy about those kids, but he wouldn't do anything like that. Not only would it be bad for them, but it would ruin his career. He's smart, and he wouldn't let that happen."

"But he did let it happen. Those kids were on the yacht."

He frowned. "I didn't hear anything about it. When did it happen?"

"The night I came close to standing you up. That was why I forgot about you."

"Then it should have been all over the news. Unless he made a deal with his wife to drop charges. They're going through a pretty bitter divorce."

"I knew they'd filed. That's why she was worried about him taking the kids. But it could be a case of he said, she said."

"And maybe she wasn't worried about the children but about not getting a gigantic settlement. Could it have been a setup? Maybe someone should talk to those kids."

"I'd go right out and do that," she said sarcastically. "Only I'm a little busy right now."

He smiled. "That's okay, it might not be an emergency. We can get to it a little later. But I know that you'll want to make certain that no one used you to do anything you wouldn't approve of."

"Or used me at all," she said coolly. "I respect your opinion, but I'll decide on my own if your friend is as saintly as you and the rest of the world think he is." She drove in silence for a while and turned just after they were within sight of the Staples sports arena. They were abruptly in an inner-city neighborhood, and she saw several children playing in the street. "We appear to have arrived."

Brice looked at the row of modest, one-story homes. "Here?"

Jessie checked her phone for the diagram Wheeler had sent her. "Yes. Ferris's car was caught on a traffic cam about a block back. He doesn't pop up again at all. It's mostly residential around here but it looks like there are some commercial buildings up ahead. We'll start here and work our way down."

"Doing what exactly?"

"Detective work. Pounding the pavement. Talking to people, keeping our eyes peeled. You've played cops. Don't you know this?"

"In my movies, it's mostly kicking ass and blowing things up."

Jessie parked at the curb. "If there's any ass-kicking to be done, let me do it. And please don't blow anything up."

She opened the door and climbed out. The houses on the street were all either brick or stucco, and several had garages. "I'll start on this side of the street and begin asking questions. You do the other side. The car we're looking for is a scarlet Lamborghini with white trim, very flashy."

"Got it." He strolled across the street. "See you at the end of the block."

Jessie nodded and climbed the three steps leading to the front door of the first house. It was opened after ringing several times by an elderly Black man in a white T-shirt, who was friendly enough but not helpful. She got the same response from the occupants of the other houses. Some of them even laughed when she described the Lamborghini. She got no answer at all from two of the houses, though she thought she saw the curtains at the window move at one place. Not a very trusting neighborhood.

She saw that Brice was now peering into one of the garages. He shook his head as he caught her glance and moved to a garage a few houses down. That wasn't a bad idea, she thought. Who said that Ferris had just passed through this area? She moved down the street to a garage on her side of the street. She stood on the step and tried to stare through the glass.

No scarlet Lamborghini.

"Are you trying to case my house?"

She turned around to see a little Black boy of about nine or ten dressed in jeans and a yellow-and-black T-shirt staring at her. She smiled at him. "No, I was just looking for a car belonging to a friend of mine."

"Yeah, I heard you." He didn't smile back at her. "Did you think my mom stole it? My mom doesn't steal. Neither do I."

"I didn't think she did. I'm just trying to find the man who owns the car. It was seen in this neighborhood." She shrugged. "But nobody I've asked seems to have seen it."

"They wouldn't have told you if they had. It's always safer not to answer questions, my mom says. That way you don't get in trouble." He was looking her up and down. "You're not a cop, are you? At first, I thought you might be, but then I didn't think you'd be fooling around with a Hollywood guy like Comet. Maybe insurance?"

She stared in disbelief. "Hollywood guy?" She lifted her head and called, "Brice!"

He ran across the street. "Find out something?" He looked down at the little boy and smiled. "Hi, how are you? What's your name?"

"Derek Eugene." He pointed to the house beside them. "I live there. We didn't steal anything from you. No one here did. Why would you care? You must have lots of cars. Though that car was kind of fancy. Maybe you should just let the insurance lady pay you for it."

"Insurance lady?" Brice repeated.

"I think that's me," Jessie said. "At first, he thought I was a cop, but he decided I was probably into insurance because a cop wouldn't be hanging around Comet."

Brice tried not to laugh. "What?"

156

"Don't ask me." She looked at Derek. "You think this is Jake Brice from the movies?"

He nodded. "Of course it is," he said in disgust. "They've just got him dressed up for some kind of role they've got him playing. They do it all the time. The other Marvel characters just play themselves, but they've always got him acting like other people until the last scene. That's pretty dumb. That's why I don't like him as much as I do the others."

Brice grimaced. "Sorry about that. I'll let my director know. They think it adds depth to my character." He glanced at Jessie. "Do you think we should let Sheree know she's failed?"

"I'm not satisfied she has. She did a terrific job. He shouldn't have been able to recognize you." She studied Derek's face. "Did you know right away that he was Comet?"

He shook his head. "Not until I saw him walking around the houses. He has a really cool walk. It was one of the only things I liked about him. He reminded me of a panther. *My* panther."

"*Your* panther," she repeated. "Who's your favorite hero, Derek?"

"T'Challa. He's better than anybody." He stopped and then corrected himself. "He *was* better. Mom keeps telling me I have to remember that I won't be able to see him anymore."

"Black Panther. Chadwick Boseman," Brice said gently. "You're right, he was better than all of us. He might be my favorite, too. I'm glad something about me reminds you of him."

"Not much." He lifted his chin. "He died, you know. But I

can still play the DVD my mom got for me. She says I've got a great memory, and he'll always be here for me."

"She's right. He'll be here for all of us."

"Yeah." Derek's voice was gruff. "Maybe you're not so dumb. Even if you did let someone steal your car."

"No one stole my car. I'm just trying to save someone who might need help." He paused. "You said it was a fancy car. Did you see it?"

Derek nodded. "The color was bright red, and that was cool, but I think the white trim at the bottom made it look kind of weird. And it wasn't big but it was slick and it roared. I looked it up on my computer later, and it was Italian."

"When did you see it?"

"Where?"

He motioned to them to follow him, and he led them to a spot down the block. "He left it parked there most of the afternoon. But it was gone when I looked out the window before I went to bed. He's never been back. Is that all you wanted to know?"

"Yes, you did great." Jessie handed him one of her cards. "If you see the car again, can you call or email me? Your mom is right. You have a terrific memory."

"Of course she's right. She's very smart. Almost as smart as me."

Brice nodded. "And maybe if you can think of a superhero you *do* like, I can arrange an introduction."

Derek thought about it. "I kind of like Thor."

"Then I'll set it up."

"But it might be nice if you're around, too. Maybe I can tell that director how they're going wrong with you."

"I'm sure they'll appreciate it," Brice said. "You'll be hearing from me."

Jessie was smiling as they walked down the street. "You were very patient with him."

"He's a good kid." After a few more yards, Brice nodded toward an industrial building across the street. "What's that?"

Jessie compared the location with Wheeler's map on her phone. "We're about at the edge of the traffic cam dead zone. That looks like an automotive repair shop. Let's take a look."

They walked across the street and saw that the facility occupied the better part of an entire block, with roll-up doors that exposed the large shop to the open air.

Brice pointed inside. "Are those . . . street sweepers?"

Jessie looked at the two tall, boxy vehicles being serviced close to one of the entrances. "Either that, or a pair of Zambonis. But yeah, I'd lay my money on street sweepers."

They walked into the busy garage. There were perhaps twenty workstations, with about half of the vehicles elevated. There was an animal control truck, three lifeguard jeeps, a parks and recreation SUV, and a sedan with fire department markings.

"Can I help you?" A young man with a clipboard approached. He wore a cloth name tag with KENNY stitched on it.

"Maybe." Jessie raised her phone and showed him a photo of Ferris's car. "Kenny, have you seen this Lamborghini in here in the last week or so?"

He gave the phone only a quick glance. "Uh, no. We don't get cars like that in here often." He smiled. "Or ever."

"Don't sell yourself short." She motioned around the garage. "You have an interesting mix here."

"We have a contract with the county. Government workers don't usually tool around in cars like that one. If they did, I might consider a career change."

Jessie watched as one of the street sweepers was raised on a hydraulic lift. "One thing to keep in mind is this car wasn't necessarily brought in for service. It may have just driven by or been parked nearby. It doesn't ring a bell at all?"

"Sorry. A car like that would attract a lot of attention around here. I'm pretty sure it hasn't been around."

Jessie swiped to a photo of Ferris. "How about this guy?"

Kenny looked at the photo. He didn't dismiss it as easily as he had the car photo. "Can I ask . . . what this is about?"

"Do you know him?" Brice asked.

"I'm not sure. What's this about?"

Jessie held the phone closer to his face. "This man has been missing for almost a week. His name is Carl Ferris. He has a kid who misses him. Can you help me find the guy?"

Kenny stared at it for a moment longer. "He looks familiar. I may have seen him."

"Where?" Brice asked.

"I'm . . . not sure."

"We don't need you to be sure," Jessie said. "I'd settle for a good guess."

"Listen, how about if I took your phone to my manager?"

Kenny pointed to a Plexiglas-enclosed office in the corner. "He might be able to help."

Jessie shrugged. "Good. We'll all go."

"He wouldn't react well to that."

"Why not?"

"Trust me. Let me show him the picture. The phone will never be out of your sight. You can watch from here."

Jessie handed him the phone. "If your boss recognizes him, please ask him to step out here for a moment."

"I'll be right back."

Kenny walked back to the corner office. They watched as he pushed open the Plexiglas door and spoke to a chubby bald man with a goatee. He stared at the photo and then held the phone for a better look. He said something to Kenny, who turned and pointed back toward them. The manager shoved the phone back toward him and turned his attention back to a stack of papers on his desk.

Kenny left the office and walked back toward them. He handed Jessie her phone. "Sorry, he didn't recognize him."

"Really? Because from here, it looked like he might have."

"Nope."

"Interesting," Brice said. "Then we can get back to talking about where *you* might have seen him."

"Actually I haven't."

Jessie smiled doubtfully. "A minute ago, you said—"

"He did look familiar to me, but no. I was mistaken."

Jessie shot a glance at Brice before turning back to Kenny. "So is this something you realized yourself, or did your boss just convince you of it?"

"The more I looked at that picture, the more I realized I didn't recognize him. Sorry. Good luck to you, though. I hope you find him."

Brice clenched his jaw in frustration. "Well, *I'm* sorry, Kenny. Because we really need to talk to your boss."

"I'm afraid that isn't possible. Mr. Moran is a busy man."

"We're busy, too." Brice took a step forward with a belligerence that made Jessie think he might be about to kick Kenny's ass, movie-star-style.

Kenny wasn't cowed. "You didn't show me a badge when you came in here. You're not police."

Jessie smiled. "Unfortunately, this dress doesn't have pockets. Otherwise I'd be able to show you my private investigator license."

"Not the same as a badge."

"Agreed."

"Meaning I don't have to talk to you."

"You wouldn't have to talk to me even if I was a cop. It's all a matter of how good a citizen you want to be."

"I'm afraid I've already told you everything I can. Like I said, good—"

"Good luck, yeah, got it." Jessie grabbed Brice's arm and pulled him away. "Let's go."

"Wait a minute. I'm not finished talking to Kenny here."

"Yes, you are. Come on."

"Jessie, I—"

"Now!" She pulled him out onto the sidewalk and ran. "This way."

He kept pace with her as she turned the corner and ran

around to the other side of the building. "What are we doing?"

"Keep up."

They ran into a rear parking lot, where a silver Lexus peeled out and roared down the street.

Jessie stopped. "Damn."

"Was that—?"

"It was the manager. His office had a back door that opened to the outside. I just saw him leave. You didn't catch that?"

"Afraid not. I was too busy trying to intimidate young Kenny."

"It's okay. If we decide we want to talk to the manager, we know where he works, and we know where he lives."

"We do?"

She nodded. "License plate. I'll have his address in less than two minutes."

"Man. I didn't catch that, either."

She grinned. "Just stick with me, kid."

"That's what I've been trying to do. Haven't you noticed? So far, it's been a little discouraging. I haven't blown up any-thing all day." He looked back at the automotive shop. "And I really wanted to let loose back there."

"I could tell." She pulled him back toward the street. "But Kenny wouldn't have been up to your speed. It's better to go for the big guy. Once I get his address and personal informa-tion, I'll call Wheeler and see if he can give me anything else on the guy."

"Then we go after him?"

"Not right away. We'll look for known associates and

anything that can link him with Ferris." She was dialing her phone. "But first things first."

"And then I can blow them up?"

"We'll discuss it over dinner. It might take a while." She walked toward her SUV. "But watching Owen nibbling on those crab cakes at that buffet made me hungry. Do you know anywhere we can get good carryout to take home?"

"Home? I still haven't had a chance to try out this disguise. When are you going to let me loose in a real restaurant?"

"It will come. I have research work to do later." She glanced at him. "But I can drop you off at your house."

He shook his head. "Just a question." He paused. "Home. Actually I like the sound of that. I'm beginning to get very familiar and comfortable with your place." He suddenly smiled. "And I know a restaurant with a chef who makes great crab cakes."

CHAPTER

7

S o where are we going today?" Brice asked as he got into
the passenger seat. "I'm in a kick-ass detective mood this
morning, so I hope we're going back to that automotive shop
to talk to that manager. I'm pumped."

"Pumped?" Jessie gave a mock shiver. "Then we'd better
do something a little less combative. The plate number tells
us that the garage owner's name is Paul Moran, a resident
of Altadena. There's no obvious connection with Ferris, but
that doesn't mean one doesn't exist. While we wait to see if
Wheeler can give us any more info on him, we'll go in a
different direction."

His brows rose. "A kick-ass direction?"

She shook her head. "Sorry." She smothered a smile. "We're
visiting a grieving widow."

He sighed. "Definitely not kick-ass. Oh well, I'm good with grieving widows. I think they associate Comet Man with something celestial or angelic."

"Angelic?"

"You know, stars, comets, angels. Same general heavenly beings."

"I don't think so. I've always believed your character definitely had a dash of mischief."

"So do I. Some fans see what they want to see. I just accept it." He frowned. "But your grieving widow won't be able to recognize me as Comet. I'm not sure this disguise will be as reassuring. What do you think?"

She chuckled. "There's nothing angelic or celestial about you at present. You're mysterious, magnetic, a little wicked."

"That's not so bad." He tilted his head. "I can build on it. Interesting? Sensual?"

He was casting out a strong aura of both qualities right now, and Jessie found it was having an effect on her. She needed to change the subject. "My widow's not likely to care one way or the other. She's Gordon Laney's widow, and he was blown apart by a barrage of bullets."

"He was Sackler's partner? The one who masterminded that failed robbery that sent Sackler to prison?"

"That's what I was told. But I have a problem believing crooks unconditionally when they tell me anything. It's difficult enough when I'm expected to believe anyone with no record. I want to hear what Gordon's wife has to say."

166

"I've noticed you're something of a skeptic. Where do we find this grieving widow?"

"She lives in a trailer at a park in Acton." She looked at the GPS. "It's about thirty minutes from here." She smiled. "Sorry it's not going to be a kick-ass kind of day. I'm sure you're going to be ready to go back to being Comet Man when this is over."

"Nah, it's been a nice balance." He leaned forward and found music on her radio. "Busy enough to feel like maybe I'm needed to keep the bad guys at bay. Followed by an evening that was relaxing and damn nice." He glanced at her. "The crab cakes weren't the only thing that was terrific last night." His eyes were suddenly twinkling. "But I could have built on that, too. Just give me the chance." He held up his hand. "Buddy plan, I know. It wasn't perfect, but it was really good."

"If you like the simple life. All we did was eat crab cakes and research, and then you played some of Dee's DVDs."

"I thought she should have some part in the evening. She provided me with my new facade. Besides, she's your friend, and I wanted to become more familiar with her work. I'd never seen her concert performances. She's dynamite."

"Yes, she is." And it had been a very nice evening. No pressure, just good food and an amusing companion with whom she was completely in sync. Which was dangerous in itself. But she wasn't going to think about that. She would put it aside until this short period with him was over. "She likes you, too."

They were slowed by heavy traffic on the 14 freeway, but they soon reached their destination. Jessie looked down at her GPS. "The trailer park should be right ahead. I called her last night after you left, and she seemed willing to talk." She corrected. "Well, almost eager."

"That's a good sign," Brice said. "Or maybe she's just lonely."

But when Jessie pulled up in front of the small, white mobile home a small, gray-haired woman came out on the stoop. She was perhaps in her sixties or early seventies, and her blue eyes were still snapping with vitality. She watched Jessie get out of the SUV. "You're that private eye? I was afraid that you'd change your mind. Nobody seems to want to talk to me." She turned to Brice. "Who are you?"

"Rick Desmond, my assistant," Jessie said quickly. "Rick, this is Pat Laney. Gordon Laney's wife. I told you about Sackler's testimony."

"Lying son of a bitch," Pat Laney said. She pointed to a few outdoor chairs beside the front door. "Would you like to sit down? My house is kind of messy, so I won't invite you in. It doesn't seem worthwhile keeping it neat when there's only me to see it. Everything's different now that Gordy's gone."

"Thank you." Jessie sat down. "We'll try not to keep you long. Just a few questions."

"I don't know much. Gordy didn't like to talk business with me. He tried to keep me away from that part of his life."

"What types of things was he involved in?" Brice said.

"He never did anything that was really bad. He never cheated his partners. He never hurt anyone. He never beat me like my sister's husband beats her." Her eyes were tearing. "He was real good to me. We had such a good time. And now I don't have anyone."

"I'm sorry," Jessie said. "How long were you married?"

"Twenty-two years. And I'd still have him if he'd never gone into that deal with Sackler. He had doubts about it, but he wanted to pay off this trailer, and it was supposed to be good money. Sackler said all Gordy would have to do was stick to the plan and he'd have money to burn. It sounded too good to be true. When Gordy was blown away, I wanted to murder that bastard."

"It sounds like Sackler ran the operation," Jessie said. "How did your husband get that tip about the weekly infusion of cash at the investment firm?"

"He didn't know anything about it," she said bitterly. "That was another lie Sackler told everyone after that security guy killed my Gordy. My husband was dead, and Sackler was alive and had a bunch of high-priced lawyers telling him what to say and do. He pled out the case, and there wasn't even any trial. Sackler will probably find a way to get out early, and no one will remember Gordy." Tears were running down her cheeks. "But I remember him, and he was a thousand times better man than Sackler."

"Can you tell me anything else about the deal?"

Pat shook her head. "I told you, he wanted to keep me out of his business."

"Then I guess we're finished. Thank you for your time."

She got to her feet and gave the woman her card. "If you think of something, please call me."

She nodded. "I will. Though you'll probably forget about me, too. I don't want much. I just want the truth to come out. There were so many lies, and I think Gordy was caught in the middle. I want everyone to know the truth. Though they probably never will."

Jessie felt a sudden pity for the woman. Who knew what kind of life she had lived? But she'd tried to carve happiness out of the shoddy life she'd had with a far-from-perfect husband. And now all she wanted was truth instead of lies.

She leaned over and took her hand. "You're wrong," she said quietly. "Everyone will know the truth. I promise you, Pat."

———◆———

"It seems things are a bit different than Sackler told you," Brice said as they drove back to the highway. "If the widow was telling the truth. And if her husband was telling *her* the truth. Either way it appears the web is growing. What do you think?"

"I have no idea. But I do know who I want to hear the truth from. So I think I'll go back to Twin Towers and have another talk with Sackler."

"You felt sorry for the grieving widow." Brice reached out and pressed her hand on the steering wheel for an instant. "For a tough lady, you're remarkably softhearted."

"Maybe it's just that I don't live in a bubble, either," Jessie said. "And our lives are all different and we have to make adjustments for whatever hands we're dealt."

"True." He paused. "That jail is perfectly secure?"

"It's a jail, Brice. They take me directly to Sackler." Her eyes narrowed on his face. "Why?"

"You probably aren't going to want me around while you're cross-examining Sackler. I was wondering if you'd mind dropping me off at the Lakers training facility where Lamar Wood is practicing, then pick me up after you finish your third degree? I want to talk to him in a place where it seems casual if anyone is watching him."

"Sure." She paused. "You're worried about him. You really think his ex is doing a number on him?"

"I told you that he's a good guy. He loves those kids, and he loves the game. I don't want to see him hurt. If that yacht was a setup, it would be a king-size dirty trick."

"Yes, it would." She frowned. "And I'd be part of the setup. I wouldn't like that. By all means, go talk to him. I want to know. I assure you I'm not going to need anyone to do any ass-kicking at Twin Towers. I'll pick you up after I'm through." She suddenly chuckled. "But what's your friend Lamar going to say when he sees your transformation? I'd like to be there for that."

◆

TWIN TOWERS CORRECTIONAL FACILITY
DOWNTOWN LOS ANGELES

"Hello, Ms. Mercado. I've been sent to take you back to Mr. Sackler. How nice to see you."

Jessie whirled to see the guard who had spoken.

Shane Winston was standing at the door with a smile on his face. "If you'll just come this way, Mr. Sackler is waiting."

She didn't move. "What are you doing here?"

"I work here, remember?" He started down the hall.

She hesitated and then moved after him. "I never saw you before when I talked to Sackler."

"I was busy somewhere else, and I didn't think it necessary to be here when you were talking to him. But now I know you, and I thought we should understand each other."

"When I left you, I believed that was already done. You seemed very cordial after talking to Brice."

"I was a little confused. I couldn't understand how you'd be a problem if you were involved with him. But when I got to thinking about it, I realized that I said a lot of things to you. Things you might try to use against me." They reached the isolated meeting room, and he turned to face her. His lips were suddenly curled in a feral grimace, and she automatically braced herself. "So I decided to come and have a talk with Sackler. He didn't know anything about Brice. He said you were a private eye and thought it must be some kind of a joke." His voice lowered. "It was no joke to me. I told you things that could make me lose my job. I won't let that happen. I knew you were a bitch the minute I saw you."

"So what are you going to do about it?"

His eyes were glittering as he took a step toward her.

"Anything I want to do. We're alone here, and I don't give a damn about Sackler. I do care what happens to me. Do you know how easy it would be for you to have a fatal accident at Sackler's hands? Then I'd be forced to put him down. What a shame, but after all it's my job. What else could I do?" He shrugged. "It's a story no one could question."

She studied his face. It could be a bluff to intimidate her. But it could just as well be a legitimate threat. He was enjoying this a little too much. He might have even talked himself into it. She'd stall a minute while she chose the strike points if she had to attack.

"Your employer wouldn't like it," she reminded him. "It's confusing, I know. Which employer? And for that story to hold water, you'd have to use your gun. And if that's the case, I wouldn't give much for your chances, Winston. That fatal accident could be yours. I'm very good at defending myself. Remember how easily I took you down in the parking lot?"

"You took me by surprise," he snarled.

"Then you'd better pick a time and place where that can't happen. That wouldn't be here and now. I'd have all kinds of options."

"The hell you would," he muttered. "This isn't the end." But he was clearly uncertain, and then he whirled and strode out of the room.

Five minutes later, he shoved Sackler ahead of him through the doorway. He threaded his handcuffs through the iron table loop, fastened them on his other wrist.

Then he backed away, still facing Jessie.

"That will be all, Officer," she said.

He didn't move.

"Thank you, Officer. You can go now."

He stared at her for another moment then turned and left the room, locking the door behind him.

Jessie drew a relieved breath and switched her attention back to the prisoner. "Hello, Sackler. I told you I'd be back."

"But you didn't tell me that you'd also disturb my friend, Winston here," he said warily. "He was full of crazy stories about you and some movie star. I still need him to protect me."

"And he needs you. Don't worry. He won't leave you in the lurch. I just had to ask him a few questions."

Sackler grimaced. "I don't think he likes you."

"He has his reasons."

"Trust me, you don't want to get on his bad side."

"Too late."

Sackler leaned back as far as his cuffs would allow. "So what brings you back here?"

"Well, I figured it would be my last chance to see you before you're shipped off to Tehachapi state prison. You'll be gone in the next couple of days, right?"

"So I understand. Too bad. I've gotten comfortable here."

"Mamertine Consultants made sure of that. I wouldn't worry about it. I'm sure they've already started greasing the wheels for you in Tehachapi."

"You think?"

"It's what they do."

He nodded. "Good. Any closer to finding Mr. Ferris yet?"

"Afraid not. And I still haven't found out who's paying your tab at Mamertine."

"What difference does that make?"

"As far as what happened to Carl Ferris, maybe no difference at all. Or maybe all the difference in the world. I won't know until I find out."

"If that's why you're here, I'm sorry to disappoint you. I still have no idea."

"Yeah, that's what you told me. But you also told me your dead partner in that robbery was the one who roped you into it."

He averted his gaze. "Yeah?"

She leaned close to him. "We both know that isn't true."

"Sure it is."

"No. It was your idea, not Gordon Laney's, to hold up that investment firm."

"Do your homework. Read my police statements. Take a look at the indictment that the prosecutor submitted."

"I've read them all. It doesn't matter how many times you repeat a lie, it still isn't true. Your partner was dead, so he wasn't around to dispute it. You pled out quickly, so your story was never thoroughly investigated. But I know he didn't recruit you for this job, Sackler. You recruited him."

He paused for a long moment. "Who in the hell told you that?"

"The truth has a way of bubbling to the surface. But you lied to me about it."

"It was that crazy wife of his, wasn't it? She was lying through her teeth."

"I don't think so. I need to know who else was involved. Who else were you working with?"

"I told you, it was just me and Gordy."

"Who *really* told you about the cash being delivered to that firm every week?"

His expression had turned cold. "I think we're about done here."

"I'm back to thinking it may be the same person who's paying so much to make sure you're being kept comfortable while you're in prison."

"You can think whatever you want."

Jessie leaned back and crossed her arms. "You forget I'm working for Mamertine now. And I could be in a position to make things extremely uncomfortable for you."

"Are you threatening me, Miss Mercado?"

"I'm only making you aware of your present situation."

"Sounds like a threat."

"Take it how you want. But as comfortable as Mamertine Consultants can make things for you when you're behind bars, what if they can pull those same levers to make things worse for you?"

Sackler smiled. "You really think they'd do that?"

"If the life of one of their own is at stake, why not?"

His smile had become an ugly smirk. "Tell me, Miss Mercado. What makes you think you're really working for Mamertine?"

She had been trying to provoke a response, but she hadn't expected anything like this. "Oh, I don't know. The identifier on the electronic funds transfer into my agency bank account?"

"Maybe that doesn't tell the whole story."

"Yeah? So fill in the blanks."

He looked away. She could tell he wanted to say more, to strike back with a blow of his own after her not-so-veiled threat. It was a tactic that often worked with men. He was pissed, and he was dying to put her in her place. Maybe if she rubbed a little salt into that open wound . . .

"I didn't mean to scare you," she said in her most patronizing voice.

"You think I'm scared?"

"You seem a little rattled."

Now he was definitely pissed. He raised his right cuffed hand and pointed a long finger at her. "If anyone's scared, it should be you."

She leaned back and smiled arrogantly. "Why's that?"

Whatever it was he was hiding, it was killing him to keep it in. After a long moment, he swallowed hard and spoke in a low, controlled tone. "Let me give you some advice. Stay in your lane and do what you need to do to find Ferris. But keep out of my business."

"Your only business is sitting in jail for the next decade or so."

He threw back his head and called, "Guard!"

The door immediately opened, and Winston came into the room. Sackler never looked back at her as the guard unlocked his cuff and escorted him from the room.

Brice was waiting outside the training facility when Jessie's car pulled up. He ran across the street and jumped in the passenger seat. "How did it go? Have any trouble without me?"

She wasn't about to tell him about that chilling few minutes with Winston. "Why should I? Like I told you, it's a jail. Lots of guards around to save me."

"Disappointing. I wanted to feel needed." He fastened his seat belt. "What about Sackler? Did he back up anything our grieving widow said?"

"No, he said she was crazy and lying through her teeth." She paused. "I believe he was the one who was lying, but I can't prove it."

"And?"

"I'm going to prove it." She smiled. "We're going to visit the investment company they tried to rob and see how their story lines up with Sackler's. We're on our way there now. There aren't any court records of witnesses because he pled out as soon as they arrested him. Which was very convenient, wasn't it?"

"Exceptionally. Do you think I'll have to kick ass at that investment company?"

"I doubt it, but you can always hope." She glanced at him. "How did your visit with Lamar Wood go?"

"Well enough. Once he got over laughing at my new persona. He kept calling me James Bond. He thought I looked like a 'nineties Pierce Brosnan."

"Interesting."

Brice looked at himself in his sunshade mirror. "I can kind of see it."

"Me too."

Brice stopped smiling. "Anyway, I was right. Wood's wife, Tiffany, set him up. She paid their nanny to take the kids to the yacht and told them their daddy had arranged to take them for a weekend in San Francisco. Once he was arrested, she inserted a pricey blackmail clause in the divorce settlement."

"And she used me to go and find the kids." Her lips tightened. "I won't let her get away with it."

"And how are we going to stop it?"

"I'll start by calling Tiffany and impressing upon her the legal trouble she could be in. I still have her number." She mused, "She must have thought she needed insurance to get that fat settlement. Now why was that?" She glanced at Brice. "Why were they breaking up?"

"He didn't tell me. He never talked about his marriage, only the kids. I know he tried for a long time to keep it from falling apart."

"Again, for the kids." She shook her head. "Divorce cases are usually pretty simple. Who's cheating on whom? Who wants what? Who gets the kids, and for how long?"

"It doesn't sound simple."

"Not to anyone emotionally involved. But I try to remain on the outside."

"Until you get used in the process."

"Then I do get emotionally involved." She looked down the street for the building that housed the investment company. She found it and swung the car into the underground garage.

"This job is much cleaner. Let's go see if we can prove Pat Gordy didn't lie to me."

———◆———

Ten minutes later they were shown to the office of Robert Mailer, the branch manager of One World Capital Management. He was a fortyish man with a receding hairline, and he came out of the office with a polite smile on his plump face. "My assistant told me you were interested in asking me a few questions, Ms. Mercado? Something to do with that unfortunate robbery attempt?"

"Yes, thank you for seeing us," Jessie said.

"I don't have much time, but I'll try to help you. I admit, we're trying to put that behind us. We were very grateful that it all appeared to be resolved so quickly. I hope there's not going to be any more publicity regarding the incident."

"Not as far as I know. I'm only interested in the details of the robbery."

"It was only an attempt by a couple of bunglers to rob us. It probably could have been resolved without incident if one of them hadn't turned around with his gun. It was unfortunate."

"Particularly for the thief your security officer blew away," Brice murmured.

"Our officer was up against two men with assault rifles," Mailer said defensively.

"I'm not arguing that," Jessie said. "It's just incredible that things went so wrong for them, in terms of both the planning and the execution. They came expecting to find cash, and there was none."

"That's true."

"Do you know where they might have gotten the idea that you had a lot of cash on hand?"

"No. I realize they came under that assumption, but that's never the case here."

"Never?" Jessie said.

"Never. This isn't a cash business. It made no sense."

Brice glanced back at Mailer's open door. "If you don't mind me asking... Why would you have an armed guard on staff if you don't keep cash around?"

"In the course of a day, our clients can win and lose vast fortunes. If someone loses hundreds of thousands of dollars in the market, he can become quite upset and come here looking for someone to blame. For the safety of my staff, we always keep security on hand." He looked at his watch. "Now, if you'll excuse me. I have an appointment."

"Yes, of course," she said. "Thank you for your time." Jessie and Brice walked out of the office and moved toward her car. "That was a surprise. But I'm not buying the inept-bungler narrative."

Brice shrugged. "Seems pretty inept to me."

She thought for another moment. "Something else was going on. What in the hell was Sackler really trying to pull off here? It doesn't make sense, and I—" She broke off as she looked down at her phone. She was receiving a text. "It's from Wheeler."

"Any news?"

"The lab has been taking a closer look at the traffic cam footage they pulled of Ferris's car. They've found something interesting. He says he'll show it to me if I want to swing by."

"Ah, the cooperative Detective Wheeler," Brice said as he got into the passenger seat. "Evidently he must think a lot of you if he wants to share his findings. You said usually the relationship wasn't that cordial with the police." He snapped his fingers. "But what am I thinking? He's the one who had you in cuffs. That's a sure way to guarantee a very warm and lasting bond."

"Very amusing." Jessie started the car. "But I'm grateful for any information no matter where it comes from. I'm going to go see what he's talking about. Do you want to go with me?"

"Of course I do. I've already broken the buddy rules once today. You're not going to get rid of me." He reached over and turned on the radio. "And I need to meet this Wheeler and size him up if he's going to be around."

"Totally unnecessary. It's not as if this is a permanent arrangement." She frowned. "And I'm not sure it would be wise. Wheeler is an experienced cop, and he's very sharp. There's a chance he might see through that disguise."

"I'll take the chance. I trust Sheree."

"So do I. But I don't know if I want to take the chance."

He grinned. "Go on. Live a little." He added with mock sadness, "You don't know how depressing it is to know how ashamed of me you are. You never want me to meet your friends."

She wanted to hit him. "You blow it, and we're done."

His smile faded. "I won't blow it. It means too much." He leaned back in his seat. "Take me to meet your detective, and I'll be incredibly convincing."

Jessie texted Wheeler from the police department's underground parking garage, and he was waiting for them when they emerged from the elevator near the fourth-floor A/V lab.

Wheeler smiled. "Have you been camping out downstairs, waiting for my calls? I *just* texted you."

"We were in the neighborhood." She gestured to Brice. "My associate, Rick Desmond. Detective Wheeler."

"Desmond." Wheeler shook his hand as he glanced at Jessie. "Since when do you work with an associate? The only person I've ever seen you working with is Kendra Michaels."

"Ms. Mercado and I seldom work together," Brice said quickly. "I run a video production house a few blocks from here. She thought I might like to take a look at whatever you found." He smiled. "I hope you don't mind. I have a good deal of experience enhancing video, but your people are the experts."

"They are." His gaze narrowed on Brice's face. "You look familiar. Have we run into each other before?"

Brice shook his head. "I don't think so." He smiled. "I

sometimes give seminars for law-enforcement officers in the Bay Area, but not in L.A."

"Seminars? Then you must be an expert, too."

Brice made a face. "That's what they call me. I know my job. Silicon Valley keeps bringing out new technology, and we just have to keep up with it. Your techs work miracles sharpening fuzzy videos every day."

Brice was in fine form, Jessie thought. He was exuding competence, charm, and modesty. She almost believed in him herself. But he might get into deep trouble if anyone decided to test that competence. She said quickly, "And I'd like to see that traffic cam video right now, if you don't mind. What did your people find?"

"I'll show you." He opened the door to the A/V lab and gestured to a console where a tech was seated in front of a large monitor. Wheeler patted the tech on the shoulder. "Run it again, Larry."

Larry rotated a wheel on the console and then pressed the PLAY button.

Wheeler spoke over the assembled traffic cam clips of Ferris's car on the city streets. "I've already sent you the route he took just before the car disappears. This morning, we discovered something else. It's a three-point-eight-mile trip but for a few blocks of it...there's someone else in the car with him."

"Really?" Jessie stepped closer to the monitor.

"Yes. Larry caught it after a bit of digital sharpening."

"Here," Larry said as his fingers flew across the keyboard. "I'll put the clips on a loop."

Jessie watched as three clips played back-to-back. The zoomed-in images were blurry, but they clearly showed someone in the seat next to Ferris.

"We think it's a woman, but the image is too soft to make any kind of positive ID," Wheeler said. "It appears that he picked up the person and dropped her off just a few blocks later."

Larry pressed a button to freeze the picture. The passenger image looked like mush.

Wheeler shook his head. "See? It difficult to make out anything."

"Can you isolate the blocks where he picked her up?" Jessie said.

Wheeler consulted his pocket notebook. "Already done. She appears only on the Olive Street cams between Eleventh and Fourteenth Streets." He turned to Brice. "I'm sure you'll have no problem getting a great picture from that," he said sarcastically.

Brice was still staring at the blurry, diffused image. "Maybe."

"I'll believe it when I see it," Larry said.

"There may be something I can do," Brice said. "I'll make a few calls and get back to you." He smiled. "But you may have the problem solved before that. Look what you've done already."

"Not enough." He turned to Jessie. "But I thought you'd want to see it."

"I did. Thanks, Wheeler. Will you let me know if you find a way to identify the woman?" Jessie said.

He nodded. "We could always ask Owen Blake if he has any idea who Ferris was keeping company with."

"I will. But there wasn't anyone special on the list he gave me but Jennifer Dayton."

"A man who runs around in a Lamborghini probably has his choice of any number of women." He turned to Brice. "Don't you agree?"

"I agree that Lamborghinis are very nice cars. But personally I prefer more interesting modes of transport." He winked at Jessie. "Like motorcycles."

"Yeah, they're interesting enough." He was studying Brice again. "I'd swear I've met you before. There's something about—"

"Rick, it's time we left," Jessie interrupted. "I promised I'd get you back for that appointment." She turned to Wheeler. "Thanks for giving me a call. I've been feeling like I've been going down blind alleys lately. At least we may have a chance at finding that woman."

"You're welcome. I'll keep in touch."

Brice cleared his throat. "Nice to meet you, Wheeler." He was heading for the elevator. "I'll remember to make those calls for you."

Jessie caught up with him at the elevator. "Stop laughing," she whispered as she got in. "It was very nice of him to think of me."

"Oh, he has no problem with doing that." His face was still convulsed with laughter. "He has a king-size crush on you. I could feel his hackles rise when he saw me with you. I was not a welcome addition."

"I didn't notice." She got off the elevator and headed for the glass exit doors leading to the parking lot. "I was too worried about him recognizing you. You came on a little strong in there."

"Nothing to worry about. It was just another role to play. Just like the ones that little Derek hates Comet playing." He was still chuckling. "And you do notice how he feels about you. Admit it."

"If I'd noticed, I would have had to do something about it. And I prefer not to be in that position."

"Poor guy. I felt sorry for him when I saw the way the wind was blowing."

"There's nothing poor about him. He's a smart and attractive man."

"Hmm. Now I'm getting hackles."

"Not likely." She frowned. "And you shouldn't have offered to give him a hand with that video. That wasn't honest."

"Yes, it was. I wouldn't have offered if I wasn't going to follow through."

Her brows rose. "So suddenly you're a digital video engineer?"

"Well, that wasn't true, but I'm going to call someone who is. I'll bring in one of the most skilled video techs in the world. If he can't help, no one can."

"And who is this genius?"

"His name is Peter Norris. He works on the digital effects team on some of my movies. He scanned me and created my digital double for some of the most amazing stuff you see in those films."

"Funny, your colleagues always go on and on about how you do everything yourself."

"That's Hollywood. We don't want to destroy the magic."

"Or your ego."

"Hmm. In any case, if there's anything to be teased out of that blurry video, Peter's our man. He's Leonardo da Vinci with ones and zeros."

"Are you sure? This seems like it's a little out of his wheelhouse."

"He can do it, trust me. If you need anything technical done, go to the entertainment industry. They pay top money for top talent. That's why you can almost always find the best people there." He leaned back in his seat. "But our immediate concern is to decide what food we want to order for takeout tonight. We'll have a wonderful meal like we did last night. Then you can do your research, and I'll get on the phone and try and convince Peter Norris to come down here and take a look at the traffic cam videos."

"You think he'll do it?"

"I'll negotiate. Some people owe me favors."

"The story of your life."

"Better than owing the favors." He smiled. "Doesn't that sound like a great evening? Just like last night."

"Very efficient. Very productive."

"Then can we go home?"

He had said he liked the idea of going home with her. She had liked that evening, too. There wasn't any reason why they couldn't repeat the experience as long as they accomplished what was needed.

"No way." She smiled. "Not until we decide what we're going to eat for dinner."

———◆———

Jessie had just stepped out of the shower at seven thirty the next morning when she received a call from Owen Blake.

"What on earth are you doing, Mercado?"

"Right now, or with my life in general? This could be a long conversation, Owen."

"I hired you to find my partner. Instead, I hear you're out there threatening one of our clients."

"Sackler."

"Yes. I thought you were just going to Twin Towers to ask him a few questions. Now I hear you threatened to turn my firm's resources against him. Just so you know, that isn't great customer service."

"I did ask him some questions, and I didn't like his answers. I only pointed out that actions sometimes have consequences, and he should be grateful for the treatment he was getting at Twin Towers."

"And hinted that the treatment might be withdrawn or even turned against him."

"Sometimes it helps to apply a little pressure."

"Well, stop it. Find another way."

Jessie smiled. "It didn't take them long to come crying to you. Which one did it, Sackler or Winston?"

"Winston, the guard. Evidently he's not happy with you, either."

"I can live with that, but why do you care? It was Ferris who cut the deal with Winston, right?"

"Right. He cut lots of deals. And if I don't continue them or otherwise keep these people happy, they might start talking. It wouldn't be good for business, trust me."

"Okay, fine. By the way, did you ever get me a copy of your firm's security video to see who hired you to take care of Sackler?"

"It doesn't exist. Evidently Ferris never met this person in the office."

"Unfortunate."

"Just keep investigating and try not to destroy my firm in the process, okay?"

"I'll work on it. I'll talk to you later, Owen." She cut the connection.

She hadn't told him about her trip to the investment house or to the A/V lab. These had been deliberate omissions. It might be just as well not to give him another report until she was closer to finding Ferris.

In the meantime, she had to hurry and finish dressing. Brice was due to arrive at eight, and he was never late.

And he wasn't this time, either. He rang the bell, and when she opened the door Brice stood on her stoop beside a red-haired young man with a spattering of freckles on his nose and the most piercing gray eyes Jessie had ever seen.

"Hi," Brice said. He gestured to the man beside him. "Jessie Mercado, this is Peter Norris, digital effects artist extraordinaire. He returned my call after I went back to my place last night. He's going to find our mystery woman in Wheeler's video cam. I thought I'd bring him here and introduce him before I sent him to work in that A/V lab."

She glanced at him in surprise. "You're sending him there this morning?"

"I wanted it that way," Norris said quickly. "I'm curious. I want to know what I'm facing."

Jessie smiled and stepped aside, welcoming them in. "I'm glad to meet you, Peter. Thanks for coming so quickly."

"Brice is an extremely persuasive man. He knows damn well that he can get me to do whatever he wants. But I gotta tell you, my first sight of him was a big shock. That was worth the trip. He tells me that you're responsible."

"I can't take the credit or the blame for that." Jessie led him into the kitchen and poured coffee into a cup. "And if you're friends, you should have become accustomed to him showing up in weird costumes and makeup." She handed him the cup. "But I'm responsible for needing you to help us out, so thank you."

"No problem." He frowned. "Though identifying that woman might be a problem if the police lab team are having trouble. It might take me a few days."

"No longer that that?"

"Hey, what can I say? I'm a genius."

She hesitated. "You might have trouble with the lab tech officers. Brice didn't tell them the truth. I'll call Detective Wheeler and have him clear the way for you, Peter." Jessie smiled. "I think they'll be happy to have your input."

—◆—

"Skyscrapers." Jessie looked up in dismay at the four tower-ing buildings. This was the last thing she'd wanted to see. There were two on each side of the boulevard, fairly new, and were each at least fifty stories. She got out of the car in the parking lot of the one nearest to the lights on the corner. "It couldn't be any more difficult to track someone, could it?"

"Not easy," Brice said as he watched the people go in and out of the entryways. "Not like we can knock on a door and have her magically open it and invite us in for a drink. This block is like a small city. I liked Derek's neighborhood much better."

"Well, there's nothing much we can do but check at the reception area of each building and see if we can get a feeling for the tenants and businesses of the inhabitants," Jessie said. "Unless you have a better idea?"

"I'll pass." Brice started to cross the street. "I'll take the skyscrapers on that side. You take these two, and I'll meet you back here at the car to compare notes. I don't imagine it will take very long, unless we get lucky."

Jessie didn't, either. But they had to try. She turned and entered the glittering glass doors of the Carmody Building.

—◆—

Jessie was leaning against the door of the car when Brice strolled back across the street to her. "You win. I gave up ten minutes ago. No startling revelations. Just an extremely busy hub of California humanity and business enterprise. I checked out all the businesses in the directories and they ranged from accounting firms to law offices to a wig broker."

"You made up that last one."

"Nope. I Googled it on my phone." She crossed her arms. "What about you?"

"About the same." He got into the passenger seat. "But you never can tell. Maybe something we saw today will click down the line."

"That's what I should be saying. Because I know it can be true." She got into the driver's seat. "But I doubt it this time, unless Peter can give us a photo to show to all those people who were giving me blank stares."

"He will. He's incredible. Give him a little time."

"I will. I have no choice." She started the car. "I'm just pissed off because I thought this might lead to a break." She backed out of the parking lot. "So let's go get a breakfast sandwich at the Pantry Café and then move on to the next step."

"Sounds like a fine plan." He smiled. "What's the next step?"

"We go back to that automotive shop and make ourselves obnoxious to the manager who flew the coop the last time."

His smile brightened to brilliance. "And that sounds even better."

"I thought it would. It's good to realize that such simple things please you."

"Not only simple things." The smile was now edged with sensuality. "Didn't you notice how I also embrace the complicated?"

Yes, she had, and she lost her breath as she remembered how completely he'd done that in the gym that night. She didn't look at him as she drove down the street toward the Pantry Café. "I noticed. But I prefer you focus on that automotive shop."

He laughed. "No you don't. But I'll do it anyway. I'll repeat it over and over to myself. The automotive shop. The automotive shop. The automotive shop."

"Be quiet." She pulled into the restaurant parking lot. "We'll be there soon enough."

⬥

There were no other children playing on the street this time when they drove through Derek's neighborhood. But they could see him standing at the far end of the street looking out at the field. She pulled over beside him. "Hi, Derek. How are you?"

"Okay." He looked at Brice. "I didn't see that car again."

"That's not why we're here. But I'm glad you're keeping an eye out for it."

He shrugged. "I wasn't." He pointed out to the field. "I was looking out there. It's gone."

"What?"

"The auto shop. Olympic Automotive. The building's locked up tight, and it's empty. I looked in all the windows. All the cars and equipment aren't there anymore."

Jessie stared in shock. Brice muttered a curse and started at a run across the field toward the automotive shop.

Derek was right. The building had been cleared out; even the signage was gone. There was no trace of the repair center they had just visited.

"Wow," Brice said.

Jessie nodded. "Wow is right. Things have a habit of disappearing on this street."

CHAPTER

8

Detective Wheeler was just as surprised to hear about the shuttered auto shop when Jessie called him. He texted back after fifteen minutes.

Jessie stared at the text from Wheeler. "This is interesting."

"Interesting how?"

"He says all the vehicles that were at Olympic Automotive are now at a storage garage near Exposition Park. The owners were all notified that their vehicles would be there only *after* the shop closed down. Apparently, they were all driven or towed there, and the on-site management of the facility has the keys and paperwork and is releasing the vehicles to their owners."

"Okay, I suppose that qualifies as interesting. What do you propose we do with that information?"

Jessie didn't even have to think about it. "We're going to

visit the fine people at Jefferson Vehicle Storage. Unless your special-effects guy has managed to work his magic on those frame grabs in the past few minutes, I can't think of a better use of our time."

———◆———

In less than half an hour, Jessie and Brice were standing in the main entrance of the vehicle storage facility, located on Jefferson Boulevard near the USC campus and several of the city's largest and most popular museums.

Brice looked around at the RVs and small boats on trailers stored on the ground floor. "I used to store some of my cars in a place like this."

"You don't anymore?"

"Nah. My collection's grown too much. Now I just lease a hangar at Santa Monica Airport."

"Boys and their toys."

"I'll take you over and show you sometime." He grinned. "It's not only boys who love their toys. I've seen you on that motorcycle."

"Have you got any motorcycles?"

"Fourteen. But only eleven that are currently in working order. There are only so many hours in the day, you know?"

"It must suck to be you."

An elderly man with a white beard and a potbelly approached them. "Picking up or dropping off?"

Jessie shook her head. "Neither. I want to talk about the vehicles from Olympic Automotive."

"Are you from the county? We talked on the phone this morning, right? I'm Wade Cole."

"I thought I'd come down and take a look at things myself," she said without answering his question. "Were you here when the vehicles were brought in?"

"Some of them. We were told that the automotive shop was going to have to close for maintenance issues, and we got a contract to keep the vehicles here and handle the return to their owners. The department of water and power was just here to get a couple of their trucks."

"Who at the shop did you deal with?"

"The manager."

"Do you remember his name?"

Cole motioned for them to follow him to a small office adjacent to the entrance. "I got the paperwork in here. I thought it was funny they were closing down so suddenly. I thought there might be something the shop wasn't telling us, like maybe they were going bankrupt or having to skip town to avoid creditors."

He picked up a red binder covered with Post-it Notes. He looked at one of them. "Here it is. The guy's name was Paul Moran."

Jessie exchanged a quick look with Brice. "Of course. We . . . *almost* met him." She pulled up Ferris's photo on her phone and showed it to him. "How about this guy? Have you seen him?"

Cole shook his head. "No."

"Positive?"

"Yeah, I'm sure. The manager was the only one we talked

to. He gave us this binder with info on all the vehicles he left with us." Cole flipped through the binder, which was filled with pages of ink-jet-printed photos of county vehicles, along with typed contact info for each one. Several of the photos had black tape over them.

"What's the tape for?" Jessie asked.

"We put that there whenever a car is picked up. About half of them are already gone."

Jessie reached for the binder. "May I see?"

Cole handed it to her. She flipped through the pages, which showed county and municipal vehicles like those they had seen during their visit to the auto shop. Some of the photos appeared to be taken inside the shop, while others were on an outdoor lot.

Jessie froze. "*This one.*"

Cole and Brice leaned over to look at the photo in front of her. "It's an animal control truck. Dogcatcher," Cole said.

"No. Behind it, in the background." She pointed to another vehicle parked several yards away. It was a white minibus with lettering on the side that read DEPARTMENT OF CORRECTIONS.

Cole shook his head. "They didn't bring that one here. I would have remembered it."

"But this means they had it in their shop."

He shrugged. "I guess."

She turned to Brice. "That's a prisoner transport bus. They're moving Sackler this week. Any day now."

"It could just be a coincidence."

"But what if it isn't?" Her mind raced. "I need to find out." She stepped away from the puzzled Cole and used her phone to call Twin Towers. It took her almost five minutes and two different operators to tell her what she needed to know. She finally whirled back to Brice. "He isn't there. He's being moved." She grabbed his arm. "We gotta go!"

"Go where?"

She turned and headed back toward her car. "Tehachapi."

———————◆———————

Colin Sackler shuffled through the concrete tunnel that would take him to the jail parking garage. Escorted by two guards, his legs were in irons with his hands cuffed in front of him. Today, finally, he was being moved to Tehachapi Correctional Institution eighty miles northeast of L.A.

The prison transport minibus was running and ready in the jail's lower-level garage, just feet from the long concrete tunnel. The guards led him through the bus's open door and up two steps to the narrow aisle that ran through a metal gate. The aisle went back five rows of seating, but Sackler was placed in the first row. He watched as one of the guards attached an in-line lock on the chain to a module on his seat.

He craned his neck to look at the uniformed driver. No one he'd ever seen before, like the guard standing in front of him.

"I guess there aren't any snacks on this flight," Sackler cracked.

"Won't need it," the guard said. "You'll be there in less than two hours, and I hear the chefs at your new home are already hard at work whipping up a seven-course meal for you."

"You're a funny guy, Dobbs," Sackler said, reading the name tag on his uniform. "Am I the only passenger today?"

"You're it. Do you like country music?"

"Nope."

"Too bad. That's all we listen to here." The guard closed the steel mesh gate, which automatically locked with a loud click. He sat in the front passenger seat and buckled up as the driver put the bus into gear and pulled out of the lot with the stereo blaring some god-awful twangy tune Sackler didn't recognize.

They left the city and headed north until the urban sprawl gave way to a series of country roads west of Mojave. The guard only occasionally looked up at the large observation mirror mounted over the windshield to check on him.

Sackler looked out at the desert brush as he reached down to the metal piping that formed the rim of his seat. He pulled on it, trying to slide it from left to right.

It didn't budge.

Shit.

He pulled again.

Nothing. Had something gone wrong?

Out of the corner of his eye, he could see the guard looking at him in the mirror. Sackler faked a yawn. When he was sure he was no longer being watched, he tugged again at the rim.

The piping slid away.

Perfect!

He reached inside the pipe with his forefinger and slid out a key and a plastic-wrapped substance about four inches long. He looked down at it. The packet was exactly as it had been described to him, with a green string protruding from one end.

Could this possibly work?

They turned onto a dusty two-lane highway. Almost time...

———◆———

Jessie sped up as she exited from the 14 freeway onto State Route 58. Wheeler was on speaker. "Jessie, the department of corrections can't get through to either guard's phone."

She and Brice shared a tense look. "How is that possible?"

"I don't know. They say that shouldn't happen. But they've alerted the highway patrol to pull them over when the bus is spotted. They should almost be at the prison by now."

"Us too. We're already in Kern County."

"I'm also on my way up there. If you see the bus, don't engage. Just call with the location."

Jessie drove in silence for a moment.

"Don't engage," Wheeler repeated. "Do you understand? The guards won't know who you are. You could get yourself shot."

"I understand. We'll evaluate the situation when the time comes."

"Dammit, Jessie..."

"I'll be in touch." She cut the connection.

Brice nodded. "He sounded a bit annoyed."

"He'll get over it," she said. "What's our next turn?"

Brice looked at the maps app on his phone. "Left on Highline Road. That'll take us most of the way to the prison. The transport should be between here and there."

"Then keep your eyes peeled."

———◆———

"I haven't been able to get online this entire trip." The guard looked down at his phone. "Can't even get a damn signal."

"I had the same problem," the driver said. "I tried to check email back at the jail, and it wouldn't load. Must be a problem with the network."

Sackler smiled. Yeah, that was it. A problem with the network. He looked out the window as he gripped the plastic-wrapped packet in his hands. Shouldn't it have happened by now? It would be just his luck to have it fouled up.

Suddenly the bus's engine went quiet. There was no sputtering, no indication that anything was wrong; one second the engine was chugging along, the next there was only the whistling of tires on the pavement.

The guard whirled to the driver. "What the hell's happening?"

"Don't know. Shit." The driver steered the bus to the side of the road as it coasted to a stop. "It's dead."

Sackler looked out the window. They were on a lonely stretch of road, miles from any home or commercial building. They had passed what appeared to be a broken-down jeep on the side of the road, but other than that there was nothing to see but thousands of acres of scrub brush in each direction.

"Oh, man." The driver picked up his phone. "No signal at all. You?"

The guard checked his phone. "No. And I know damn well there are towers out here."

Sackler laughed. "At least you guys can't play that shit-kicking music anymore."

"Shut up," the guard said.

The driver opened his door. "I'm gonna look under the hood."

"Okay." The guard stood and took his position standing in front of the gate while the driver climbed out and walked around to the engine compartment.

"It's freakin' hot out here," Sackler said. "What is it? A hundred? A hundred and five? Maybe it overheated."

"Maybe."

"I'm pretty good with engines." Sackler leaned forward and gripped the metal gate. "I can take a look."

"Just sit down. He knows what he's doing."

Sackler released his grip on the gate, leaving the small packet affixed to the lock. He quickly glanced up. The guard hadn't noticed.

They watched as the driver lifted the hood and leaned inside.

BAM!

There was a loud pop, followed by a fizzing sound. The driver screamed and stumbled backward. His face was covered in what appeared to be blood.

"My God, Hawley!" the guard yelled.

The driver was still screaming. The foamy liquid on his face was slightly pinker than blood, Sackler realized, but whatever it was, it was causing excruciating pain to the man's skin and eyes.

Sackler used the key to quickly unlock himself from the module and then leaned forward and pulled the green string from the packet. He threw himself on the floor, several feet behind the seat.

BOOM!

The explosive material blew the gate, sending shards of metal into the guard's chest and neck. The man fell backward, unconscious. Sackler kicked the gate open and grabbed the guard's gun. He sprinted through the open door and ran past the still-screaming driver, who was now on his hands and knees.

Tough luck, buddy.

Sackler bolted toward the old jeep about fifty yards back. As he'd been promised, the ignition key was under the floor mat. A black box with two short antennas was on the passenger side floor. That device, he knew, triggered the kill switch that had been placed in the bus's engine compartment.

Sackler started the jeep and spun out, heading back in the direction from which they had just come. In less than a hundred yards, he turned off the road and sped across the open desert.

———◆———

Brice leaned forward in his seat. "Is that...?"

"That's the prison transport." Jessie accelerated. The bus

was about a quarter mile away, resting on the side of the road. As they drew nearer, she could see a bare-chested man using his uniform shirt to wipe his face. His red-stained cheeks were streaked with tears and snot.

Jessie pulled over, and she and Brice jumped from the SUV. "What happened?" she yelled.

"Prisoner escape." The driver still didn't look up. "Check on the guard. He's hurt."

Jessie jumped into the bus and saw the wounded guard. "Shit. It's bad." She turned back toward the driver. "Did you call 911?"

"It just happened. And our phones aren't working."

Jessie pulled out her phone. "Zero signal bars."

Brice checked his. "Same here."

Jessie ran a few yards away and checked again. "I'm good over here. There must be something in the bus that's jamming our reception." She called 911 for medical assistance and to report the escape, passing along details as dictated by the driver. She hung up and called Wheeler.

"Sackler's gone."

Wheeler cursed. "Which way was he headed?"

"The driver thinks he took off in a white jeep. But it was only a couple minutes before I came on the scene, and I sure didn't see him heading back my way. And I seriously doubt he was heading toward the prison."

"Then where'd he go?"

Jessie turned and looked around. There, miles in the distance, was a single brown plume moving across the landscape. It could be from a tractor, or maybe . . .

"See you when you get here." She hung up on Wheeler and pointed toward the dust cloud. "There."

Brice turned toward the driver. "Could that be him?"

He struggled to see with his still-watering eyes. "Hard to say. Maybe. It's only been a few minutes."

Jessie ran back to her SUV. "I'll check it out."

"I'm going with you," Brice said.

"No!" She spun around. "Apply pressure to the guard's wounds. Do CPR if he needs it. Can you do that?"

"Of course. But I'm not just going to let you—"

"Not your choice, Brice. Help them!"

Jessie started her SUV. She spun the wheel and sped back down the road until she saw fresh skid marks where a vehicle had recently left the pavement.

That had to be it.

She cut the wheel hard right and followed the skid marks into the desert brush. Her SUV shook from the bumpy terrain. She engaged the four-wheel drive as she tried to look for places where the vegetation had been disturbed. There was no easy trail, but she could still see the dust plume in the distance.

She gripped the wheel harder as the shaking became more intense. This would definitely be easier with a jeep, especially if it was equipped with off-road tires.

She swerved to avoid a boulder and then again to narrowly miss a large cactus.

Where in the hell could he be heading? She tried to visualize an overall picture of the area based on her recent use of Google Maps on her phone. As far as she could remember, there were no highways or major roads up ahead, at least for several miles.

The dirty plume was higher in the sky. She was catching up.

Let it be him and not just a piece of farm machinery. She powered down her window, but she couldn't hear anything over the sound of her own struggling engine.

After a few minutes, Jessie looked up. The plume was dissipating, fading into the afternoon sun. Whatever caused it had stopped. She reached into her jacket, unsnapped her holster, and pulled out her nine-millimeter automatic. She placed it on the seat beside her.

She was on an incline now, climbing a small ridge. Up ahead, she heard a distinctive engine roar, accompanied by a hydraulic whine.

What in the hell?

A helicopter roared over the ridge, directly in front of her!

Jessie jammed on the brakes, grabbed her gun, and leaped from her SUV. She saw the white jeep at the bottom of the ridge, driver's side door still open, next to the flat expanse where the helicopter had obviously been waiting.

BLAM–BLAM–BLAM!

Gunfire rained from the helicopter. Jessie took cover behind her vehicle.

BLAM–BLAM!

The helicopter banked right and roared away. Jessie holstered her gun, pulled out her phone, and called Wheeler.

"You hung up on me, Mercado."

"He's in a helicopter. It looks like an old Robinson R22,

like the news stations used to fly. It's white with faded blue trim."

"You get a tail number?"

"Afraid not. It's been mudded over."

"Okay, I'll call it in. Are you all right?"

"Fine. Better if I'd been able to catch the scumbag."

"We'll get him."

"I'll see you at the bus. I'm headed back there now."

"Okay. Good work, Mercado."

"Yeah, sure," she said in disgust. "He still got away."

———◆———

A paramedic unit and a highway patrol officer were already on the scene by the time Jessie arrived back at the prison transport bus. The guard had regained consciousness, his wounds had been cleaned, and he was being administered a painkiller. The driver was given an eye flush, and both men were quickly driven away to the hospital.

As the paramedic unit left, Jessie looked under the bus's open hood. "There was a small charge planted here. It sprayed something in the driver's eyes. It's all over the place in here."

"Planted by who?" Brice said.

"One guess," Jessie said. "Most likely a recently closed L.A. auto shop."

She walked around and climbed into the bus's open door.

"Ma'am, I can't let you in there." The trooper stepped toward her. "It's a crime scene."

"Then you'd better come in here with me. Make sure I don't disturb anything."

"My orders are to secure the scene."

"And you're doing a bang-up job." Jessie crouched next to the gate and inspected the blown lock. "Where in the hell did Sackler get this stuff?"

The officer leaned into the bus. "Ma'am..."

"I'm not touching anything." Her eyes went to the seat, where she immediately spotted the missing section of piping. "That's where." She stood and exited the bus.

It took Wheeler almost an hour longer to reach them, and the crime scene techs arrived a few minutes after that. Jessie showed them the charge under the hood, the blown lock, and the piping where Sackler had obtained the key and explosive putty. She also pointed out what she assumed was a kill switch activated by a timer or a nearby triggering device that caused the sudden breakdown.

"This bus was in that auto garage," Jessie said. "They did this."

Wheeler used his phone to snap photos of the kill switch. "I think you're right. We need to find them. The driver and guard were taken to Adventist Health hospital. I'll go there and see if I can get statements, but I probably won't get anything more than what you got."

"Probably not," she said absently. Her gaze was still on that red explosive powder. It was familiar..."I'm heading back into town. Need anything more from me?"

Wheeler shook his head as he turned away. "I'll let you know if we find that copter."

"Good. Thanks, Wheeler."

She suddenly stopped short.

A very familiar red powder.

Brice nodded toward him. "You don't want to go with him to the hospital? That guard might be able to talk now."

"I don't need to talk to the guard," she said sharply. "I need to talk to my damn client."

Wheeler obviously had been too busy to make the connection with the red powder they'd found in that vacuum cleaner at Ferris's house, and Jessie whirled toward Brice and grabbed his arm. "We're out of here. Let's get going." She didn't wait for an answer but strode over to the SUV and jumped into the driver's seat.

Brice followed at a slower pace but was buckling his seat belt a minute later. "What's the hurry? This was a very interesting crime scene. And I think I was just beginning to bond with Wheeler. He only yelled at me twice to get out of his way."

"Well, he'll probably do it again after he catches up with us." She backed up and then took off down the highway. "So you'll have your opportunity to explore the possibilities. But I had to get out of there fast so I could decide if I wanted to let Wheeler arrest my client."

"I think I should call attention to the fact that you're speeding. Client? Owen?"

"I know I'm speeding." She was dialing her phone. "I don't have that much time before Wheeler identifies that red dust." She let it ring until it went to voicemail. "Owen's not answering. I want to talk to him before the police do. We'll start with his house."

They arrived at Owen's Pacific Palisades home just in time to see his gray Cadillac Escalade backing out of the driveway.

Jessie screeched to a halt, blocking the vehicle.

Owen jumped out of his SUV. "What are you doing, Jessie? Get out of my way."

"I don't think so." She looked at the packed bags in the back compartment. "Going somewhere?"

"What if I am? Just a little trip out of town. None of your business."

"I believe it could be. We just came from an escape from a prisoner transport. It was your client, Colin Sackler. Two guards have been hospitalized. Evidence will show your missing partner may have been responsible. There was a red component in an explosive compound hidden in that prison bus. I saw it at Ferris's place, and the police saw it, too."

"I don't know what you're talking about."

"What about the fact that the bus's carefully choreographed breakdown was almost certainly orchestrated by the automotive garage where Ferris's car was recently seen? Talk to me, Owen. Tell me what's happening."

"I can't do that. It's all Ferris's fault. I had nothing to do with it."

Jessie motioned to the luggage in the backseat. "Then why were you trying to skip town?"

"Okay, I might have heard about the escape from one of the guards at Twin Towers. I want to get away and plan my next move."

"While I'm out here twisting in the wind. Owen, it appears that your firm arranged a prisoner escape."

"Not the firm. Carl Ferris. I had no idea what he was doing."

"Then you'll have to convince the police of that."

Just then a squad car and Wheeler's SUV tore around the corner.

"Wheeler," Brice murmured.

Jessie nodded. "I'll handle it."

Wheeler climbed out of his car and stared at Jessie for a long moment. "The red powder," he said.

"Yeah, I saw it, too. Owen says he doesn't know anything about it."

"Maybe he should tell *me*," Wheeler said. He looked at Owen's car at the bottom of the long driveway. "But thanks for blocking him in." He looked up at Owen. "Looks like you were going somewhere."

"I had nothing to do with that escape," Owen said. "But I suppose I'd better call my lawyer."

"That might be a good idea," Wheeler said as he took his arm. "And I think you'd better come along with us for a little discussion." He smiled at Jessie. "Thanks for helping out. See you later?"

She nodded.

Before they put him in the squad car, Owen glanced at Jessie and said under his breath, "Yeah, thanks a lot."

"I guess I'm out of a job?"

"Hell, no," he muttered as he ducked into the squad car. "I need you to find Ferris more than ever. Find the bastard!"

◆

When Jessie and Brice walked into the police station an hour later, she saw Wheeler coming out of the elevator talking to a well-dressed, expertly coiffed man. "The lawyer," she murmured to Brice as she watched Wheeler shake hands with him. "He must have been waiting for Owen. Though Wheeler is being awfully cordial with him."

"Because it's Josia Fenton," Brice said. "He was probably at that reception the other day, and he's good friends with the chief of police you met."

"You know him, too?"

"Yes, but not as well as I do Rand. He might not recognize me." He shrugged. "But I won't take the chance. You don't need me to stay here while you talk to Wheeler anyway. He'll be much more at ease with you if he doesn't have to worry about competing. Tell him I asked you to drop by here so that I could go to the A/V lab and see if Peter was performing satisfactorily, since I recommended him." He turned toward the elevators. "Call me when you're finished."

"That lawyer's leaving," she said. "And your other excuse was pretty lame. Wheeler is an adult and a professional."

"Then maybe it's me that's afraid of competing." His eyes were twinkling. "Anyway it's still a good excuse and you needed one." He brushed by Wheeler as he got on the elevator. "Good to see you again, Wheeler. On my way to check out Peter Norris in the A/V lab. Has he been doing a good job for you?"

"A great job, according to the A/V team. They say he helped write some of the software they use."

"Thank Jessie. Always glad to help her on a case." The

door was closing. "And she told me what a total pro you are, Wheeler. See you later."

Wheeler turned to Jessie as the elevator doors shut. "I didn't expect to see you this soon."

And Brice had been right about her needing him as an excuse, she thought in resignation. "It's a surprise to me, too. But Rick has been so worried that Norris might not be performing to your satisfaction that I gave in about coming here when I would have much rather have gone back to that crime scene. He said by the time I had a cup of coffee, he'd be back, and we could get on the road." She headed for the coffee machine. "Don't let me keep you. I know you must be busy with Owen."

"Doing what?" he asked sourly as he put coins in the coffee machine. "Black, isn't it?" When she nodded, he punched the selection. "I barely had time to get him settled in an interrogation room when his fancy lawyer was knocking on the door. I had ten minutes of asking him questions about Sackler and his partner, who now looks guilty as hell, before his lawyer stopped me from harassing the poor man."

She took a sip of coffee. "Any answers?"

"He punted. Completely innocent, of course." He frowned. "But you know, I have a hunch he might be telling the truth about not knowing that Ferris might have set up the escape plan."

"Really? I didn't know you believed in hunches."

"I don't. But I believe in my own judgment, and it's the same thing."

"There's a lot to be said for instincts." She took another

sip of coffee. "Did he say anything in the squad car coming here?"

"Nah, nothing about the escape. I asked him about Jennifer Dayton, though, and if she might have known anything about him planning it."

She saw where he was going. "The marriage? You don't know why he'd ask her to marry him and then ask her not to tell anyone? That was weird as hell. You're thinking she might have been in on the planning of the escape and that's why he wanted the secret marriage? A wife can't testify against her husband." She shook her head. "I'd swear she was honest with me."

"So would all the other people I interviewed," Wheeler said. "I ran it by Owen to see what he thinks. He doubts that she really had anything to do with Ferris's schemes, but it's possible he told her something about what he was doing."

"What about the automotive garage? Could he tell you anything about that?"

"Total blank," Wheeler said. "Which is where my entire department is right now. We've talked to several of the shop's employees, and they have no clue what happened. The owner, who was responsible for closing it up, has disappeared." He checked his watch. "But we have a lead we're following up on. I'm supposed to get a call soon."

He looked up and smiled. "You're the one who tipped us off about the garage. I'll be sure to let you know when I get the word."

"Thanks. I'd appreciate it."

It was almost 10:00 P.M. when Brice walked Jessie to her front door. He lightly brushed her cheek. "You did good work today. I can see why you're so good at your job."

"My client isn't so thrilled."

"Your client may be a crook."

He leaned close to kiss her, but Jessie's phone buzzed in her pocket. She pulled it out and read the screen. "It's Kendra."

"Which means that's my exit cue." His hand dropped away from her face. "Damn. She may be brilliant, but she has lousy timing." He stepped back and turned away. "Answer her. I'll see you in the morning. Remember to lock the door behind you." Then he was gone.

She drew a deep breath as she punched the talk button. "Kendra? It's good to hear from you. Are you having a good time?"

"I'm learning a lot. I guess that's good enough. It's beautiful here, but I miss home. I'll be glad to get back. How have you been doing with Owen?"

"Not much progress finding his partner. There have been...difficulties."

"What kind of difficulties?"

"I'm not quite certain. I'm still exploring."

"You sound like you're walking on eggshells." She paused. "Did I saddle you with a situation you're uncomfortable with?"

And if Kendra got even a hint of that, she'd be on the next plane. "Don't be silly. I took the job, and I'll work it out. It just may take a little longer than I thought." *Distract her.* "Why does everyone think I need someone to hold my hand? Let me tell you what Dee did."

She proceeded to tell the story of Dee sending her bodyguard team to Jessie complete with the Pink's meal and how Jessie had been tearing her hair out to think of a way to send them back without hurting their feelings. She made it as exaggerated and as humorous as possible without mentioning Brice or why Dee had been that concerned about her. Evidently, she did a good job because Kendra was howling with laughter before she'd finished.

"Good Lord, what did you do to her?" she gasped.

"What could I do? It was Dee." Jessie added, "But she finally decided I didn't need those giants, and she's happy now." Then she changed the subject, and for the next fifteen minutes, she kept the conversation as light and amusing as possible. When they finally said goodbye, Jessie felt as if she should draw a breath of relief. Well, if she'd kept Kendra from worrying about her, that was the main objective. If she'd had to explain Jennifer Dayton's death or the attempts on her own life, Kendra would have returned home immediately.

Jessie headed for the bedroom to shower and get to sleep. She usually enjoyed talking to Kendra, but tonight's call had unsettled her. It brought home how far she was from finding Carl Ferris and how deadly this missing persons case had become. She was filled with dread, not optimism, and she hoped tomorrow would change that feeling.

CHAPTER

9

Tomorrow brought an early-morning call from Wheeler. It rang three times while Jessie struggled to become wide awake enough to reach her phone on the bedside table and recognize the ID. "Wheeler? Why am I being honored at this hour of the morning?"

"Stop bellyaching," he said gruffly. "Because I made you a promise, and I'm trying to keep it. Informants don't always work nine to five. I got the message two hours ago, and I've been trying to call him back ever since. I just got through to him."

"Informant?" She sat up straight in bed. "What promise?"

"I told you that I'd let you tag along with me when I made contact with Paul Moran, the manager of that automotive garage."

"You found him? Where is he?"

"I didn't find him. But I put the word out, and my informant said that he'd heard from one of his mechanic buddies that Moran was trying to score some cash by selling off some of his expensive diagnostic equipment. He's supposed to meet someone in the business to close the deal early this morning so that he can get the hell out of town."

"When?"

"Five. And I've got to get out to the storage facility where they're meeting before Moran skips out. Do you want to come or not?"

"Of course I want to come." She was on her feet and heading for the bathroom. "Text me the address, and I'll call you when I get close. Okay?"

"Okay. It's on Whittier." He rattled off the address.

"I'll see you out there." She cut the connection and started to throw on her clothes. Five minutes later, she was heading for the door.

She stopped. Brice. He probably wouldn't be pleased. Too bad.

◆

She met Wheeler a couple of blocks from the storage facility. He was alone in his unmarked vehicle. "Just in time." He was moving down the street toward the complex. "No vehicles on the street. But they might be inside the yard."

"It looks deserted," Jessie said. She followed him quickly. "You're sure your informant had the right info?"

"I'm told he's reliable." Wheeler checked out the storage

unit. "It's unlocked." He lifted the gate. "Stay here. I'll go ahead and see what's going on."

Jessie ignored his words and ducked around him. "Well, he must have been here." She was looking at an assortment of gear lying on the ground. "I'm sure I saw this stuff at the automotive garage." She froze. "And that's Moran's car over there."

"You're sure?"

"Oh, yes. I was very pissed off when he peeled out of that shop instead of talking to us." She edged toward the car as she lit the flashlight on her phone. "Why would he leave it here? I guess he could have sold it with his other equipment, but that would have been—"

She broke off because she knew why Moran had left that car.

He was lying slumped in the passenger seat with a bullet in his head.

———◆———

8:05 A.M.

There wasn't much more she could do here, Jessie thought as she watched the medical examiner's van pull out into the street. Not that she'd accomplished very much in the past couple of hours. But she'd been lucky that Wheeler had let her—

"Good morning," Brice said as he ducked under the crime scene tape and strolled toward her. "I hope I didn't miss anything." He handed her a cup of Starbucks coffee. "I was right on time but somehow I missed you. I wonder how that happened." He was pissed.

"I left you a note."

"I read it."

"And I sent you a text fifteen minutes ago. I was busy or I would have done it before that."

He glanced at the van that was departing with Paul Moran's corpse. "I can see how you might have been." He took a sip of his own coffee. "It didn't occur to you that you should have called me when Wheeler dragged you out of bed to come here? That I might have a right to know when you were going to take a risk like that?"

"No, Brice. Time was short, and I didn't want to miss out on possibly seeing Moran. This is my job, and I knew I could handle it, no matter what it was. Okay?"

"But it ended up with you 'handling' a murder victim." He held up his hand as she opened her lips. "I know I don't have any right to be pissed. I was just worried. The thought of you getting hurt scares the hell out of me. But I know I have to tread very carefully around you or you'll throw me off the case."

"I do appreciate what you've done for me, Brice. Of course there are going to be risks in what I do. But I can't let you get in the way of me doing my job."

"Fine. I'll keep that in mind." He glanced around. "You seem to have been deserted by Wheeler. Where is he?"

She shrugged. "I have no idea. He took off about twenty minutes ago after he got through talking to the M.E. It's not as if he had any responsibility for me. He gave me a chance to make contact with Moran, and he let me go around with him to canvass the neighbors. That's more than I could expect from him. He kept his promise. It just didn't work out as we both thought it would."

———————◆———————

They had just climbed back in her SUV when Jessie finally got through to Owen. He sounded distinctly frazzled and a little ill tempered. "It's about time you got in touch with me. Toss me into that detective's hands and just walk out of my life."

"I wasn't sure you really wanted to continue our arrangement." She paused. "And I wasn't sure that I wanted to go on when I felt you weren't helping me."

"I meant what I said. I need you to find that bastard, Ferris. He's making my life miserable."

"Then I need direct access to your company's files. All of them, not just the names of your clients. Everything. I want it right now, and no excuses."

"Shit." He was swearing under his breath. "Okay, but Ferris didn't keep complete records for his special clients, maybe on purpose. If you want to take a look, though, you'd better get down here damn quick while there still is a firm."

"What do you mean?"

"There are cops and U.S. Marshals swarming all over this place, tearing into everything, trying to find any info about Ferris. You might as well join them." He cut the connection.

———————◆———————

When Jessie and Brice arrived at the Mamertine office, they saw that Owen hadn't exaggerated. It appeared to be under siege as agents seized computers, office files, and employee phones. Wheeler was in charge, giving orders to the agents while Owen stood helplessly looking on.

"Your territory," Brice murmured. "Ask your questions, and I'll wander around and try to pick up on anything."

Wheeler glanced at Jessie as she walked into the room. "If you have any influence with this dude, you'd better tell him to talk to me. He doesn't realize what kind of shit he's in."

"I have talked to you," Owen said. "Just like I've talked to Jessie. But I can't discuss what I don't know."

Jessie pointed to a group of U.S. Marshals. "That's a new development."

Wheeler nodded. "Sackler's escape falls under marshals service jurisdiction. Since it's looking like Ferris may have helped arrange the escape, they're on his trail, too."

"Ferris," Owen said. "Not me."

Wheeler crossed his arms. "You can help yourself by helping us find him."

"I'm already doing that by paying her." Her jerked his thumb toward Jessie. "She's been taking my money searching for the bastard and she hasn't been able to find him, either."

"I'm asking you," Wheeler said. "Another possible participant in this escape has turned up dead, and your partner may have had some connection with him. If I were you, I'd try harder to help us." Wheeler strode away toward the reception desk, where agents had collected the confiscated laptops.

A woman's voice called out from down the hall, "Come on, give me ten seconds!"

Jessie looked up to see a group of marshals rolling out the freestanding bulletin boards she'd seen during her previous visit to the office. Ferris's young assistant, Sienna, was running after them with her phone, trying to snap pictures of the client information boards. "Please, guys. I need this to do my job."

The marshals didn't even slow down.

Jessie dropped to her knee in front of the first board, blocking the marshals' path out. She pretended to adjust the cuff of her pant leg.

The deputies stopped. "Ma'am?" one of them asked.

Jessie didn't look up, but she could hear Sienna's camera phone clicking away behind them. "Just a second, guys."

"If you wouldn't mind..."

Jessie stood and backed away, allowing the marshals to roll the boards toward the elevators.

"Thanks," Sienna said as she checked the photos on her phone. "I needed to get these."

"Don't you already have everything in your client files?"

"Yeah, but Mr. Ferris has those pages color-coded on his boards to show the status of every client's stuff. Some of them are more up to date than the computer files. This will make it a lot easier for me. Thank you."

"Anytime."

Sienna walked away.

"Yes, thank you," Owen said. "Though it may not make a difference if the firm goes under."

She turned toward him. "This is bigger than your firm, Owen. Do you have an alibi for last night?"

"Yes, I was on a Zoom call with a producer in Taiwan for most of the night. But that cop didn't care. He's sure I know something." He was cursing again. "I could kill Ferris. He's destroying everything I've worked for here."

"I wouldn't talk about killing anyone right now if I were you," she said. "It's very bad timing."

"And I'm even angrier that I have to worry about word choices when I'm not guilty of anything."

She pulled him to one side. "Then tell me what you know about that investment firm robbery Sackler was convicted of. It's almost a sure bet that whoever engaged your firm on his behalf was the same person who orchestrated his escape. Tell me that and we're halfway to an answer."

"I know. That detective pounced on me the minute he came in today. You have to believe me when I tell you that I didn't have anything to do with this. Ferris set it up."

She studied Owen with narrowed eyes. Was he telling the truth? She probed a little deeper. "You have to think about it. It's dangerous not to realize the position you're in. Remember that both Jennifer Dayton and Paul Moran were murdered because they probably knew something that someone didn't want them to reveal. For all we know, Ferris could be dead, too. You could end up with a bullet in your head if you're hiding something. It's not worth it to take that kind of risk."

"Ferris isn't dead. I know he isn't. He's just trying to hang all this blame on me. Maybe he got himself in trouble and he doesn't know how to get out." His voice was suddenly harsh. "All you've got to do is find him. I'll pay you anything you want to drag him back here. But I don't want you to turn him in to the police until I get a chance to talk to him privately."

"Why?" Jessie asked.

"The son of a bitch has destroyed my business and my entire life. I have a right to have him standing in front of me to tell him that and ask him why." His expression turned hard. "That's what I'm paying you for. Do you understand?"

Jessie nodded. "You're making yourself clear."

She didn't know what to think of Owen. It could be rage that was causing him to ignore everything but his anger toward Ferris. But she'd thought she'd seen just a flicker of fear when she'd spoken about the deaths of Paul Moran and Jennifer Dayton. It could be that he felt as if he was being drawn closer into that deadly circle but was afraid to confront it.

"Goodbye, Owen." She turned away and made her way toward Brice, who was waiting at the door.

"Anything?" he murmured as he fell into step with her. "He looked...upset."

She nodded. "And I think he might be scared."

———◆———

Jessie whistled when Brice walked into the kitchen the next morning. "Very nice." Her gaze slowly traveled over his beautifully tailored dark suit and crisp white shirt. "I wasn't expecting it. Sophisticated businessman instead of a dashing playboy."

"It's a multifaceted role you've chosen for me." He shrugged. "I can't be Zorro or James Bond all the time. When you told me we were going to Jennifer Dayton's memorial service this morning, I decided I had to honor her." He looked at Jessie's black sheath dress and her hair pulled away from her face. "Just as you're doing. It's a good look for you."

She nodded. "It's difficult thinking of going there as business, even when I realize that Ferris or even the murderer might be there. I didn't know her well, but I got the impression that Jennifer was a good person." Jessie looked away. "And I was there when she had her life torn from her. Her killer tried to take my life, too. It could have been my memorial service you were going to today."

"Shut up," he said. "Do you actually believe I didn't think about that while I was driving here? I remember that night." He pulled her to her feet. "Let's get out of here. May I drive?"

"No," she said flatly. "I was afraid you'd want to take over when I let you drive yesterday."

"I didn't think I'd get lucky, but I had to try." He held the door open for her. "So we sit in the back of the chapel and be respectful and keep our eyes open. Is that the plan?"

She got in the driver's seat. "And maybe take a few photos if there's anyone interesting."

◆

Jessie saw someone interesting the minute they entered the Westwood United Methodist Church. Wheeler was standing under the balcony at the far side of the huge room and nodded to her as she and Brice sat down in the back pew. Then he was crossing the chapel toward them.

He nodded at Brice. "Hello. Good to see you. Somehow I thought you'd be here."

"And here I am." Brice smiled. "I suppose you're here for the same reason as Jessie?"

He nodded. "And so are those two U.S. Marshals sitting over there near those stained-glass windows. Jennifer Dayton has a nice crowd here. I'm sure she wouldn't mind that she has a few people who are trying to find a reason she ended up the way she did." He hesitated and then took a step to the side. "Can I have a word with you, Jessie?"

"Sure." She stood and slid past Brice into the aisle. "A problem?"

"Maybe. I just wanted you to know I appreciate the help you've given me, and I respect the fact that you're a good P.I. This has nothing to do with either of those things."

She tilted her head. "Go on."

"But it's gotten a little difficult lately. I'm not going to be able to feed as much information as I have been on this case. Ferris is a prime suspect in a prisoner escape. The U.S. Marshals Service has taken over that part of our investigation, and I can't step on their toes by openly feeding you information, especially when the suspect's own firm is your client."

She smiled. "You've been very generous, Wheeler. I've enjoyed working with you. Perhaps another time?"

He sighed with relief. "You bet." He glanced at Brice. "And you're not entirely on your own."

"Actually, I am. He's not like us. He's an outsider who might not be around long. So any tips you throw my way will be appreciated." Her smile widened. "Good luck, Wheeler." She turned and slid back into the pew and dropped down beside Brice.

"Am I allowed to know what he said?"

"He more or less fired me. He's nervous about the U.S. Marshals. We might get a crumb of information from him from now on, but it won't be much."

"You didn't look like you were being fired."

"I didn't want him to feel bad about it. That would be a sure way to have him step farther away. Now he'll remember that I was understanding and cooperative, and I thought the same about him. He's much more likely to work with me again. That's the name of the game when you're a P.I."

He chuckled. "Did I ever tell you how sharp you are?" He paused. "He was looking at me once. Did I enter into the conversation?"

"I told him I couldn't count on you as I did him," she added bluntly. "That you might not be around long."

"Ouch. I don't like that."

"Tough. It's the truth, Desmond."

"We'll see." He leaned back. "The pastor is coming to the podium. Time to start checking out the guests."

During the service, Jessie watched the other attendees more than Jennifer's friends and relations speaking about her from the podium. Studying their reactions. She could see Wheeler and the other law-enforcement officers doing the same thing. She tried to memorize the faces of everyone who was more interested in the other attendees than the service itself.

About midway through the service, they ran a projected photo montage set to music. There were several photos of Jennifer and Ferris at a beach house somewhere, during several different visits at different times of year, judging by their dress. Jessie took note. She raised her camera and snapped photos of several different slides, including one of Jennifer and Ferris near a beachside cotton candy vendor.

"The beach?" Brice asked as the service ended. "You might ask Owen, if we can catch up to him. I saw him standing in the vestibule watching from there."

"We'll catch him." She turned and almost ran outside and down the steps. Owen was just getting into his Escalade when she caught up with him. "I wasn't expecting you to be here, Owen. You were pretty bitter when I spoke to you yesterday."

"Those cops would have probably thought I killed her, too," he said. "And I liked Jennifer. Ferris didn't deserve her." He looked at her. "Were you here to see if he'd come?"

"Among other things." She showed him the beach photos on her phone. "You probably saw these on the screen. Do you know where that place is?"

He glanced at the photos. "I have no idea."

"Did you ever hear either one talk about a beach trip?"

He shook his head.

"Why did I know that would be your answer?"

"Because Ferris screwed me over every way he could." He climbed into the SUV. "Find him."

The next moment he drove away.

Brice was right behind her. "No luck?"

Jessie shook her head. "It's not my day. But at least *he* didn't fire me." She sighed. "Though I'm beginning to wish he would." She pulled out her phone and worked her way through a few different screens.

"You really need to wean yourself from that Candy Crush addiction."

"Candy Crush?" She stifled a giggle. "What decade are you from?"

"Dated reference?"

"A little. I think I played that in elementary school."

"Ooh." He made a face. "You know, it's really not cool to go after an actor's age."

"I wasn't implying you're old, just . . ."

". . . ridiculously out of touch?"

"Bingo."

"I guess I can live with that."

"Good." She flipped back and forth between a photo and a web screen. "The game I'm playing is called 'track the business license.'"

"What?"

"In that photo montage, on the same day Ferris and his girl-friend were at that house, they were also near a cotton candy cart on the beach. A business license number was stenciled on its side."

"How do you know it was the same day?"

"They're both wearing the same clothes, and Jennifer Dayton was also wearing her hair the same way, with those same daisy hair clips."

"You have a source who can give you info on that business license?"

"Yeah, the state of California." She held up her phone. "It's registered in Ventura. Wanna go to the beach?"

———◆———

Less than an hour's drive up the 101 freeway, Jessie and Brice parked on the pay lot at Ventura Pier Beach and walked across the paved bike path. Jessie pointed to the white cart serving up cotton candy to two children. "That's it. We're in the right place."

Brice looked around and then pointed to a cluster of beach houses about half a mile south. "Those look like the house in the picture. Should we head down there?"

"Definitely."

They walked down the beach until they reached the group of almost-identical attached beach houses with wooden balconies. Most were adorned with deck chairs, small tables, and hanging flowerpots.

Jessie compared the decks with a photo she'd snapped at the memorial service. She pointed at an end unit. "That one."

"Are you sure?" Brice tilted his head. "They look a lot alike."

"Look at the design on the hanging pot. And the trim around the door is rust-colored, just like in the picture."

Brice nodded. He gripped the balcony railing and swung himself over with the power and grace of an Olympic gymnast. Jessie followed him with just as much power, but substantially less grace.

Brice snickered. "If you like, I can show you how to smooth out that move."

"No, thanks. It must be exhausting to constantly care how you look when you do things."

"You have no idea. I can't tell you how many retakes I've had to do for picky directors."

She moved to the sliding glass door and peered through a narrow opening in the curtains. "Doesn't look like anyone's here." She turned toward Brice. "Tell you what. Before I knock, go around to the other side and make sure no one slips out."

"And if someone does?"

"If it's Ferris, tackle him. We didn't come this far for him to get away from us."

"Got it." Brice executed another graceful swing over the porch railing and ran around to the front side.

She looked through the window opening again and rapped on the glass.

No reply.

She tried again. Still nothing.

Brice walked back around. "No dice, huh?"

"No." Jessie looked around to see if anyone was watching them. "I'm going inside. You might want to wait back at the car."

"Why?"

"Because if we get caught, your mug shot is going to be on the evening news all over the world."

"Hey, I'm trying to save a man's life. Who would blame me for that?"

"Ventura PD might."

"Don't worry about that. Want me to break the lock?"

"No." She moved to a horizontal sliding window next to the door. "No alarm sensors here, and I didn't see any motion detectors inside." She placed her hands flat against the windowpane and tried to slide it across. It didn't budge. "Locked."

"Want me to break that one?"

"No." She smiled with amusement. "You really want to break something, don't you?" She pointed to the visible swivel sash lock halfway up the window. "Watch."

She placed both hands on the pane again and quickly moved it up and down in the frame. It gave less than a quarter inch, but the movement was enough to put pressure on the sash lock. As she continued, the sash lock slowly swiveled downward.

"No way." Brice stepped closer to get a better look.

Jessie continued the up-and-down movement of the window. "Just a little bit more . . ."

The sash lock continued its downward swivel until it reached a full-unlocked position. She pushed right to slide the window open.

"Wow," Brice said. "It's scary how easily you just did that. I hope my stalkers don't know that trick."

"Invest in some better locks. And maybe a few broomsticks."

She climbed through the open window.

As Brice followed, Jessie glanced around the small living room and kitchen area. "No photographs or anything that connect it to Ferris. Nothing personal at all. It could just be a rental."

She looked in the kitchen sink, where food-encrusted dishes were stacked. "These have been here for a while. A few days at least."

She moved toward the bedroom and bathroom. The bed was unmade, and there were a few men's toiletries next to the sink. She recognized the same brand of aftershave, toothpaste, and shampoo she'd seen at Ferris's house.

She stepped back into the common area to see Brice rifling through a stack of papers on the dinette table.

"Anything there?" she asked.

"Mostly junk mail and local newspapers addressed to 'Occupant' and 'Our Neighbor.'" He lifted a yellow sheet of paper. "But here's something."

"What?"

"It's an invoice." He looked closer. "And it has Ferris's name on it."

Jessie took the paper and glanced at it. "A rental agreement for a truck. Dated for the day he disappeared."

"A moving truck? You think maybe he packed up his stuff and skipped town?"

"It says it's a white medium-size box truck. I think those are used mostly for cargo. The rental company is here in Ventura." Jessie pocketed the receipt. "Let's go talk to them."

Ventura Equipment Rental was a surprisingly large company for a beach town, but the manager, George Caber, was more interested in the crossword puzzle he was working than helping them when he found out that the only thing they wanted was information. Jessie persisted, and he reluctantly examined the card file. "It's a truck rental. It hasn't been returned yet."

"When is it expected back?" Jessie asked.

"Two days ago. But we got a call from him extending the rental period a week."

Jessie turned to Brice. "Why would he have needed a truck? Was he going to move out of town?" She turned back to Caber and showed him a photo of Ferris on her phone. "Was this the guy who rented it?"

He looked at the photo and shook his head. "Sorry, I don't remember." He went back to his crossword puzzle.

Brice was looking at the wall. "You have a security video camera. Could you find out?"

Caber didn't look up from his puzzle. "There's probably a law against giving out information on my customers. I wouldn't want to get in trouble."

"We wouldn't want that, either." Brice reached into his pocket and pulled out his wallet. "All we want is for you to stir your memory a bit." He put a sizable stack of twenty-dollar bills on top of Caber's crossword puzzle. "I'm sure you don't see anything wrong in that?"

Caber smiled as he picked up the cash. "I'll see what I can find on the hard drive. I'll be right back." He ducked into the adjacent room. He came back only a few minutes later. "Funny, you were right, that did stir my memory. That *was* the guy who rented the truck."

It was Ferris!

"*Yes*," Jessie said. Now, this was progress. She pointed to a LoJack decal on the store counter. "Is the truck equipped with that tracking technology?"

Caber nodded. "All the vehicles are equipped. My boss doesn't trust anyone. We just don't activate it unless the rental is late. This truck isn't late."

"Unless you didn't get the message extending the lease." Brice reached into his wallet and pulled out another stack of cash. "I'm certain that happens a lot in a busy place like this."

Caber nodded eagerly. "More than you'd think." With a few swift keystrokes, he pulled up the location of the truck. "It's nearby." He wrote down the address and handed it to Brice. "Do you want to know anything else?"

"No, I believe that will do. Thank you."

Caber smiled. "You're welcome. Anytime."

"You're smirking," Jessie told Brice as she got into the driver's seat of the SUV and headed for their destination. "And it doesn't become you."

"It's not a smirk. It's a smile of happiness that I could be of use to you." His smile deepened. "I finally felt like a team player. And you have to admit that I did help big time with getting that information from Caber."

She couldn't deny it. "Yes, you did. But then most of my clients aren't multimillionaire movie stars with that kind of cash to throw around."

"It's only money. I've always believed in contributing whatever I could to the common good," he said lightly. "And this time it was into Caber's wallet so that he'd give us what we needed. Now stop trying to pop my bubble when I'm feeling so happy about helping you."

"I will." She smiled back at him as she pulled a U-turn across Harbor Boulevard's lanes of traffic. "Maybe I was just feeling guilty that I couldn't contribute as much this time. Okay?"

"Was that an apology?"

"Perhaps." They entered the downtown business district, less than a mile from the beach house they had visited earlier. She looked for the address Caber had given them. Suddenly she caught a glimmer of something white near the end of the street. "There it is! White, medium-size box truck." She jerked the invoice out of her jacket pocket and handed it to Brice. "Check the license plate against this." She pulled in behind the truck and jumped out of the SUV.

Brice waved the invoice. "That's it. We've got it!"

Jessie had already made her way around to the driver's side window. She stood on the metal ladder step and peered inside.

"Anything?" Brice asked as he came to stand beside her.

She stepped back to the street. "No, it's empty. We need to see what's in that storage compartment." She strode around the vehicle, checking doors. "Damn, it's locked up tight." She tried the cargo compartment. "Cargo, too." She walked back to her SUV, opened the back hatch, and pulled out a long pair of bolt cutters. "I need to know what's inside."

"Go ahead." Brice was grinning. "I'll be on the lookout for the cops like a good team player."

Jessie ran back to the truck's rear door and positioned the bolt cutters over the heavy padlock. She cut the lock loose and pulled it free. "Got it!"

Brice ran to help her lift the gate.

A gleam of silver and scarlet lit the darkness of the interior.

"What is it?" She climbed into the back of the compartment. "It's looks like—"

"Wow." Brice's phone light pierced the dimness. "It's a red Lamborghini."

Jessie nodded. "This is it. Ferris's car."

CHAPTER

10

Brice couldn't take his eyes from the Lamborghini. "Excellent taste."

"This is how the car disappeared from the traffic cams." Jessie thought for a moment. "It was parked on that street in downtown L.A., then driven up the ramp and into the truck after dark." She slid between the car and the cargo compartment wall. She peered inside the Lamborghini. "Nothing suspicious looking." She added reluctantly, "And I'm afraid it's time to let Wheeler in on this."

"Must we? We're doing so well."

"Yes. I realize you're enjoying the game, but they can pull prints and DNA. I have to show I can work and play well with others."

Brice took a step closer and put a caressing hand on the roof of the car. "Why the hell would he leave a beauty like that parked out here in a truck?"

"Maybe he didn't have his own palatial warehouse in Santa Monica to store it in. A few of us have problems like that." Jessie was once more peering into the interior. "I really would like to know what's in that glove box."

"Now you're talking. Whatever you say." He prepared to break the driver's side window. "It's just a shame to—"

Jessie had already opened the passenger door. "Yes, it would be. When it isn't even locked, Brice."

"What an anticlimax. You'll do anything to get top billing."

"I suppose he thought the car would be safe enough unlocked since the entire vehicle was locked up tight in the cargo compartment."

"Or maybe he was in a big hurry, frantic to get away, and just didn't think to lock it." He tilted his head. "I think I like my explanation best, much more drama."

"It could go either way," she said as she examined the interior. She tried the narrow glove box. "It's locked."

He sighed. "And that would stop you?"

"I could lose my license if I broke into it. I might try it if it was a life-or-death case. Otherwise, I have to be careful not to do anything that would interfere with the authorities working the case." She glanced around the dashboard. "That's an interesting cup holder." It was an unmarked cup, but with a unique design at the base. Jessie took photos of it with her phone. Then she saw something else, the small metal object on the dash. "That's a transponder. Like the FasTrak ones use to bill motorists on toll roads and California freeways. But it's not a toll road transponder. I've never seen one like this."

"Neither have I," Brice said. "How do we find out what it is?"

"We either steal it and investigate..." She grimaced. "Or we call someone who will be able to find out legally."

"I believe the fun is about to vanish from our day. You're still going to call Wheeler?"

She nodded reluctantly. "He's been good to me on this case. We have to notify him about what we've found."

"But he told you he wasn't going to return any favors."

"And he might not. That's sometimes the luck of the draw. But he does have a sense of fairness. He might still feel grateful enough to let me know what he finds out."

"And if he doesn't?"

"I have photos. We'll do it ourselves. It will just take longer. But we'll take a glance in the trunk first." She pulled the trunk release and got out of the vehicle. The next moment, she and Brice were pulling up the trunk lid.

"Empty," Brice said. "That's a disappointment. No precious diamond stash. No dead body. Who would leave us flat like this?"

"Someone who lives in the real world." She took out her phone and punched in Wheeler's number. "Why don't you go up to the truck cab and see if that truck glove box is open while I talk to Wheeler?"

"Right." He went toward the front of the truck and slid back the panel. "Back in a minute." He ducked into the cab. But she was talking to Wheeler now, and she made the conversation as quick as she could.

She'd just hung up when Brice came back into the cargo space. "How did it go?" he asked.

"He wasn't pleased to hear from me. But he's on his way." She tilted her head. "The glove box?"

He shook his head. "Out of luck. That was locked up, too. Next order?"

She sighed impatiently as she glanced up and down the street. "We can ask around and see if anyone here knows how that truck appeared miraculously in their neighborhood. Or anything else they can tell us. But it's a business district, so most places are closed now." She shook her head. "I'm a little disgusted that we struck out when it looked like we were going to get somewhere. I wanted to get *something* out of our sunny trip to the beach."

An hour later, Wheeler drove down the street and parked behind Jessie's SUV. He was with another man in a U.S. Marshal's uniform that Jessie remembered seeing earlier that day at the memorial. He was in his early forties with a receding hairline and a lean, muscular body. He was frowning as he followed Wheeler to where Jessie was sitting in the cargo compartment of the truck.

Wheeler wasn't frowning, but his expression was distinctly rueful. "Hello, Jessie. This is Marshal Elrond Patton. We're working the case together. I didn't expect to see you this soon."

"Why not? I had a job to do. It was natural we'd run into each other." She turned to the marshal and held out her hand to shake. "I'm Jessie Mercado. I noticed the beach scenes at the Dayton memorial this morning and thought we should follow up on it. We found something interesting and decided we should share it."

"The Lamborghini."

She nodded. "I did break into the truck, but I did nothing else that would impede your investigation."

"Detective Wheeler speaks highly of you. And the fact that you beat us here justifies that opinion. I saw the same slideshow this morning and didn't make the connection."

"You might have later," Jessie said. "Sometimes it happens like that."

"Where's Desmond, Jessie?" Wheeler asked.

"He's still asking questions at some of the businesses on the street. There are two restaurants and a coffee shop that are still open." She pointed to a print shop next to the truck. "I talked to a manager locking up over there, and he says the truck just appeared one night." She made a face. "And he'd like it to be gone."

"It will be as soon as we impound it," Wheeler said.

Patton glanced around. "You don't think Ferris has been staying around here somewhere? He could be watching us right now."

"Everything within sight is a business," she said. "It's only a ten-minute walk to the beach house where Ferris had been staying, so he probably just parked here and hoofed it back there. But judging from the mail, giveaway newspapers, and menus stuck in the front door, he hasn't been there for a few days."

Wheeler jumped into the truck. "Let's take a look at that car. Coming, Patton?"

"In a minute. You go on." His gaze was on Jessie's face. "I'd like to ask her a few more questions."

"Sure." Wheeler shrugged and disappeared into the truck.

Jessie's eyes narrowed on the marshal's face. Trouble? His expression was mild, even friendly, but his dark eyes were cool and sharp. She could tell he was a hard-ass, but that didn't mean she couldn't deal with him. Still, some law enforcement could be difficult. "Questions?"

He smiled. "I believed Wheeler when he said you were a good P.I. He's generally a good judge of character." He shrugged. "Though he can be a little naive on occasion. But when I heard a rumor that you were privy to certain facts in the investigation, I decided to take a long look at you."

"Yes," she said warily. "And?"

"I didn't see anything I didn't respect," he said. "But you have a good many unusual friends, and that could be awkward. I didn't realize how unusual until I saw you with the man Wheeler called Desmond at the memorial. Then I became very curious."

She raised her eyebrows. "'*Called*' Desmond?"

"Because he's not, of course. He's Jake Brice. In my younger days, I worked undercover a lot. I learned every trick in the book to disguise myself. Whoever did the work on him was an expert. I might not have known except Brice is one of my favorite actors."

Shit!

He chuckled. "Don't panic. I'm not going to ask you

248

what kind of game the two of you are playing. Maybe he's researching a role."

"I'm just doing my job, and Brice is finding it amusing to help out. It was easier to have him incognito."

"You're probably right about that. As long as it doesn't interfere with my investigation, I don't have a problem with it. In any case, I won't tell Wheeler unless I have to."

"It won't be a problem."

"I believe you." He jumped into the truck. "Now I'll take a look at that Lamborghini." His eyes were twinkling as he looked back over his shoulder with the faintest smile. "When Brice shows up, tell him I'll be delighted to meet Rick Desmond."

———◆———

"Well, what do you think about Patton?" Jessie asked Brice as soon as they got on the road back to L.A. "I couldn't make up my mind about him, but he seemed decent enough."

Brice chuckled. "Yeah, and he likes me better than Wheeler does. That's definitely a plus." He thought about it. "I think he's sharp and probably goes his own way no matter what anyone else thinks. This time, it's working in our favor. I'll vote for that. Why were you worried about him? What was the problem? You didn't like him?"

She shook her head. "No, I do like him." She paused. "I guess I was just worried about him knowing who you were."

"What are you talking about?"

"He saw through your disguise immediately."

He turned toward her in surprise. "How do you know?"

"He told me. He's a big fan of yours."

"He didn't say anything to me."

"That's because he didn't want to give away your secret to Wheeler. And he's probably not crazy about dozens of paparazzi getting in the way of the investigation, which is exactly what would happen if your involvement became public knowledge."

"Wow." Brice leaned back in his seat. "I had no idea."

"To be honest, I've also been feeling a bit protective of you where the paparazzi are concerned. I've seen how they can twist things. They'd love to make you out to be an idiot actor playing detective."

He placed his hand over hers on the steering wheel. "I'm touched you feel that way."

"Don't let it go to your head." Jessie took her hand away. "I guess I just became accustomed to protecting Dee from paparazzi when I was taking care of her, and it became a way of life. You should have seen some of the stories they concocted about her. I had to go after a couple of the dirtbags who did it."

"And you'd do that for me?" His eyes were twinkling. "This is getting better and better."

"Shut up," she said. "You can take care of yourself, and I wouldn't lift a finger for you."

"Liar. The old instincts would kick in, and you'd ride to my rescue." He leaned back. "And I believe I'm liking Patton even more than before since he was the trigger that made you confess."

"You're crazy. I didn't confess anything."

"I won't argue with you. What are we going to have for dinner? We haven't eaten all day. What about Chinese? We haven't had that this week."

"I don't care. Whatever you like."

Brice was looking through the menus in the glove compartment and finally pulled out one from Mao's Kitchen. "Give me your order. I'll call it in, and it will be there by the time we get home."

Home. She didn't question him this time. The conversation had been too unexpectedly intimate, and she didn't want it to continue in that vein. "That sounds good. I am hungry."

"I figured." He was still looking at the menu. "And after dinner, I'll give you your present."

"Present?"

"Yes, but we won't talk about it now. I don't want to give it to you while you're hungry. I want you in a good mood."

"And I wouldn't be if I was hungry?"

"It could go either way." He was punching in the number on his phone. "Now, what do you want from Mao's?"

———◆———

Jessie put the last dish in the dishwasher and pressed the switch. Then she turned to face Brice. "We're done." She braced herself. "When do I get my present?"

He chuckled. "Don't be so wary. What are you expecting? I'd never give you anything that I thought wouldn't be good for you. You're acting as if you think I'm going to hand you a cobra in a basket."

"You're a wild card. I don't know what you'd consider a decent present." She frowned. "And I don't want gifts from you. It could be . . . awkward."

"I promise this one won't be awkward. It will only help build our relationship to a more interesting level." He took her hand and led her toward the living room. "You'll see what I mean. I left it in my jacket pocket." He released her wrist and picked up the jacket he'd taken off and thrown on the couch when he'd walked into the house. "But first, did you like Mao's magnificent cuisine? Are you happy and satisfied?"

"Very. I order from there all the time. Are you stalling?"

"Then I have nothing to lose." He reached into his jacket pocket, pulled out a credit-card-size object, and handed it to her. "I only ask you to consider the possibilities."

She looked down at the plastic object he'd put in her hand. "What?" she said blankly. "It's the transponder. How did you get it? Did you steal it?"

"It depends on how you look at it. It's not *the* transponder that you found in the Lamborghini. It's *a* transponder, one that's identical, that I found on the dashboard of the truck when you sent me to check the glove box."

"So you did steal it."

He shook his head. "I don't steal. I merely borrowed it. I knew you wanted it, and you had scruples about taking it." He beamed at her. "And now you didn't take it, I did. We'll give it back when we're finished with it. If the marshal tries to arrest me, I'll tell him that I have a hopeless addiction to transponders and I couldn't resist. Everyone knows movie people are crazy."

"Don't be ridiculous. This isn't funny. No one is going to believe that I didn't do it."

"Yes, they will. I'll tell them to hook me up to a lie detector." His voice lowered. "Stop fighting, Jessie. You're not interfering with Wheeler's investigation. He's got his transponder that he can follow up with. The only difference is that we have one, too." His fingers gently stroked her cheek. "And you're much more clever than Wheeler, and maybe you'll have the answers before he does. What's wrong with that?"

"Plenty."

"Maybe a little legally, but not morally. And since the sin is mine, I'll shoulder the burden."

"You think I'd let you do that?"

"No, probably not. You're too honest. If we're caught, you'd probably confess and get both of us thrown in jail."

"No. The risk should be mine, not yours."

"My choice." He leaned forward and kissed the tip of her nose. "As happy as I've been with our arrangement on this case, I've been dying to bring more to the party." He rubbed his cheek slowly, sensuously, back and forth against hers. "Jessie, you *wanted* this transponder. You want to know where it will lead us." He whispered, "So do I. So let's go find out."

She didn't speak for a moment. She closed her eyes as she felt the heat move through her. The temptation was almost irresistible. *He* was almost irresistible. In that moment, Brice was everything that was sexy and electric.

"Am I going to get my way?" he whispered. "Will you take the transponder?"

"I'll take the transponder."

He backed away and looked down at her. "And is it time for me to go home?" he asked softly.

"Why would you do that?" She began to unbutton his shirt. "This *is* your home . . . for tonight."

CHAPTER

11

Jessie set the transponder on the dash of the SUV after she got behind the wheel and shot a glance at Brice. "Here we go. For what it's worth." She backed out of the garage. "I did some research on these things. Unlike the FasTrak transponders for toll roads, this looks like a commercial model. You need one to get through a security gate in office buildings or factories. When we get close enough to the installation that issued this, it should beep."

"Okay, where should we start?"

"We're going to swing by the Mamertine building, then by the building where One World Capital Management is. If neither of those gets a hit, then we go downtown and start with the path that Ferris took on the day he went missing." She raised her phone. "It's already been programmed into my GPS app."

The Mamertine and One World buildings were non-starters, and the downtown area wasn't looking any better.

"Where do we go if this doesn't work?"

Jessie shrugged. "Back to Ventura? I can't think of any other—"

A faint beep!

She slowed down. The beep grew louder as they drove past two tall buildings. It was strongest as they finally reached the Ten Wilshire Building. She stopped, and they lingered in front of it while Jessie scrambled to look up the tenants. "It's all pretty much one tenant," she said. "Gauntlet Industries, a conglomerate of security-related companies. Let's see who— whoa!"

A fleet of black security SUVs were streaming out of the parking garage and surrounding them. Ten uniformed security guards swarmed out of the vehicles and around them.

"It seems that transponder is two-way," Brice murmured. "And I don't like the look of these guys."

Jessie was already getting out of the car. But the security guards were all heading toward Brice's side of the car.

One of them yelled as he started to pull his gun. "Get out of the car, Ferris. Now!"

Brice opened the car door. "No problem. But I'm not Ferris."

"Back off." Jessie ran around the SUV and stood next to Brice. "We're getting back in the car and leaving. This is a public street. I don't know what you think you're doing here."

"You're not going anywhere." It was the guard who had yelled at them to get out of the car. He was looking at a photo on his phone. "No, he's not Ferris, but we need a word."

The other guards lunged toward Jessie and Brice.

"No way," Jessie said as she grabbed the arm of the first guard who reached for her. She pulled him around and twisted his arm behind his back. He yelped in pain.

Another guard ran to help, but Brice clotheslined him with a strong forearm across his throat. The guard fell flat on his back on the sidewalk.

Jessie and Brice whirled to face the others, but the guards suddenly froze in response to being yelled at from the leader, a man in a black business suit. "Hold off! Stand down!"

The lead guard was now smiling politely at Jessie and Brice as he tapped his earpiece. "Ma'am, sir...I'm sorry. I'm chief of security for Gauntlet Industries. There's been an unfortunate mistake."

"You think?" Jessie said.

"I'd like to extend our apologies and ask you both to come inside."

Jessie took a deep breath and brushed the hair out of her eyes. "And why would we do that?"

"Our CEO wants to meet you, Miss Mercado."

"How do you know my name?"

"I don't. She does. Natalie Durand would very much like to meet you. Will you join me?"

Jessie and Brice looked at each other.

"Fine," Jessie said. She looked back at her SUV.

"We'll take good take care of your vehicle, ma'am. If you'll come with me . . ."

The security officer escorted Jessie and Brice across the building's grand foyer, a breathtaking conglomeration of marble and glass. He motioned for them to enter an open elevator door. He stepped inside after them, inserted a gold card into a slot, and pressed a starred button on the panel.

The elevator picked up speed, rapidly ascending the sixty-story building.

Jessie smiled. "Are we gonna crash through the ceiling, like Willy Wonka's elevator?"

The security chief ignored her.

"Come on. It was a *little* funny."

He sighed and checked his watch.

"Okay, maybe not."

The elevator stopped, and the doors opened to reveal blinding sunlight and a warm breeze. The man waved them outside. They were on a rooftop patio and garden, centered by a majestic fountain and several seating areas.

"Make yourself comfortable," the security chief said. "Miss Durand will be here shortly."

He disappeared back into the elevator.

Brice looked around. "It's beautiful."

"Stunning," Jessie said. "But I'd appreciate it more if I knew they weren't going to try to throw us over the edge."

"I wouldn't worry about that. Plausible deniability is diffi-cult to maintain when *two* blood-splattered corpses are on the sidewalk outside their front door."

"You have a way of painting such horribly vivid pictures with your words."

"That's why I get paid the big bucks."

"I thought it was because you look so good with your shirt off."

"Now you're confusing me with Chris Hemsworth."

"Ha. You *wish* you could be confused with Chris Hemsworth."

"Hmm. This conversation's taken an ugly turn." He stepped toward a seating area backed with a fully stocked bar. "Any idea who our host is?"

"Natalie Durand? I've heard the name. I think maybe she killed someone once."

Brice smiled, but the expression faded when he realized Jessie wasn't joking. "That's comforting."

"It happened when she was a kid. Someone was attacking her mother. I think the creep had it coming."

The elevator chimed, and the door opened to reveal Natalie Durand. She was slender, attractive, and slightly angular in appearance. She extended her hand to Jessie. "Ms. Mercado, a pleasure to finally meet you."

Jessie shook her hand. "Finally? You know who I am?"

"Of course. I know you've been trying to find Carl Ferris, which is something I have an interest in as well." She turned to Brice. "But I'm afraid I don't know anything about you. Though I understand you also gave my men a bit of a challenge."

"My associate, Rick Desmond," Jessie said quickly. "And he has a tendency to respond that way when attacked."

"I believe we all noticed that." She shook Brice's hand. "Evidently, I should always arrange to be on your side. You're not looking for a job, are you?" Jessie noticed that Natalie's Southern accent seemed even more pronounced when she spoke to Brice.

Brice smiled back at her. "Not at the moment. I'm finding life quite satisfying at present."

"I see." She motioned toward the bar. "Have something to drink?"

"No, thanks," Jessie said. "Why don't you just tell us why we're here?"

Natalie poured a glass of water from a lemon-filled pitcher. "I could ask you the same question. You're the one who turned up at my doorstep, Ms. Mercado."

"Maybe I was just passing by."

"With one of my company transponders, checked out to a man who's been missing for more than a week. When it popped up on our screens, my security force had every expectation that they'd rush down and find Ferris."

"Did they think they'd need an entire squadron of gun-toting guards?"

Natalie stepped away from the bar with her water. "They weren't sure what was waiting for them down there. It could have been Ferris, or it could have been someone who took him. It was a disappearance, remember?"

"Instead it was just us. What a disappointment."

"Not at all. I appreciate you accepting my invitation."

"With that kind of welcome party, how could I resist?"

Natalie smiled. "My security team may seem overzealous,

but I don't apologize for them. They're the best there is. They're extremely protective of me and this company."

"As they should be," Jessie said. "I know a thing or two about that."

"Of course you do. You were once Delilah Winter's head of security. Then you'll understand why I can't let my guard down for a second. One mistake could be disastrous, especially if your entire company is based on the concept of security."

Brice crossed his arms in front of him. "Pardon me for asking, but what *is* your company?"

"I'm CEO of Gauntlet Industries. You've probably seen the Gauntlet name on most armored cars in this country, and in many others throughout the world. That's how the company got its start, and when I joined it eight years ago, that's all they did. We've expanded into an entire range of security services, both commercial and consumer." She smiled. "Though lately we've been concentrating on the more volatile areas around the world."

"That explains the goon squad," Jessie said. "But not why you're so interested in my case."

Natalie shrugged and leaned against the railing. "I recently engaged Mamertine's services. I spent some time with Carl Ferris in the weeks before he disappeared."

"You were a client," Jessie said. "You think there may be a prison stint in your future?"

Natalie laughed. "Hardly. I was making arrangements for a former employee."

"Like one of the overzealous security guards we met downstairs?"

"No, nothing like that. For someone who worked for us a long time ago."

"Do you mind telling us who?"

"Of course not. Ask whatever you like. I owe you something for the inhospitable way we greeted you." Natalie sipped from her glass. "But I understand it's someone with whom you're familiar."

"Colin Sackler?"

"I'm afraid so. I was as surprised as anyone to hear that he escaped."

"Sackler was an employee of yours?"

"Years ago, he drove a Gauntlet armored car in Tucson. He was wounded in a robbery of his vehicle. While in recovery, he became addicted to prescription painkillers and his life kind of spun out of control." She shook her head. "A sad story. He obviously couldn't work for us anymore. The next time I heard about him, he was involved in that pathetic robbery attempt here in L.A. We felt bad for him. After he was convicted, I reached out to Mamertine to at least make his life a little more bearable."

Jessie's eyes narrowed. "So you were the one who paid them to take care of Sackler. Why all the secrecy?"

"He was involved in a holdup that left a man dead. I wanted to help him, but I had my company's reputation to think about. I thought it best to keep Gauntlet Industries' name out of it."

"So that's it? You just felt bad for an old employee?"

Natalie smiled. "That's right. We take care of our own here at Gauntlet."

Jessie stepped toward her. "Yet we have evidence that Carl Ferris may have helped engineer Sackler's escape."

Natalie straightened away from the railing in surprise. "Why on earth would he do that?"

"I have no idea. I was hoping you might tell me."

"Assuming that's true..."

"It is," Jessie said. "I assure you."

"Then you must realize that's nothing I'd ever ask for. I'd have no possible reason."

"Are you sure? I've discovered that Mamertine is willing to perform an amazing range of services that can't be found on the company website."

"Like breaking inmates out of prison?" Natalie scoffed. "I find that hard to believe. Whatever Mr. Ferris's motives may have been, they had nothing to do with my business arrangement with him."

Jessie nodded. She was beginning to admire the woman's composure. Natalie was keeping her cool, even when confronted with such a serious accusation. Time to step it up. "When was the last time you saw Ferris?"

"I'm not sure. Probably a couple of weeks ago."

"Where?"

"One of the restaurants at L.A. Live, I think. That's where I arranged for his services and paid him."

"In cash."

"Yes. Like I said, I didn't want it to be traced back to my company."

"I remember you mentioned that." Jessie hesitated and then decided to go for the bluff. "But I happen to know you may be the last person who saw him before he disappeared."

Natalie didn't bat an eye. "What makes you think that?"

"Traffic cams. He picked you up on this very street and dropped you off a few blocks away. It's clearly you in the passenger seat."

"Really?" Natalie gave her a sly smile. "If that was true, I'm sure the police would have spoken to me about it by now."

"I'm sure they will. We brought in one of the world's foremost digital effects artists to upscale and sharpen the traffic cam footage. He delivered his work very recently. It's clearly you in the passenger seat."

Natalie frowned as she considered this. "I believe I do remember. I didn't realize that was the day he disappeared. He had just visited Sackler in jail, and he gave me an update. I didn't want him calling or coming up here, so we spoke in his car. I'd issued him two transponders, one for each of his cars. When he approached the building, he didn't even have to call for me to know he was here. I came down and spent a few minutes with him."

Jessie stared at her in silence. Sharp, very sharp. Even when caught in a lie, Natalie was lightning-quick with a reasonable explanation.

Natalie put down her glass. "If there isn't anything else, I'm afraid I have a roomful of people waiting for me at a conference table downstairs."

"No. Thank you for talking to us."

Natalie reached into the breast pocket of her jacket and produced two embossed business cards, which she presented to Jessie and Brice. "If there's anything I can do, any information I can provide to help find Carl Ferris, don't hesitate to contact me."

Jessie pocketed the card. "Miss Durand...one more thing. Have you been in touch with Colin Sackler since he worked for your company?"

"No. I never knew him even when he was an employee. But at Gauntlet, we do try to take care of our own. Is that so wrong?"

"Not at all."

Natalie motioned toward the elevator. "Your car is parked on the street. One of my guards is with it to make sure it isn't towed. Good luck with your case." She flashed a dazzling smile toward Brice. "And if you ever get bored, Gauntlet's opportunities are limitless."

"I'll keep it in mind." He got on the elevator with Jessie and punched the button. "A pleasure, Miss Durand."

He was grinning as the elevator started to zoom downward. "At least she appears to appreciate my alter ego."

Jessie shook her head and put her finger to her lips.

She didn't speak until after they'd existed the elevator and were heading for the SUV. "The elevator was probably bugged. It would be smart to do it and be able to listen to any conversation after we left her." They were almost at the car. "And I think she's very smart. In fact, she's probably had time to have a bug planted in the SUV. Let's wait until I can take a look and maybe get home before we discuss her."

He nodded. "Works for me." He was still grinning. "After all, you're the brains. I'm just a pretty face."

Jessie put her SUV into gear and pulled away from the curb.

"Now?" Brice asked.

She shook her head and once again placed her index finger over her lips. She turned at the corner and headed north on Grand Avenue until they found a block with metered parking. Jessie pulled over, climbed out, and threw open the hatchback. She rooted around in a black canvas case until she came up with a device with a fixed antenna.

"What's that?" Brice whispered.

"An RF signal detector. Let's see if it picks up any listening or tracking devices."

She swept it over and around her SUV. She found a device magnetically affixed to the underside of her left rear wheel well. A quick scan inside revealed a tiny microphone in the passenger seat. Jessie rejoined Brice on the sidewalk and held up the devices. She dropped them to the ground and smashed them with her heel.

"You were right," he said.

"One was to track us; the other was to listen to us." She looked down at the smashed devices. "We were meant to find those."

He acted as if he hadn't heard correctly. "What?"

"They clearly wanted us to find these things."

"Why would you think that?"

She was still staring down at the sidewalk. "This is cheap stuff. A P.I. operating out of his car in Bakersfield might use those devices, but not a multinational security company. I sure as hell wouldn't use them. Gauntlet's security people obviously thought that if I was suspicious enough to sweep, this would be enough to convince me I'd found every-thing. I'm not buying it." She raised her phone and typed a message.

"Who are you texting?"

"Someone with all the hardware and know-how to find the Gauntlet devices I *couldn't* locate." Her phone chimed as the text was answered. "He's going to meet us around the corner from my house. Let's go."

———◆———

They didn't speak for the entire ride back to Jessie's neigh-borhood, instead filling the SUV with music from satellite radio. Jessie drove past her house and parked around the corner, where a rotund older man was waiting next to a black van.

Jessie jumped out and fist-bumped the man. "Rick, this is Charlie Dalbert. He's an expert at both data security and surveillance equipment."

Brice nodded. "Delighted."

Jessie turned back to Charlie. "Work your magic, Charlie. There could be some high-level surveillance gear in here. It may have been placed by agents from Gauntlet, if it makes any difference."

Charlie's face tensed. "It does. They use government-spy-agency-caliber stuff. The kind that shuts down whenever it detects a sweep. Tough to locate."

"But not impossible."

Charlie grinned. "Not for me."

"That's why I called you."

"What do you want me to do with any gear I locate?"

"Destroy it. And send me a big fat bill for your services. I'll be passing it along to my client, for whom I'm not feeling all that warm and fuzzy right now."

"Got it. It'll be a refreshing change after all the government work I've been doing lately. There are some cheap bastards holding the purse strings at the DEA these days."

Jessie fist-bumped him again and walked with Brice back toward her house.

"Handy person to know," Brice said.

"He's the best. I've known politicians and intelligence agents who won't even check into a hotel until Charlie has scanned the room from top to bottom. If Gauntlet has put something else on my car, he'll find it."

In less than fifteen minutes, there was a knock at her door. Jessie opened it to see Charlie holding up a clear sandwich bag containing pulverized electronic parts.

"You weren't kidding," he said. "They knew what they were doing. Two interior microphones, one lodged in the driver's side air vent, the other on the back passenger side door handle."

"Any trackers?"

"One. Stuck to the underside of the hood. All top-shelf stuff." His expression was suddenly dead serious. "You gotta be careful, Jessie. These guys are serious about keeping tabs on you."

"Thanks, Charlie."

He presented her with a handwritten invoice. "I hope you

were serious about the bill. I charged you what I do for my corporate clients."

Jessie glanced at the total: fifty-five hundred dollars. She smiled. "It's fine. He'll pay. Thanks for coming on such short notice, Charlie."

"Anything for you, Jessie."

Jessie closed the door and turned back toward Brice. "Did I hear a snicker?"

"Maybe a tiny one. It amazes me how you manage to attract such a varied collection of men to do your bidding." He gave her a small salute. "Including me."

"It was easy. I paid him fifty-five hundred dollars." She shrugged. "And we're both working stiffs who have to earn our daily bread. It makes a difference. I can't answer for you. I suspect you're a little nuts. Besides, I'm not the one Natalie was zeroing in on." She suddenly frowned. "But maybe that was a little unusual when you look at her background and character."

He chuckled. "And now you're hinting that my fantastic face and gorgeous physique weren't enough to bring Natalie running?"

"Just thinking." She opened the door and preceded him into the kitchen. "I'm trying to get a handle on her, and she's . . . complicated. I believe she's playing a role, and it probably changes minute by minute." She tossed the plastic bag of destroyed devices on the kitchen table. "She gives us a hint and then yanks it back, and then makes it almost impossible to find any bugs without going to an expert." She smiled. "Though I'm sorry that I insulted your star power. It just occurred to me that maybe she actually needed you for something else besides your body."

"Ouch." He went to the refrigerator and got himself a beer. "You really know how to hurt a guy." He went to the cabinet, poured her a glass of wine, and brought it to her. "But here's your reward for a job well done. Let's go out on the patio and watch the sun go down and talk Natalie." He held the door open for her. "Unless you think she might have managed to infiltrate our happy home with another bug."

"*My* happy home," Jessie corrected as she went out and settled in one of the yard chairs. "And I wouldn't put it past her. I don't believe I've ever run across anyone sharper. She had an answer for everything. And in the end, we still didn't know anything more."

"We know she was the woman in his car that day." He chuckled. "You bluffed your way through that. I was surprised she didn't call you on it."

"So was I. I just took a chance. But you notice how quickly she bounced back. Maybe she was too busy trying to build a logical story to worry about denying it." Jessie replayed the exchange in her mind. "But she knew about me and my connection with Sackler, and she couldn't have found that out from Ferris."

"Owen?"

"That's my guess. It would have been too coincidental for her to just stumble on the fact that I was investigating his disappearance." She took a sip of wine. "And that means we've been fed bullshit from the beginning. He has to know Natalie Durand and what she's up to."

"So are you going to bow out?"

"Not yet. I don't like being used. I'm royally pissed off." Her lips tightened. "I'm going to find Ferris, just as I've been paid to do. I'm going to find out why the hell Owen and Natalie Durand want him so badly."

Brice's phone rang, and he looked down at the ID. "Peter." He answered the call and listened for a moment. "No, it's great. Just a minute." He muted his phone and looked at Jessie. "Peter's finished enhancing the traffic cam shots. He wants to bring it over and show us." He grimaced. "I really don't want to tell him you don't need them now."

"I know. Let's have him come over, and I'll tell him. Besides, we might still need it for evidence. We were just a little ahead of the game."

"Right." He went back to his phone and said, "Peter, come on over. We can't wait to see what you've done. How soon can you be here?" Brice listened. "Great. See you then." He cut the connection. "He says he'll be here in less than an hour. He's going to pack so he can leave here and go straight to the airport."

———◆———

Brice already had steaks on the grill when Peter appeared at the front door. "Hi, Jessie." He smiled and waved a manila envelope in his hand. "Here it is. Where's Brice? I need to see that bastard."

"He's on the patio barbecuing." She followed him through the house. "Why exactly is he a bastard?"

"You have to ask?"

"Why is he one right now, I mean? Show me your photo enhancements."

He glanced over his shoulder at her. "Which you probably think you no longer need. Right?"

Jessie's shoulders slumped. "Peter... How did you find out?"

"I could hear it in Brice's voice. I've known him for years, Jessie. I could tell that he wasn't excited on the phone when I told him about my breakthrough. Which meant you'd already had one of your own. That's okay. I just don't want the two of you struggling to make me feel that my time wasn't wasted." He was suddenly grinning as he added, "Because it definitely wasn't."

She drew a relieved breath. "That's what I told Brice. Evidence."

He nodded. "And other things."

"Hey, Peter." Brice was coming across the patio toward them. "You don't have a beer yet. Jessie must be—" He broke off as he saw Peter's expression. "Am I in trouble?"

"Only a little." He glanced at Jessie. "You could have been honest with me, you know. I'm a big boy. I've spent months working on special-effects shots that get cut because a test audience in Tarzana didn't like something about the scene. I thought we could tell each other anything."

"Of course we can," Brice said quietly. "I was feeling guilty."

"Good. Serves you right." He started to laugh. "But I won't forgive you if you let those steaks burn."

"We were going to tell you about it later," Jessie said. "I'll go get you that beer while Brice rescues the steaks." She turned toward the door. "And you get ready to tell us why you said your time wasn't wasted."

When she came back, the steaks had been saved, and Peter was opening the manila envelope and taking out several photos. "She's very attractive if you like cobras. Do we have a name?"

"Natalie Durand. Cobra?" Jessie asked. "I didn't notice the resemblance. And I'm sure Brice didn't. She appeared quite taken with him."

"It doesn't show up in all the photos," Peter said. "Only the last one in the set." He handed them to Jessie. "Enjoy."

She glanced down at them. "You're a genius. These enhancements are amazing." She showed them to Brice. "Peter's taken them from blurry messes to almost crystal clarity." There was no doubt the photos were of Natalie Durand. He'd even managed to reveal the expressions. One was frowning, intent. Another warmly seductive. The last was venomous.

Brice whistled softly. "She looks as if she'd like to kill Ferris."

"But I don't think he saw it," Peter said. "The camera caught her when she was looking straight ahead on this one and not directly at him. He only saw the softer expressions."

"Good work," Jessie said. "There was definitely conflict."

"Damn good work," Peter agreed. "And you didn't even notice the little bonus I gave you in the second photo. Look a little closer at the dashboard."

"Holy shit," Brice said. "What the hell is that?"

Jessie squinted as she bent closer. "It's a printed object that you managed to sharpen and magnify."

"It's a parking ticket I identified as coming from an office building," Peter said. "You think the Cobra-lady's face was difficult? I deserve an Academy Award for this ticket."

Jessie was still looking at the resolved image. "The ticket has a unique logo. I recognize it."

"Let me guess," Brice said. "The Ten Wilshire Building? We just came from there."

"No." Peter shook his head. "I did an image search. This parking company only services the Brandt Building in Beverly Hills."

Jessie looked up. "That's the home of the investment firm Sackler tried to hold up. Things keep coming back to that firm...I'll follow up on it with Owen," she said. "Has Wheeler seen these?"

Peter shook his head. "Not yet. I wanted you to get a first look at them. I'll email them to the LAPD after I leave here."

"Thanks," Jessie said. "You still managed to win the day, Peter. We'll tell you all about our experience with Natalie." Jessie motioned toward a patio chair. "But first, sit down and drink your beer and tell us how you managed to bring those traffic cam photos to life. They're amazing."

———◆———

"Thanks, Jessie. This was fun," Peter said an hour later as he walked toward the front door. "I have to catch my flight, so this is goodbye until the next time Brice decides he needs me."

She squeezed his arm. "If there's one thing I've learned about the two of you, it's that you'll stay close no matter how many miles away you are. But I hope I'll see you the next time you're in town visiting Brice."

"I'm sure you will." He grinned. "Somehow I don't think he'll be very far from you."

———◆———

The next morning, Jessie received a call from Wheeler just as she and Brice were leaving her favorite breakfast spot. "Patton brought Shane Winston in for questioning. Do you want to come in and observe?" he asked gruffly. "If you do, get here in the next thirty minutes."

"I'll be there." She paused. "But you told me that you couldn't include me in the investigation. What changed things?"

"You were the one who tipped me off about Winston." He added, "And you found that damn truck. Besides, actually it was Patton who suggested I invite you. It surprised the hell out of me. Maybe he likes you. He even invited Desmond. Can you get in touch with him?"

"Perhaps." She reached out and touched Brice's arm. "Yes, I believe I can reach him. Thanks, Wheeler. Even if it was Patton's idea, I appreciate you being on board with it. See you later."

She cut the connection and turned to Brice. "Did you hear that? We're off to watch Patton grill Winston. Wheeler thinks Patton likes me. No way. We both know that he's one of your fans. He probably wants you to see *him* give a performance. What do you think?"

Brice was silent and then said slowly, "I don't know what

makes him tick. He might be curious about me. Or he told you that he wanted to keep an eye on me. This could be his way of doing it. Maybe I'm under surveillance. That might be interesting." He opened her car door for her. "In any case, let's go see Patton perform."

CHAPTER

12

When Jessie and Brice arrived at the station, they were taken to an observation area with several other investigators. A large pane of one-way glass fronted the area, offering a view of the interrogation room, where Winston was already seated at a table.

Within a minute, Patton entered the interrogation room, sat down opposite Winston, and opened up a file. "Now let's get down to business, Winston," he said. "If I get the right answers, you might get out of this without jail time yourself."

Winston crossed his arms defensively. "You can't prove I did anything but my job. I was protecting a prisoner. I had nothing to do with Sackler's escape. And if Ferris knew anything about it, he didn't tell me. Why would he? He paid me for one thing, and that was to keep Sackler safe."

"You were a guard. You could have had an opportunity to help Sackler with smuggling in materials, preparing that bus to blow. Yet you're telling me you didn't do it?"

"That's what I'm telling you." Winston was tensing, licking his lips. "And you can't prove anything else."

"Let's go over it again. Tell me everything that you did for Sackler since he came to the prison."

He drilled down, skillfully questioning every movement he'd made until Winston started to stumble and get angry.

"He's good," Brice whispered to Jessie.

Jessie agreed. Patton was slick and sharp, remembering every statement and then trying to trip Winston when he went over them the next time. So far she hadn't learned anything new, but it was interesting watching Patton's work.

And then he did bring up something with which she wasn't familiar. "You know Sackler seems to have had a pretty rough time at Twin Towers. But then so did anyone who harassed him," Patton said. "I hear an inmate who was giving Sackler a hard time ended up in the hospital. He was beaten almost to death and is in a coma. He may not recover."

"You can't pin that on me," Winston said. "I wasn't even working that day."

"I know you weren't. But you still know who did it, don't you? Because you're connected, and you have your ear to the ground. You're not the only one there who takes money from Mamertine, and I'm not just talking about guards."

"I don't know what you're talking about."

"We know it was another inmate who beat up that guy. Jermaine Simmons. He's admitted it because he knows what's good for him."

Winston's eyes flashed in a momentary panic.

Patton chuckled. "That hit a nerve, didn't it? Maybe because you're the one who worked out the deal with him on behalf of Mamertine?"

"No!"

"Somebody did. Who better than a guard who's already on Mamertine's payroll? We'll keep talking to Jermaine. It's only a matter of time before he fills in all the blanks for us."

Winston shrugged. "I'm not going to sit here and let you accuse me of doing something I didn't do. I want a lawyer if I'm under arrest."

"You're not under arrest...yet." Patton leaned back in his chair. "You can go now. Just don't leave town. I'm going to want to talk to you again real soon."

Winston muttered a curse as he got to his feet. The next moment he left the interrogation room.

Jessie and Brice stood and left the observation area. They met Patton and Wheeler in the hall.

Patton nodded to Jessie. "Not very entertaining. No breakthroughs."

"You came close. I didn't know about that inmate."

"It's only guesswork. But something was happening at that prison." He looked at Brice and smiled. "And sometimes things and people aren't what they seem, are they?"

"That's what I've been told," Brice said. "But you'd know better than me."

Patton laughed and strolled away down the hall.

Wheeler started to follow him and then glanced at Jessie. "Patton wants to go and have another talk with Owen. He thinks he's not telling everything he knows. But you're not invited along this time."

Jessie nodded. "I get it. I'm working for the guy. Too bad. I'd like to see him work on Owen. I certainly haven't made much progress with him."

"Not this time, Jessie." Wheeler was hurrying after Patton. "See you later."

She only waited until the office door closed behind them before she was taking out her phone and placing a call.

"You're phoning Owen yourself?" Brice asked.

"You bet I am. I'm mad as hell. Every time I turn around, I find out how little I really know about what went on in that jail. This had to have something to do with Mamertine."

Owen answered on the first ring. "Jessie?"

"Okay, Owen. Now I find out you have *prisoners* on your company payroll?"

"What the hell are you talking about?"

"I just sat in on a chat with Winston, the guard your company was paying. Though I guess I should specify *which* guard, since I'm thinking he wasn't the only one. Right?"

"Calm down, Jessie."

"No. Not until I know you're being straight with me. I'm tired of this bullshit. Your client, Sackler, was getting a hard time from a fellow inmate at Twin Towers. Well, someone beat the hell out of that inmate. He may die. It looks like it was another prisoner. What do you have to say about that?"

"Things happen in jail. That's probably why Ferris wanted Sackler protected."

"It seems like a lot of things have a way of happening when your firm is involved."

"I already have the U.S. Marshals busting my balls, Mercado. I really don't need it from you."

"I know you don't. And yet you haven't fired me."

"Don't think I haven't thought about it."

"But you haven't done it. Which means you really do want to find out what happened to your partner."

"Of course I do."

"Then why are you being so coy about your firm's arrangements for Colin Sackler?"

"Because..." His voice was suddenly quiet. "I honestly didn't know what our deal with him was."

"Do you expect me to believe you could be really so clueless about something like this?"

Owen was silent for a long moment before answering. "I'm afraid so."

"How could that be possible?"

"Because Carl Ferris did this kind of thing. The things we didn't say out loud. The things that our clientele were willing to pay extra for. I honestly didn't know about those arrangements he made under the radar." His voice was suddenly harsh. "Okay, maybe I didn't want to know."

"Under the radar? Seriously? That's what you're calling it?"

"All I knew was that he made things go smoother." He

paused. "Look, my business hasn't been going well in the past few years. That's why I took in a partner. Ferris had fresh ideas, and in the beginning I thought it was a good move. He brought in the clients, and that's why I didn't question him. He seemed to be a good enough guy. I'm not that bad a judge of character. And whatever he's done, I refuse to believe that he'd actually go so far as to arrange an escape."

"Even though he's shown himself willing to bribe guards and maybe even prisoners?"

"I don't know anything about that. And I don't want to believe I'd be that much of a fool. I *liked* Ferris." Owen sighed. "That's why we need to find him and make sense of all this."

"Then maybe you can tell me why your partner was at One World Capital Management shortly before he disappeared."

"Where?"

"The investment firm that his client tried to hold up. I'm guessing you have no idea why he'd go there."

"No."

"I'm trying, Owen, but you're not making it easy for me."

"I never said it would be easy. Not from the beginning. And I never asked anything from you but that you find Ferris. It's not as if I tried to involve you in anything illegal. No one has proven that he was actually guilty of anything."

"Yet I went to a memorial service for Jennifer Dayton, who was murdered. That felt as if I was pretty damn involved."

"We don't know that Ferris isn't a victim, too. Stick with me just a little longer, Jessie."

Her hand tightened on the phone. "Not much longer. And after what I just heard, you can expect another visit from the U.S. Marshals Service."

"That won't bother me. They didn't find anything to incriminate me. I'm innocent, Jessie. Besides, they took almost everything the first time they came."

"They haven't taken you. Yet. But they'll have more questions, and you'd better work up some good answers. At least better answers than the ones you've been giving me."

She cut the connection.

Brice stepped closer. "You're still hanging in there. Why?"

"Stubborn. And he told the truth, the only thing he asked is if I'd find Ferris. The rest is collateral damage."

"Of which a considerable amount seemed aimed at you," he said. "And I thought *I* had some difficult employers."

"Any that might get you killed?"

"Actually, yes. Remind me to tell you about a certain director who thought it would be exciting to have me dangling from the side of the Fontainebleau Miami Beach during a hurricane."

The observation room door suddenly swung open, and Wheeler, Patton, and the other law-enforcement personnel poured into the hallway.

"Good," Patton said to Jessie. "You're still here."

She blinked. "What's up?" she asked.

"We're headed to Victorville. A small brush fire broke out just off State Route 18."

"We're firefighters now?"

"It's already been pretty much extinguished. But it appears to have been caused by a helicopter crash. *Your* copter. The one that carted Sackler away after he escaped."

"Are you sure?"

"No. The make, model, and color sound like it, though. Since you're the only one who actually saw it, I thought you might want to go out there with us and ID it."

"Bodies?"

"Not so far, but the fire team is combing the area for human remains. Anyway, we're going out there now. Do you want to go or not?"

"We want to go." She was already heading for the elevator. "We'll follow you."

———◆———

Jessie and Brice joined the mini-convoy of LAPD and U.S. Marshals Service agents for the eighty-mile trip to San Bernardino County, up I-15 in a stretch familiar to most locals as part of the L.A.–Las Vegas corridor. Jessie spotted smoke from the brush fire from several miles away, making it easier to track the blaze to an isolated stretch of State Route 395. The caravan pulled over at a spot marked by a fire engine and a pair of San Bernardino PD squad cars.

They parked and joined Wheeler and Patton on a small

hill on the roadside. It offered a view of hundreds of acres of burnt brush, much of it still smoldering. Patton pointed to an area several hundred yards away, where a group of firefighters and police officers were gathered. "That's it."

They made their way down the hillside and crossed the open field. There, next to a clump of boulders, was the charred wreckage of a helicopter. It was still radiating heat, and the burnt interior generated a harsh odor that made Jessie's eyes water.

"Look familiar?" Wheeler asked Jessie.

"Maybe." She walked down the length of the wreckage. "It could be." The once-white helicopter was now mostly black, and its tail section had separated from the rest and was lying almost twenty feet away. But it still held the familiar contours of the old Robinson R22 helicopter she'd seen just days before.

"Still no crash victims?" Jessie asked.

One of the firemen shook his head. "No. Our guys have been looking, but nothing so far."

Jessie inspected the tail section as a cop and another group of visitors descended from the road and walked toward them. "Look," she said as she pointed to a section of the tail largely untouched by the fire. "The number's been covered over. I thought it was mud when I saw it the other day, but up close it looks more like brown paint. And you can see the blue trim in places. It's faded just the way I saw it the other day." She turned to Patton. "This is it. I'm sure. This is the helicopter that took Sackler away."

"Good." Patton clasped his hands behind the back of his neck. "That still doesn't explain why it's here now."

"Or how it crashed," Brice said.

"It didn't crash," one of the new arrivals called out from the hill. It was a woman.

Jessie's head cocked to one side. She knew that voice. Could it be...?

"Staying out of trouble, Jessie?"

Jessie whirled to find herself face-to-face with Kendra Michaels.

"What the hell?"

Kendra smiled. "*That's* the greeting you give me?"

"Yes, when you're supposed to be half a world away." She flew across the distance separating them and gave her a hug. "What are you doing here?"

Kendra took off her sunglasses and pocketed them. "I came back a couple of days early. My flight just landed a few hours ago. I got a text from a friend in the LAPD tipping me off to your party here, so I thought I'd crash it."

"So to speak." Jessie gestured toward the helicopter wreckage.

"Yes." She looked over Jessie's shoulder at Wheeler. "Detective Wheeler, I'm not sure if you remember me..."

"Of course." Wheeler nodded. "I saw you work a couple of years ago when you helped the LAPD crack the Koreatown murders. Very impressive."

"You're too kind. But your colleagues did the hard work on that case. I was only consulting."

"That's not what they told me." He gestured to Patton,

who had come to stand beside him. "Technically, we're all crashing this man's case. U.S Marshal Patton is in charge of the investigation into Colin Sackler's escape."

"Elrond Patton." The marshal was smiling at Kendra. "I'm happy to meet you, Dr. Michaels. You have quite a reputation. We'd welcome your input."

"Thanks," Kendra said. "I'm here to keep a promise to Jessie. We'll be working the Carl Ferris disappearance together."

Jessie smiled. "Yes, we will."

"Which reminds me." Patton turned to Jessie, with a mocking smile. "Shouldn't we introduce her to your associate, Rick Desmond? Or does she already know him?"

"No, we've never met." Brice stepped forward and smiled at Kendra. "But I'm very glad that you're home. I know how much Jessie's missed you."

"Do you?" Kendra went still, her gaze fixed searchingly on Brice's face. "I've missed her, too. Strange how you lose touch when you're gone for even a little while." She glanced at Jessie. "Isn't that true, Jessie?"

Kendra *knew*. Of course, Jessie thought. Kendra's early years as a blind person had left her with finely honed observational abilities, and she was probably using her trained senses to generate a mental workup on Brice's life story. Hopefully, she'd keep it to herself for the next several minutes. And to make the situation worse, Patton was looking as sly as the cat who ate the canary. "Yes, but that just makes it more fun to catch up later."

Patton gestured toward the burned wreckage. "Dr. Michaels, why did you say this helicopter didn't crash?"

"Because two men landed it here, set it on fire, and ran up to the road where a car was probably waiting for them."

The group just stared at Kendra for a long moment.

Jessie smiled. "Okay, Kendra. Nice opening. Care to tell us how you know that?"

"Take a whiff. The smell that's coming off that wreck isn't aviation fuel. It's gasoline. It was used as an accelerant."

Patton nodded. "I smell it. But I'm not sure I could tell the difference between this and flight fuel."

"I bet you could if we had samples of both types here. Gasoline has a much more pungent odor."

"Okay," Wheeler said. "How about the two guys? You smell them, too?"

"Afraid not. But the ground is fairly soft around here. Soft enough that there are at least faint footprints for everyone at this scene. Plus several pairs of footprints for people who have come and gone. It's pretty easy to tell which ones belong to investigators and which ones belong to firefighters. Investigators are wearing dress shoes; firefighters are wearing work boots. But there are two pairs leaving the scene that are different from all the others. They're tennis shoes. And they go only one direction." She frowned. "I don't see those prints heading toward us here, just away from the wreck."

"You said they were running?" Jessie said.

Kendra pointed toward the prints heading back toward the road. "The tennis shoe prints are spaced farther apart, and they're deeper than they are down here. Both pretty good signs they were moving quickly away from the fire they'd just set."

"Good," Patton said. He motioned toward one of his men holding a camera. "Make sure you get those prints. We'll want to make some impressions."

Jessie grinned at Kendra. "Welcome to the case."

———◆———

Fifteen minutes later, Jessie, Kendra, and Brice walked up to the cars on the main road. Brice held out his hand. "Toss me your keys, Kendra."

"Why?"

"It's a long drive back to Jessie's house. It'll be a good chance for the two of you to catch up."

Kendra smiled and tossed her keys to Brice. "Thank you. That's very thoughtful."

"He definitely has his moments." Jessie nodded at Brice. "Thanks. See you back at my place."

Brice unlocked Kendra's car and climbed in. "I'll pick up dinner on the way back. Enjoy your drive."

They had only been on the road for thirty seconds when Kendra turned toward Jessie. "Two questions: Why is Comet Man driving my car, and why is he disguised as Enrique Iglesias?"

"It's complicated."

"It must be. Another question: How is movie star Jake Brice suddenly your 'associate'?"

"It was either him or a bunch of three-hundred-pound bodyguards."

Kendra laughed and held her head in her hands. "You definitely need to catch me up."

Jessie took a deep breath. "Where do I start?" She spent the rest of the drive home filling Kendra in on the case and Brice's involvement, which to her surprise also served to clarify some of the events and emotions for herself.

When they finally parked in front of Jessie's house, Kendra sat in silence for a long moment. "We need wine," she said. "Much wine."

Jessie and Kendra walked through the house and went straight to the backyard, where they enjoyed the last minutes of daylight while sitting in the Adirondack chairs facing the canal. Jessie poured them each a glass of wine and rested the bottle between them.

"I knew damn well you'd see through Brice's disguise," Jessie said. "I was afraid you'd mention it in front of everybody at the crash site."

"I wouldn't have done that," Kendra said. "I think it fooled everyone there except the marshal."

"Oh, yeah. He saw through it right away. But he's a fan of Brice's, so he's keeping quiet about it."

"It's an amazing disguise."

"We have Dee's makeup artist to thank."

"Sheree did that? No wonder it looks so good. If I ever need to go incognito, now I know who to see."

"Evidently you're also a fan of Brice's or you wouldn't have been able to identify him with the speed of light."

"I think he's brilliant. And a lot of my younger music therapy students are huge fans of his. One of them in particular might have been able to see right through him. An eight-year-old autistic boy."

"It's funny you should mention your kids. One of the only people who was able to recognize Brice was another boy about that age."

"Children sometimes see more clearly than adults." Kendra shrugged. "Anyway...You clearly got more than you bargained for with this case. I'm sorry, Jessie."

"You have nothing to be sorry about."

"Sure I do. When I tossed this to you, we thought it would be a simple missing persons case. It's turned out to be so much more."

"Just another week at the office."

"Really?" Kendra asked dryly. "Two killings, an escaped prisoner, and two murder attempts on you that came extremely close. None of which you mentioned to me when we spoke on the phone. It was no wonder Dee was worried. That's a nasty bruise you have on your neck."

"You should have seen the other guy."

Kendra laughed.

"Seriously," Jessie said. "I cut a nice bloody cross into his wrist with my fingernails. I wish I could have gotten to his jugular instead."

"Wow." Kendra held out her glass. "I believe I need more wine."

Jessie raised the bottle and refilled Kendra's glass. "It sounds worse when you put it into words." She wrinkled her nose. "Though I guess it really hasn't been easy. But I want you to know something. I'm not holding you to our agreement to work this case together."

"I'm holding myself to it."

"But you must be exhausted. You went straight from a twelve-hour plane flight into the middle of my case. Trust me, I got this."

Kendra put a hand on her arm. "I know you do, Jessie. You don't need me. You're tougher and smarter than anyone I know. But I want to be here. You've helped me more times than I can count, and I'm thrilled I can finally do the same for you."

"Are you sure? Because if I were in your shoes, I'd want nothing more than to drive home to San Diego, unpack my suitcases, and collapse."

"Then you don't know yourself. Think about it."

Jessie considered it and smiled. Kendra knew her too well. "Okay, you're right."

"I know I'm right. You're stuck with me."

"Thanks, Kendra."

"Whatever you need, I'm here for you all the way." Kendra took a long sip of her wine. "And now that we've settled that you're not going to kick me off this case, are you going to let me stay here with you?" She looked her in the eye. "Or would I be in the way of what's going on with you and Brice?"

"You're staying here." Jessie smiled. "There's nothing physical going on between me and Brice, at least not anymore."

"That's a shame."

"It's been an occasional thing with us, but I've kind of put the brakes on since he started helping me with the case. It would be far too complicated."

"But he's obviously done a hell of a lot to try to keep you safe, so there's something going on there." She held up her hand. "But that's not my business. Just so I'm not in your way."

"You're not. As I said, too complicated."

"It always is." Kendra smiled. "And on that note, I'm going to go to your guest room and take a shower. I'll see both you and Brice later."

Jessie watched her stand and head toward the guest room. What she was feeling was a mixture of relief and bewilderment. Naturally, she was happy that Kendra was here, because she would be an enormous help. And her presence would have the added bonus of keeping Jessie from becoming more deeply involved with Brice. A definite win-win.

———◆———

It was dark by the time Brice came back to the house. He breezed past Jessie when she opened the door. "Hi, I hope you've finished catching up because I'm hungry." He nodded down at several bags he was carrying. "If not, you'll just have to hold the rest until after dinner." He smiled at Kendra, who had just come from the guest room. "Tell me you like Italian. I drove to Westwood to this little restaurant that's absolutely fantastic. Pomodoro."

"I love Italian."

"Great." He carried the bags into the kitchen and put them on the bar before turning back to Jessie. "Should we set up on the back patio? It's a nice evening."

"We know," Jessie said, "we got an early start out there with a Cabernet."

Brice smiled. "Then I'll just have to make up for lost time."

———————◆———————

The meal was everything Brice claimed it to be, and he was funny and his stories fascinating in the next couple of hours afterward as they were sitting over after-dinner drinks. Jessie could see that Kendra was amused and intrigued. Who wouldn't be? Brice was in top form.

But it was a short performance. After he helped clean up and then said his goodbye to Kendra, he turned to Jessie. "Another fun night. Walk me to the door?"

"It *was* fun." She followed him into the house. "Thank you for everything."

"You'll miss me," he prompted.

"I'll miss you," she said solemnly.

"Well, not too much," he said. "Because I'll still be around."

"Around *where*?"

"Anything you need, I'll just be a phone call away. I'll call you once a day and check to make sure the two of you are doing okay." He saw her start to frown and said quickly, "Come on. Answering a call won't hurt you."

"Brice."

"This might be our last case together. I just want to make the most of it."

She sighed. "Okay. And it *will* be our last case. We're going to have that talk, Brice."

He reached out and gently touched her cheek. "I'll look forward to it...after you find Carl Ferris. You need to have a clear mind for a conversation like that." He leaned forward and brushed his lips over the tip of her nose. "I'll talk to you tomorrow."

Then he was gone.

CHAPTER

13

Jessie and Kendra were finishing breakfast the next morning when Jessie got a call from Wheeler. She pressed the SPEAKERPHONE button as he started to speak. "I promised I'd let you know about anything we learned about that helicopter," he said. "It was used as a TV news traffic copter in San Francisco back in the early 'eighties. It belonged to a private pilot in Fresno for a time, then was removed from service over a decade ago. Someone apparently brought it back in working order for this one job. We're now trying to trace where the repairs might have been done. I'll let you know."

"Thanks, Wheeler. I appreciate you keeping us in the loop."

"You guys might have saved us a little time at that wreck. Like Patton says, it doesn't hurt to return the favor."

"Oh, is that what Patton says?" Jessie asked. "Then aren't we lucky we're all on the same page?"

"Hey, I agreed with him, Jessie. He could have made

things difficult if he had any objection to you being there yesterday."

"Sorry, Wheeler. You're right."

"It's always awkward when you have different agencies jockeying for position. But Patton seems to be a decent enough guy." He paused. "We're going down to the LAPD garage this morning to inspect Ferris's car. Since you and Desmond already had a good look at it, I don't suppose you'd be interested in going along?"

Jessie glanced at Kendra, who gave her a nod. "It wouldn't hurt to have a fresh pair of eyes to look at it. And you can't get much fresher than Kendra's. We'll see you there." She ended the call and stood up. "We need to get—"

The front doorbell rang.

Kendra answered it to see Brice standing there with a smile on his face and a bag of the most delicious-smelling doughnuts on the face of the earth. "Don't panic. I'm not stalking you. I just had to pass the bakery on my way to a breakfast meeting at Patrick's Roadhouse. I thought I'd share them with you." He looked beyond her shoulder to Kendra. "Good morning. You'll love the doughnuts. Great with coffee. But I don't have time to stop and have a cup with you."

"What a pity." Kendra was smiling as she came forward, her gaze raking him from head to foot. "Maybe another time. But you've got to satisfy my curiosity. Where did Enrique go?"

"A good deal of him disappeared in the shower, but Sheree had added other enhancements that I had to dispose of."

Jessie was finally able to stop staring at him in shock. The white streak in his hair, those brilliant blue eyes... "Why?"

"You told me you liked me better as myself. I do, too."

He shrugged. "I only did this charade so that you'd feel more comfortable while you were on the job. I've learned to handle who I am with all its inconveniences." He nodded at Kendra. "But since you'll have Kendra to keep you company, and she won't cause you any awkwardness, I decided it was safe to return to normal."

He handed the bag of doughnuts to Jessie. "Enjoy. I've got to get out of here. I'll be late."

"Where are you going now?"

"I have to go to a satellite studio in Hollywood for remote interviews for the foreign release of my new film."

"Ah, that's the reason you've ditched the disguise," Jessie said.

He shook his head. "I've been delaying the interviews all week. I could have done it again. I just thought I'd do them now since I only have a couple more things to follow up on today."

"What things?"

His blue eyes were suddenly twinkling. "It's a mystery. You like mysteries, try to solve that one." He turned and headed for the car parked at the curb. "And this doughnut visit doesn't count as an official check-in," he called over his shoulder. "If you need me, give me a call. If I don't hear from you, I'll phone you later today."

Jessie watched him drive away. "He's driving a Lykan HyperSport. He'd never drive that unless he was in full movie-star mode. It attracts too much attention."

"That's his job," Kendra said. "And now we'd better finish getting dressed and go do *our* job."

The first thing Jessie noticed when they entered the LAPD garage was that the Lamborghini's door panels and floorboards had been disassembled. It struck her as being a little ridiculous. "Come on. He's not a drug dealer."

"Granted." Patton was walking toward them. "But it looks like he's masterminded a prison escape. We're turning over every rock to get every bit of evidence we can find."

Kendra was giving the car a thorough once-over. "Does Ferris ski?"

"I have no idea," Jessie answered. She looked at Patton and Wheeler. They both shrugged and shook their heads. "Why?"

"Because the tires have recently had snow chains attached to them. And there are fresh cuts on the sides of the tires and scratches in one of the wheel wells where one of the chains came loose while driving." She examined where the roofline met the doors. "But wherever he went, it doesn't look like he's ever had a ski rack attached."

Patton was obviously impressed. He turned to Wheeler. "I'm sure your people would have noticed all that eventually, huh, Wheeler?"

"Of course they would," Wheeler said.

All they needed was to get Wheeler and Patton at each other's throats, Jessie thought. She glanced at Kendra. "Do you need to see anything else?"

Kendra shook her head and closed the trunk she'd been glancing through. "I don't think so."

"Then I think we'll move on." Jessie smiled and nodded at the two men. "Thanks for your cooperation."

She and Kendra headed out of the garage. "Snow," Jessie murmured as she got into the SUV. "In sunny L.A. There's something I want to check." Jessie immediately grabbed her electronic tablet from under the seat and began scrolling through it.

"What are you looking for?" Kendra asked.

"I got Owen to send me all of Ferris's files. It's a record of each of their prisoner clients, along with all the matters that Mamertine is handling for them while they're in lockup. They handle alimony payments, property management, vehicle smog inspections..."

"...abusive fellow prisoners who may need to be roughed up..." Kendra finished for her.

Jessie smiled. "That one's probably off the books. But when we were in the police garage, I remembered one of the properties they're managing." She reached the end of the files. "That's strange."

"What is it?" Kendra asked.

"I'm sure I saw a picture of a cabin that belonged to one of Ferris's clients. There was snow around it."

"You think he could be hiding out there?"

"I don't know. It could be in Switzerland for all I know." She put down her tablet. "It's not in any of the records here."

"Where did you see it?"

"In his office. He had bulletin boards with client records all over them. The marshals service seized everything after Sackler escaped." Jessie thought for a moment. "They might let us look at the stuff, but I'm not sure I want to flag this for them just yet."

"Got any other ideas?"

"I'll call Mamertine." She picked up her phone and punched the number. After the receptionist answered, she said, "Jessie Mercado calling for Sienna."

"One moment, please."

The call was transferred to Owen's assistant, not Ferris's. "Owen Blake's office."

"Jessie Mercado here. I'm trying to reach Sienna."

"Sienna Henley is no longer with the firm. Is there something I can help you with?"

Jessie hesitated before replying. "What happened to Sienna?"

"I'm afraid there have been personnel changes here. But I'm handling Mr. Ferris's accounts, so I'm sure I can help you with anything you may need."

"I need to talk to her."

"She's no longer employed by Mamertine, but I can handle any—"

"I understand," Jessie said. "I need Sienna's phone number right now. I'll wait."

The assistant suddenly sounded nervous. "I don't think I can give that information out. You'll have to speak to Mr. Blake."

"Fine. Put Owen on."

"I'm afraid he's out of the office right now, but I can take a message."

Jessie swore as she looked back down at her tablet computer and opened a people search database. Within seconds, she read the result aloud. "One Oh Two Seven Eight Dunleer Place. Is that it?"

After a long moment of silence, the assistant responded. "Yes. One Oh Two Seven Eight and a Half, actually. She lives in the guesthouse."

"Thank you." Jessie read aloud two phone numbers, and the assistant confirmed one.

"But I have to tell you," the assistant said, "we haven't been able to get hold of Sienna since she left."

"What do you mean?"

"She hasn't answered her phone, and she hasn't returned any of our calls. We've been trying to confirm a routing number for her final paycheck."

Jessie took this in. "Thank you." She cut the connection and handed the tablet to Kendra. "This is strange. She was just in that office a few days ago." She started the car. "Let's go see her."

Jessie and Kendra arrived at the two-story home on the tree-lined street in Cheviot Hills, just a few minutes' drive from Mamertine. They climbed out of Jessie's SUV and glanced around the quiet neighborhood. Jessie pointed to the wrought-iron side gate. "Guesthouse."

They walked to the gate and gave it a tug. Locked. Jessie pulled out her phone to call Sienna, but before she could punch the number, Kendra gripped her shoulder and pointed into the backyard.

There, thirty feet in front of them, Sienna's body was sprawled in the middle of the lawn.

"No way." Jessie climbed the gate and jumped down to the other side. Kendra was a second behind her. They tore across the grass.

Sienna was lying faceup, wearing cutoff jeans and a blouse that was spread open over her torso.

"Sienna!" Jessie yelled.

Sienna opened her eyes and screamed. She pulled the blouse over her bare chest. "What's happening?"

Only then did Jessie see that Sienna was lying on a bunched-up beach towel and wearing a pair of wireless earbuds. "Oh, God. I'm so sorry."

Sienna sat up and pulled out the earbuds. "You scared the hell out of me."

"I think you scared us more."

"By what? Getting some sun in my own backyard?"

"That's not what we thought," Jessie said. "We were afraid...Never mind. It's been that kind of a case."

Sienna was still catching her breath as she buttoned her blouse. She turned to Kendra. "And you are...?"

"Kendra Michaels. Nice to meet you. And very glad you're alive."

"That makes two of us."

"Three," Jessie said. "Your office has been trying to get hold of you, by the way."

"It's not my office anymore." Sienna stood. "I got laid off. I guess that's what happens when your boss helps a guy escape from prison. Anyway, I don't want to talk to them. I figure they want my help doing things they should have just kept paying me to do."

Jessie nodded. "Well, I hope you don't mind helping me again."

"What do you need?"

"Those pictures you snapped of Ferris's client information boards the other day. I could use copies of those."

Sienna shrugged and pulled her phone from her pocket. "They're still here. One of my last official acts as a Mamertine employee. But almost all of these are in the computer files you already have."

Jessie pulled out her own phone. "I know. I just want to compare them. Can you AirDrop them to me?"

Sienna's fingers flicked across her phone screen, and within seconds copies of the bulletin board photos were in Jessie's device.

Sienna looked up. "Is there something in particular you want to know?"

"No, I'm good. Thank you. This will be helpful. Are you doing okay, Sienna?"

"I guess so." Sienna pocketed her phone. "You know, as annoyed and pissed off as I've been about this whole thing, I've mostly just been...sad. I used to work in a law firm downtown, and I didn't like it at all. At Mamertine, I thought we were helping people. Maybe not everyone deserved help, but I know their families appreciated it. But for Carl Ferris to pull this crap, it confirms every scummy thing that people said about us."

"I'm sorry," Jessie said.

"It's okay. Good luck with your case."

Jessie and Kendra left the yard and walked back to the SUV. After they climbed inside, Jessie immediately raised her phone and examined the photos of Ferris's bulletin boards.

"You didn't want to ask Sienna about the property you saw?" Kendra asked.

"No. I think she's on the up-and-up, but just in case, I didn't want to take the chance that she might tip off Ferris." Jessie swiped her finger across the phone screen, flipping through pages of files. She finally stopped. "Here. This is what I saw in Ferris's office."

Jessie turned the phone around to show her a picture of a two-story cabin perched on a snow-covered hillside.

"Stunning," Kendra said.

Jessie turned the phone back around and looked at the client information card next to the photo. "It belongs to Duane Ashland, an attorney who was convicted for an investment fraud scheme. Mamertine is handling his daughter's college expenses, taking care of cleaning and landscaping services for his two homes, and helping coordinate his appeal."

She picked up her tablet computer and glanced through the client files. "For some reason, Ferris didn't put this house in the computer records. According to the bulletin board, this cabin is unoccupied. And, it's in Lake Arrowhead, only ninety minutes from here."

"Lake Arrowhead," Kendra repeated. "Which requires tire chains at this time of year."

"Exactly. Ferris would've had access to the keys and alarm codes. He's been careful not to use his credit cards or anything that could put him on the grid. This is how he could avoid that. It looks like a fairly remote cabin where he knows no one will bother him. The owner's in jail." Jessie put down the tablet. "We know he's used those tire chains recently, maybe to go up there and check it out. We need to go there."

"Then let's do it."

Jessie started the car. "I'll give Brice a call and pick him up on the way."

———◆———

Kendra, Jessie, and Brice moved along the steep hillside that offered a spectacular view of the surrounding San Bernardino Mountains. The sun had just set, and they had parked on an access road and taken a dark and winding path to avoid being seen by any house occupants.

Brice spoke up in a tense whisper. "One wrong step and we may be impaled on one of those trees down there. You realize that, don't you?"

Jessie clicked her tongue. "Wimp. You don't hear Kendra complaining."

"She's just as crazy as you are."

Kendra's left foot slid as she rounded a clump of bushes. "If Ferris is up here, we can't announce ourselves by driving up to his front door."

"I get it," Brice said. "Though I don't like it."

Jessie led them up a steep incline. "It's actually the perfect spot for someone who doesn't want to be found."

"Including by us." Brice pointed ahead. "Is that it?"

He was pointing toward the cabin situated on a small plot of land next to an awning, a pair of patio chairs, and a snow-covered Egg barbecue grill. A Jeep Wrangler was parked nearby.

"Doesn't look like anyone's home," Brice said. "The place is dark."

"Someone's there," Kendra said.

Jessie looked the place over. "How do you know?"

"There's water moving through the pipes. Listen."

Jessie and Brice cocked their heads to hear the faint sound of water rushing through the house's plumbing. Then it stopped.

"Also, that Jeep's engine is cooling down. Hear the clicking? It's been driven here in the past few minutes."

Jessie nodded. "Okay, it's safe to assume somebody's in there. Kendra and I will knock on the door. Brice, you circle around back and make sure he doesn't try to slip out on us."

"I'd feel better if I was with you," he said quietly. "We don't know what he's capable of."

"Don't insult us. We got this."

"Famous last words."

"Now you're *really* insulting us."

He raised his hands in surrender. "Fine. I'll go around back."

Brice circled behind the cabin.

Jessie turned to Kendra. "Ready for this?"

"Yes. Here's hoping it's really Ferris."

"If it's him, he's coming with us whether he wants to or not. He's caused me too much grief."

"I'm with you."

They walked toward the cabin and attempted to peer into the first-floor windows. Shades covered them all. Jessie rapped on the front door.

No answer.

Jessie sniffed the air. "Smell that?"

Kendra nodded. "Szechwan beef. He's cooking."

"How rude not to invite us in for dinner."

Jessie rapped on the door again.

———◆———

Brice stood back from the rear of the cabin so that he could take it all in at once. He was listening in case Jessie and Kendra called out from the other side, but deep down he knew Jessie could take care of herself in almost any situation, and Kendra Michaels was no slouch herself. Hell, he might even need *them* to—

What in the hell? Someone was crawling out from the cross space underneath the cabin. It was a man, and it had to be Ferris, Brice realized. "Stop!"

Ferris froze.

"Jessie!" Brice shouted as he started to move forward. "Back here!"

Ferris scrambled to his feet as he spotted Brice. He ran toward the access road above.

Brice sprinted after him, but Ferris was surprisingly fast. The man stumbled only slightly as he leaped over a small row of hedges at the property's edge and then kept running.

Brice cleared the hedges just seconds later. He looked around. Where in the hell had Ferris gone?

Up ahead there was another row of bushes that lined the access road. He could hear movement from the other side.

"Ferris!" Brice ran toward the bushes and threw himself over. "Stop!" He hit the ground hard.

Suddenly he was bathed in blinding white light. Headlights, he realized. He looked up.

Ferris was being held by two men in paramilitary uniforms. He was struggling but was quickly subdued by a hypodermic needle to the neck.

Brice jumped to his feet but suddenly found himself faced with even more men in uniform. Half a dozen gun barrels swung in his direction.

BLAM!

———◆———

"This way!" Kendra shouted to Jessie. They ran from the cabin toward the shrubbery. They'd seen the lights only seconds before hearing what sounded like a gunshot.

"Brice! What's happening?" Jessie called out.

Kendra felt something strike the side of her head. She fell to the ground, and only then did she see that Jessie was fighting off two uniformed men. She'd punched one repeatedly in the face, and blood from his nose spurted on her hand and jacket sleeve.

"We have to take her," one of the men said. "She's wearing our DNA."

Kendra tried to sit up. "No! Jessie…"

The man jabbed Jessie with a hypodermic needle, and her body went limp.

As Kendra got to her knees, her vision fogged. "Jessie…"

A wave of dizziness hit her.

Darkness.

———◆———

Kendra sat up, struggling to steady herself.

She heard a vehicle driving away, so she suspected she'd been unconscious for only a minute or so. Her head throbbed but the dizziness was going away.

Brice…

She crawled over to where he was lying. Was he dead?

No, he was stirring. But there was blood on his shirt. He'd definitely been shot. How bad?

His eyes opened as she began to examine his wound. "Jessie? What happened to Jessie?"

"She's alive. They took her when they grabbed Ferris."

"Shit!" He tried to sit up.

"Stay still." She pushed him back down. "They shot you. I'm trying to figure out how bad it is."

"Jessie…" He winced in pain.

"I know. But you need to let me help you." Kendra pulled back his jacket and shirt. "You were wounded in your left torso. I'm no doctor, but I don't think any of your organs took a hit." She pulled his shirt and jacket back over the wound. "We need to get you to a hospital."

Brice tried to sit up again, but Kendra pinned his shoulders. "Stop it. If you're not careful, you could make things worse. A lot worse. You could bleed out."

"We have to find her."

"And we will. But first we need to get you patched up." She placed his hand over the wound. "Keep applying pressure." She sat back on her heels and pulled out her phone.

"Who are you calling?" he asked.

"Nine-one-one. Got a better idea?"

"Actually, yes." He reached into his jacket, produced his wallet, and pulled out a metallic blue card. "Call this number."

"What's this?"

"It's a concierge hospital in Pasadena. Full-service medical. I'm a member. They'll arrange to medevac me out of here. You'll come with me."

Kendra looked at the card. "Faster than 911?"

"Much faster. I'm sure they have an arrangement with medevac teams up here with all the ski resorts in the area. And it will get me in and out of their ER in a heartbeat." He made a face. "Without any leaks to the press. While we're on our way, you can call Wheeler and get him to work on finding Jessie."

She dialed the number. "I guess being a global superstar has its advantages."

"Believe me, it has less to do with that than with the membership fees I pay them every year." His gaze was raking her face. "You don't look so great yourself. Are you okay?"

"I got a little tap on the head. Otherwise I'm fine."

He looked stricken. "Shit. I'm sorry. That's the first thing I should have asked."

"You were too worried about Jessie. So was I. Believe me, I understand."

"That's no excuse. If I'm going to get checked out there, so are you. Agreed?"

She smiled. "Agreed. Though I expect I won't get the rarefied treatment you will."

"Yes, you will. I won't have it any other way." He added grimly, "Now let's just get this over with and go after Jessie."

CHAPTER

14

Y ou were right," Kendra told Brice as soon as they permitted her to go into his room. He'd been transported, admitted to the ER, and treated in record time. "I've never seen a medical facility this efficient. What did they say about the wound?"

"That it was nothing. Just like I said. I heard you checked out okay, too." He reached for his T-shirt and gingerly pulled it over his head. "Did Wheeler get back to you?"

She nodded. "He said the local police are investigating. No leads yet. They want a statement from us."

"No way." He jerked on a shirt and buttoned it with one hand. "We're out of here."

"No. *I'm* out of here. You have a fresh bullet wound in your side."

"It went in and out. Not a problem."

Kendra shook her head. "The nurse outside said that the

doctors wanted you to stay overnight for observation. So it's not quite 'nothing.'"

"Sure it is. You know these places err on the side of caution."

"I'll bet you didn't feel that way after Jessie put down her motorcycle a few days ago and checked herself out of the hospital early."

"I didn't get a vote in the matter." He saw that she was still looking at him doubtfully. "I need to be a part of this, Kendra. You've done your duty and gotten me patched up. Now it's time we concentrated on Jessie. I have a few ideas where we could start, and I think we can help each other. But no matter what you say or do, I'm leaving here and going after her."

Kendra hesitated for a long moment. "What ideas are you talking about?"

"I'll tell you after we get out of here, but in this case, all roads lead to Natalie Durand and Gauntlet Industries. She's the key."

"I agree. Jessie's filled me in."

He was heading for the adjoining bathroom. "I've got to throw down a couple of the pain pills they gave me and then make a few calls. I'll be out in front in ten minutes." He pointed to a set of keys on the night table. "Will you bring the Range Rover around?"

"What Range Rover?"

"The one I rented. It should be in the front parking lot. It was delivered here before I even got out of the ER."

Kendra picked up the keys. "How'd you pull that off?"

"The global superstar thing may have been a factor." He winced and gingerly touched his side.

"Yeah, I can see you're in great shape." She held up her hand as he opened his lips to respond. "But I won't let it bother me. You're right, the only one I should be worrying about now is Jessie. Your ideas about how to find her had better be damn good."

———◆———

"Wake up. Can you hear me?"

Someone was shaking Jessie...

And they weren't being gentle.

"Wake up!"

Jessie wanted to reach out and punch him, whoever it was. Couldn't he see she was trying to open her eyes?

"Come on!" She heard hands clapping in front of her face.

Why in the hell was this so hard for her?

She fought and finally managed to make her lids open.

Prison bars!

That jarred her wide awake.

What was happening?

Jessie sat up on the cold concrete floor. Her head throbbed, and deep, dark shadows seemed to cross in front of her. She struggled to focus on something, anything other than the bars in front of her face.

"Are you okay?"

Jessie turned. Carl Ferris was behind her, seated on what was clearly a metal prison bunk with no mattress. Her gaze flew around the enclosure. They were together in a dark jail cell, eight by ten feet, with only the two bunks and a metal toilet. She stared dazedly at the toilet.

"Commode doesn't work," Ferris said matter-of-factly. "I'm not sure the plumbing is connected yet."

"Am I still unconscious?" She took a moment and then slowly stood and walked toward the metal-bar door. "Where are we?"

"Mojave. The high desert."

"Could you get a bit more specific, Ferris?"

He shrugged. "It's a private prison. Unfinished. It was about ninety days from completion when the state legislature banned all private prisons in the state. So it's been sitting here like this for the last couple of years."

Jessie shook her head in disbelief. "I've heard about places like this. But why in the hell are we here?"

"Because Natalie Durand wants us here. This place was built with Gauntlet money. It's a multibillion-dollar industry, and she'll do anything to get their private prison program back on track."

"That's what this is all about?"

"Yep. If you don't think either of our lives is worth seven or eight billion to Natalie Durand, you have another thought coming."

A horrible thought occurred to her. "Where's Kendra? And Brice?"

"I don't know who you're talking about."

"They were with me at the cabin." Jessie looked through the bars of their cell door. She craned her neck to see down the long row of cells, situated on a dim concrete corridor and illuminated only by an occasional recessed spotlight. They appeared to be quite alone.

"You led Natalie Durand's people to me," he said bitterly. "This is your fault, you know."

"I was doing my job." Jessie inspected the cell door. It was a manual slider that engaged with a single-lock mechanism in the steel doorframe. She turned back toward Ferris. "I'm a private investigator. My name is Jessie Mercado. Your partner hired me to find you."

"Owen? That's just great. Well, you're the only one they dumped in this cell with me. There was some guy chasing me behind the cabin. But then I was caught and jabbed with a needle. That's the last thing I remember."

"Did you see a woman? Kendra?"

"Afraid not. I didn't even see you until I woke up here." He shook his head. "I'm telling you, it wasn't my partner who was so damn anxious to find me. It was Natalie Durand. She was pulling his strings. She's the one who wanted me found, and you did it for her."

He appeared to be stuck on that track, she thought. It was clear she wasn't going to get anything more from him about Brice or Kendra. Forget that she was almost frantic with worry and get what information she could.

She stepped toward him. "Gauntlet built this place?"

"They financed it, but most people don't know they have anything to do with it. At least not yet."

"What's Natalie Durand's problem with you?"

"Because I know something that could get her in a lot

of trouble. And she probably thinks you're at least close to knowing it, too."

"She's right about that, because you're going to tell me everything right now."

"What if I say no?"

She leaned into his face. "Do you really want to go down that road? Because after what my friends and I have been through today . . ."

Ferris turned away. "Okay, fine. Let's not turn against each other."

"That's entirely up to you." Jessie sat down on the bare bunk across from him. "So what in the hell is going on?"

He paused a long moment before launching into it. "Natalie Durand reached out to me a few months ago, right after Colin Sackler was arrested for that stupid armed robbery. She had this story about him being a poor former employee who just took a wrong turn in life."

"She told me the same story. Did you actually buy that?"

"At the time, yes. She wanted our standard services, but she also knew about our arrangements with some of the guards to keep clients safe. She wanted that for Sackler, too, and was willing to pay for it. I might have questioned that, but her money was good. Very good." Ferris's jaw tightened. "Things started to go south when she wanted more from me. More than I'd ever thought about doing for a client."

"Like arranging an escape?"

"Yeah. I thought she was kidding at first, but Natalie Durand doesn't joke around. She kept coming back with more money and more threats about revealing the sensitive parts of our arrangements. If she'd gone public about our payoffs to the guards and inmates, she might have put us out of business."

She frowned. "It doesn't make sense. No way Gauntlet would do all this for some random former employee."

"They didn't, and I knew that. I spent time with Sackler in my visits to the jail, and I eventually got him to tell me what was going on. It took a while, but he finally spilled it."

"Tell me."

Ferris leaned wearily back against the wall. "He was in the catbird seat because Natalie had hired him to rob that investment firm."

"What?"

"Yeah. It was all her plan. She didn't want anyone who could be traced back to her. She knew Sackler's story, knew he needed the money, and she reached out to him. He took the job and brought a buddy along to help out."

She shook her head. "Why in the hell would she do that?"

Ferris waved his hands around. "For this damn place. And dozens more like it. And for the billions in government contracts these places will earn for Gauntlet. Because they weren't robbing that investment firm for cash. It was for the blackmail photos and documents in their safe, stuff that can be used against our governor. As it turns out, he has some dark and nasty appetites he's often crossed the southern border to satisfy."

Jessie just stared at him in stunned silence.

Ferris shrugged. "Sick, right? It was stuff that belonged to a certain Mexican politician who furnished the governor with his pleasures. This politician could be run out of his country any day now. He's a client of that investment firm, and the blackmail material is basically meant to be his retirement fund. Apparently it was being held in the safe there."

"And that's what Natalie Durand was after?"

"Yes. She wanted that material to strong-arm the governor to push through the idea of private prisons in our state again."

"How did she even know about this?"

"Gauntlet provides security for the politician and his staff on their U.S. visits. During one tequila-soaked evening, his staff told the Gauntlet bodyguards all about it. Naturally, the word got back to Natalie."

"Of course."

"Sackler and his partner raided the investment company and got the nasty pictures. His partner got killed, and Sackler got away just long enough to ship the blackmail material to Natalie via a FedEx box down the street. He was captured before he even made it home. Naturally, One World Capital didn't want to admit what they had in their safe, so they stuck with Sackler's story that he came out empty-handed."

Jessie thought about how smoothly the investment firm manager had lied to her. "So, Natalie Durand hired you on behalf of Sackler as a token of her appreciation? She could've had him killed just as easily. She doesn't seem squeamish to me."

"She isn't. But if there's one thing you can say about Sackler, it's that he's a survivor. He insisted that he'd made arrangements to have the details of her plans released in case anything happened to him. All it would take is a scheduled email that would be sent if he wasn't around to stop it. Who knows if he really did it? But it was enough for her to want to keep him happy. And close. I saw him out in the corridor a few minutes ago."

Jessie stood and paced across the small cell. "So did all that help Gauntlet's plans for these prisons?"

"I'd say so. Suddenly the governor is on board. You may have noticed that he's now pushing through loopholes a mile wide that allow private prisons. Like if they have a certain amount of square footage and personnel devoted to vocational training, that kind of thing. As soon as the legislation is signed, this place and two others will finish construction and go on-line. And several more will be on the way."

Jessie shook her head. "Incredible. Did your partner know about all this?"

"Owen didn't want to be in the loop about a lot of the stuff I did. He never wanted to get his hands dirty. He didn't even know who was paying for Sackler's services, which is just the way Natalie wanted it. That's why she paid me in cash, so none of this could be traced back to her."

"I happen to know you recently visited the investment company that your client tried to rob."

"How do you know that?"

She decided not to tell him about the parking ticket that Peter helped her see on the car dashboard. "Never mind. What were you doing there?"

He shrugged. "My job. There was a rumor that this Mexican politician may have some pull with certain prison gangs. We were afraid they would harm Sackler as revenge for stealing that valuable blackmail material. I was hoping to negotiate a settlement with One World Capital Management as a go-between, but that went nowhere. That's when we knew we had to get Sackler out before he got to Tehachapi."

"Okay, so you planned Sackler's escape. Whose idea was it for you to disappear?"

"My own. Natalie was furious that Sackler told me as much as he did. But eventually she filled in the details I just told you. Then I noticed I was being followed and my phones were being tapped. I'd finished making the arrangements for his escape, and I had a bad feeling about the way things were going. I knew my life might not be worth much once Gauntlet got what they needed from me. So I decided to disappear for a while. I asked my girlfriend to marry me. Once she did that, I knew she wouldn't have to testify against me for anything I'd done. I even thought maybe she'd go away with me."

"But you didn't tell her that. You proposed and just wanted her to keep it secret."

Ferris nodded. Even in the dim cell, she could see that his face was flushed and his eyes were watering. "Pretty dumb, huh? But it was for her own safety. I thought the less she knew, the better. But I guess Natalie thought she knew more than she did. I still can't believe it. When I found out she'd been killed, I considered turning myself in and telling the cops everything."

"Why didn't you?"

"What good would it have done Jen? And it would've meant the end of my business, my freedom, maybe my life. I had one final meeting with Natalie in my car after I saw Sackler at Twin Towers. I parked near the auto shop and finalized my arrangements with them. I came back after dark, loaded my car into the back of a rental truck, and drove it up to Ventura. I hid out at a friend's vacation home before I paid an Uber driver three hundred bucks off the books to take me to Lake Arrowhead. I knew my client's house was vacant, and he was storing his Jeep there." He added sadly, "I hated leaving Ventura. Jen and I had some nice times in that place."

And it had gotten that innocent woman killed, Jessie thought. He might be feeling sorry now, but it was obviously just as much for himself as for Jennifer Dayton. Selfish to the core, and the last person she wanted to have to count on to help her get out of here.

She suddenly didn't want to look at him. She turned her head and glanced out through the bars. "How many people do you think are watching over this place?"

"Not many. Maybe half a dozen. They're all Gauntlet security people."

"And what's on the other side of the prison wall?"

"Just desert. Miles of sand and scrub brush."

"Killer view, huh?"

"Trust me, people won't be coming here to sightsee," he said.

"But someone will be coming to pay us a visit, or they wouldn't have brought us here. They could just have cut our throats while we were out cold."

He flinched. "Did you have to say that?"

"I call 'em the way I see 'em." Jessie turned around to face him. "But I have no intention of not coming out of this in one piece, so if you want to come along then stop whining and do what I say. Understand?"

Ferris frowned. "Who are you to talk to me like I'm some kind of—" He broke off as he met her eyes. "I understand."

"Good. Then give me a little time to decide what to do. That drug they gave me is still blurring my thinking a little." She leaned against the door. "One thing's for sure. First order of business . . . We need to get the hell out of here."

"Like I said, Natalie Durand is the key." Brice raised the binoculars he'd just purchased. "And she's inside that building."

He and Kendra sat in the Range Rover, parked half a block from the Gauntlet Industries building. They were facing the garage exit. "Jessie told me about your meeting with her here," Kendra said. "It'll be tough to make anything stick to her."

"Doesn't matter. I know she has Jessie and Ferris. The team that took them was beyond professional. You saw them, military precision. It had to be her people. And we already know she was trying to follow Jessie's every move. They probably tracked us and snatched Ferris and Jessie." He shook his head. "I don't know why they took her."

"Something's just come to me," Kendra said. "Right before I lost consciousness, I heard one of them say he had to take her because she was wearing his DNA."

Brice wrinkled his brow. "What does that mean?"

"She beat him up pretty good. His blood was splattered all over her clothes."

"That's our Jessie." Brice smiled. "For whatever reason, Natalie Durand wants Ferris. I think there's a good chance that either he'll be brought here or she'll go to wherever they're holding him. I'm hoping Jessie is with him. In either case, this is where we need to be."

"Are you sure Natalie Durand is even here right now?"

"I just got a report from my man inside. He said her car is still in the garage."

"Your man inside?"

Brice pointed to what looked like a gray-haired homeless man on the corner. "Meet Charlie. Probably one of the best surveillance techs in the world. Jessie used him to find Gauntlet's trackers and bugs in her SUV. I called him before we left the hospital, and he couldn't volunteer to help fast enough. That's his van parked on the street in front of us." Brice raised his phone. "He just sent me a text. Natalie's car is in the garage, but he couldn't get close enough to plant a tracker. Her chauffeur was hanging around too close."

"So what's he going to do?"

"He's going to loiter by that garage exit and plant a tracker on her car if she leaves."

"That could be dangerous for him."

"He knows what he's doing."

"Are you sure?"

"He's just as worried about Jessie as we are."

"That doesn't answer my question. Why don't we call Wheeler and suggest he put a couple of his men on surveillance? It's their job, not Charlie's."

"I called him before I called Charlie. He was more interested in getting statements from us than anything else. I don't have proof that Gauntlet is responsible for any of this, so Wheeler's not totally buying in to this yet. Until we get some proof, we're on our own."

Kendra didn't disagree with anything Brice had just told her, and she sympathized with his desire to help Jessie at all costs. But Brice's take-charge attitude was suddenly tempered by his ashen complexion. "You're looking a little pale," Kendra said. "Maybe you should go back to the hospital."

"That's not an option. I'll be fine. I just need to—" Brice leaned forward in his seat and raised the binoculars. "Wait, that's her."

Kendra turned to look. Natalie Durand, accompanied by four of her dark-suited employees, had exited the building and was walking toward the crosswalk. The group crossed the street just thirty yards in front of them. "Where are they going?"

"I'm not sure. It looks like they're heading for that building across the street."

As they watched her, Kendra became aware of the sound of a helicopter nearing them. They looked up and saw a sleek white corporate helicopter with the Gauntlet logo emblazoned on the side.

"Oh, no," Brice said. He pointed to the orange-and-white wind sock flapping on the building's roof. "There's a helipad up there. We're going to lose her!"

Charlie had obviously come to the same conclusion and was running back toward his van. Kendra and Brice climbed out to meet him. "She's about to get on that helicopter," Brice said. "Got any ideas?"

"Change of plans." Charlie threw open the back doors of his van, grabbed a handheld monitor, and gave it to Brice.

"You two wait in your car and be ready. This may or may not work."

"What are you doing?" Brice asked.

Charlie grabbed a long leather bag and slung it over his shoulder. "No time to explain." He nodded to Kendra. "Nice to meet you. Get ready to move!"

He ran across the street mid-block, dodging the approaching cars.

"Let's do what the man says." Kendra opened her door and climbed inside just as the helicopter touched down on the building across the street. Brice climbed in five seconds later, looking at Charlie as he ran inside a parking structure next door to the helipad.

"Any idea what he's planning?" Kendra said.

"None whatsoever." Brice looked at the monitor in his hands, which showed a digital map of the downtown area. He trained his binoculars on the parking structure. "Charlie's running up the stairwell. For a heavy man, he can *move*."

"It may not matter. I think she's boarding the helicopter now."

Brice was still looking through the binoculars. "Wow."

"What is it?"

He handed her the binoculars, and she used them to find Charlie on the second-from-the-top level of the parking structure. He had unzipped the leather bag and was quickly assembling a compound crossbow.

She looked at Brice. "That's his plan?"

"I like it."

Kendra looked back into the binoculars to watch Charlie as

he placed something on the crossbow's track and raised it to his shoulder. The helicopter lifted off and swung over the parking garage. In that moment, Charlie fired the crossbow and a projectile found its home just above the left landing skid.

The tracking monitor came to life in Brice's hands with a loud beep. The screen flashed, and a green pulsing dot suddenly appeared, tracing the helicopter's flight path.

"We're on!" Brice said. "Straight ahead and turn left when you can."

CHAPTER

15

Kendra gripped the wheel harder as she weaved through the congested downtown traffic. "Which way?"

Brice looked at the tablet. "Get on the 110 when you can. She's heading north."

"But how far north? She's in a helicopter. We may never catch up."

"If she was headed to San Francisco or Seattle, she'd take a private jet. We just need to stick as close as we can. Wherever that copter goes, we'll know it."

Kendra cut the wheel left to turn onto the I-110 entrance ramp and was immediately greeted by a sea of brake lights. "Dammit."

Brice held up the monitor. "It's okay. She's still in our sights."

After more than half an hour navigating the bumper-to-bumper freeway traffic, they reached a less-congested area where they could pick up speed. They followed the signal for another ten miles before Brice leaned over the tablet screen. "The signal just stopped. I think she's landed."

"Where?"

"Looks like the middle of the high desert."

"Are you sure that's not just where you lost the signal?"

"I don't think so. The signal still looks strong."

"What's there?"

"I'll check." He pulled out his phone and checked the location on a map. He tried again on a different app. "Nothing, according to these maps. Google maps has a satellite image over a year old. It looks like a construction site, but there's no listing. It's funny... It isn't far from where that old news copter was ditched."

Kendra shook her head. "Still nothing concrete enough to go to the police with."

"You're right. But that can't stop us. And we'll need help." He thought for a minute, his eyes still on the map. "That's why I believe I'll reach out to a few friends of mine." He pointed to a place on the map. "I'll have them meet us in Cactusville. It's pretty close to there."

"What friends, exactly?"

"You'll like them," he said, his fingers flying over the keyboard of his phone. "I'll send them a text right now and tell them what's going on."

"And I suppose they're just sitting around waiting for orders from you?"

He was still absorbed in his message. "Actually, yes."

Kendra shook her head. "Okay...But you're going to have to tell me how to get to Cactusville."

He didn't look up from his texting. "You got it."

———◆———

Jessie sat up from her bunk. It had been over two hours since she'd regained consciousness, and for the first time there were sounds emanating from the area outside. An outer cell door clanged open, and several sets of footsteps were coming her way. She also heard a familiar voice. "I believe Empress Natalie is approaching," she said sarcastically to Ferris. "Maybe we'll finally get some idea what they have in store for us."

"I don't know if I want to know," he said. "Why do you think I was hiding out?"

"Yes, why were you hiding out, Ferris?" Natalie asked as she came into view. "When we were all so worried about you?" She smiled as she stepped before the jail door. She was accompanied by three of her agents, all suited up in the same tactical gear they'd worn at the cabin.

Natalie nodded to one of the guards, who unlocked the jail door and slid it open. The others leveled their automatic weapons at Jessie and Ferris. Natalie stepped forward and spoke in a voice that was velvet-smooth. "I thought we had an understanding, Ferris. And then you just disappeared. Do you think I enjoyed depending on Jessie to hunt you down? You've caused me a great deal of trouble."

"Sorry," Ferris muttered. "But you said a couple of things

that made me extremely uncomfortable. I wasn't sure you were still happy with our arrangement."

"Why shouldn't I be happy? You gave Sackler everything he needed. You arranged his escape." She looked over her shoulder, where Sackler himself had just stepped from the corridor. "Where would he ever get an idea like that, Sackler? You didn't say anything, did you?"

"Nah, he never did anything bad to me," Sackler said. "And he did get me out of that prison."

"No, I got you out," Natalie said coldly. "Remember that, Sackler. You'd be rotting there right now."

"Of course," Sackler said quickly. "And I'm grateful to you, Miss Durand. I'll always be grateful."

She was suddenly smiling again, and her Southern accent deepened. "Pay attention, Ferris. That's the kind of respect I appreciate." She glanced at Jessie. "But you haven't been very respectful, Jessie. I'm not at all pleased."

"Is that why you had me thrown in this cell?" Jessie asked. "All I did was the job I was paid to do. I found Ferris here, which is something you sure as hell weren't able to do."

Natalie's voice was ice-cold again. "I told Owen he had to keep control of you. He blundered, and now I'm afraid you have to pay for it."

Jessie half expected one of the gun-toting guards to open fire on her, but after the expected barrage didn't materialize, she took a step toward Natalie. "What happened to Brice and Kendra? What did you do to them?"

Natalie's smile was catlike. "You don't know?"

"Tell me."

334

Natalie pretended to think. "No, I don't believe I'll tell you at the moment. If you ask me nicely later, I might let you bargain for them." The group turned and left the cell, which one of the guards locked behind him.

Ferris silently swore as the group's footsteps receded into the distance. "I thought we were dead."

"That's what she wanted us to think. She gets off on it. But in the end, I can't see her letting us leave here alive. She's one nasty piece of work, and she's already killed before." Jessie's lips tightened. "We don't want to be next in line."

"What are we supposed to do?" Ferris asked roughly. "These bars are an inch and a half thick."

She nodded. "I'm thinking about it. This prison is only half built, and there aren't that many guards here. Maybe we can find a way to use that."

His eyes widened. "Or maybe you'll get us both killed."

"No, that's what I'm trying to prevent." Ferris would obviously be no help at all, she thought in disgust. She was clearly on her own. "Just keep out of my way, okay?"

She sat on the concrete floor and pulled off one of her boots. She reached inside and peeled back an adhesive sole insert. She held up the insert and tossed the boot aside.

"What do you think you're going to do with that?" Ferris asked.

"We'll see." She started at the heel and tore a two-inch strip from the sole insert. She stretched the black rubber piece between her fingers.

She smiled at Ferris. "This might actually work."

———————◆———————

BARROW STREET

CACTUSVILLE, CALIFORNIA

Brice looked up from the tracking monitor and pointed ahead. "His place is down there, just past the intersection."

Kendra looked around at the dark storefronts. "Are you sure we're in the right place? It looks like a ghost town."

"Welcome to Cactusville, California. There's a bit more activity during the day, but not much. I'm surprised you didn't know about this place."

"Why's that?"

"Jessie's father lives here. I met him just a few days ago. He's quite a guy."

"Really? No, I didn't know that he lived anywhere close. Jessie never talks much to me about her past. She always seems to live pretty much in the present." She gave him a glance. "So you rated the parental introduction. You and Jessie must be more serious than I thought."

"It wasn't her choice, trust me. But I can be fairly determined when I'm worried." He smiled as he saw the four huge men standing in a parking area in front of one of the buildings. "Oh, good. They're here."

"Friends of yours?"

"They definitely are now."

She looked them over. "They're absolutely enormous."

"Yes. And some of the most bighearted guys you'll ever meet. They're on loan from Delilah Winter. It's her security squad. Jessie said she told you how I inherited them. Pull over here."

Kendra parked at the curb, and they climbed out of the car. The hulking men surrounded Brice, assailing him with hugs and fist bumps. Brice gestured toward Kendra. "Gentlemen, this is Dr. Kendra Michaels." He rattled off their names: "George Keller, Bob Kosack, Bill Lewis, Zach Dacksano. Kendra is a friend of Jessie's and Delilah's."

Then George, the blond-haired man, stepped toward her. "Nice to meet you, ma'am. Don't you worry. We're gonna get Jessie back."

The others nodded in agreement, and two high-fived each other.

"*If* she's there," Kendra said.

One of the other men stepped forward with a worried frown. "You think she may not be?"

"She's there," Brice said quietly. "I'm sure of it. Why in the hell else would that company CEO fly out to the middle of nowhere at this exact moment?"

A voice called out from the parking lot. "I could think of a few reasons."

The group turned toward the figure limping toward them in the shadows.

Brice whispered to Kendra, "Jessie's dad."

James Mercado heard him. "Damn right I am. What are you whispering about? And why the hell did you send this team of giants to invade me?" He stopped in front of Kendra. "You're Kendra Michaels."

"Yes, sir. I was with Jessie when she was taken."

"She told me about you. She trusts you." He glanced at Brice. "If you're so sure she may be out in the desert, why aren't the police here?"

"We don't have proof," Brice said. "But we know Natalie Durand has an intense interest in this case. She had your daughter's car bugged, and she tried to track us. Then, just hours after Jessie and Ferris were abducted, a Gauntlet helicopter took Natalie Dorman out to a construction site about twenty-five miles east of here."

"That's the Sierra Ridge prison. The project's been abandoned." James shrugged. "Maybe this woman is just looking it over to buy it, or partner on the thing."

"Look it over at night?" Brice shook his head. "You can hardly see your hand in front of your face out there. I promise you, there's something else going on."

James thought about this and then nodded. "You're no fool. Maybe you're right."

Brice changed the subject. "The last time I called, you said you'd finished the job I gave you?"

James motioned for the group to follow him. "Yeah, they're all here in my garage." He reached into his pocket and produced a gray key fob. He pushed a button, and two large roll-up doors rose along the front of his building. There, perfectly displayed in his workshop, were seven vintage motorcycles.

Dee's security guys hooted and hollered, clapped, and whistled.

"Those are beautiful," Kendra said. "Are they yours?"

Brice nodded. "I just had them trucked out here the other

day for James to tune them up for me. I didn't even tell Jessie I was doing it. I was going to try to persuade her to borrow one."

"I finished the last one just a few hours ago," James said. "Some nice machinery you have here."

"You're a magician, James." He shook his head. "Good thing, because I really didn't think I'd be using any of these so soon."

"Well, what are you going to do with them?"

Brice turned toward the four security men, who were now gathered around the bikes and examining them. "If you guys are up for it, I thought we'd use my bikes to go to that prison. We'll stay off the roads, and when we get closer, we'll kill the headlights. The moonlight should be enough for us to make our way."

The men nodded. George, the group's sharpshooter, patted Brice on the arm. "You told us to come prepared for anything, and we have Kevlar vests and tactical kits in the van. We brought some extras if you want 'em."

James Mercado stood up straighter. "If you think Jessie is really out there, I need to be there with you. I'll take the Triumph."

Brice shook his head. "No, James. It could get rough out there."

He glared at him. "You think I can't keep up with you guys?"

"It isn't an age thing," Brice said gently. "You're probably the toughest guy here. It's that bum leg of yours. Sorry, but it could get in our way. You wouldn't want that to screw things up for Jessie."

James swore under his breath. "Okay, I get it. You're probably right."

Brice made a face. "Besides, Jessie would kill me if I let you get hurt."

"Yes, she would." He was still scowling. "She's too damn protective. We've talked about it before. But I won't be left out of this. I'm going with you. I'll just have to figure out something else."

"What?" Brice asked. "You can always hold down the fort here with Kendra."

"Excuse me?" Kendra cocked her head to the side.

"I just thought—"

"You thought nothing." She grabbed one of the several black nylon bags George had just brought out from their van. She slung it over her shoulder and said in a low voice, "And while you're so busy deciding who should be allowed to go, maybe I should tell your friends why it might not be a great idea for you to be bouncing over the desert on a motorcycle."

"No, I get your point." Brice shrugged. "I didn't even know if you could ride."

"Then you should have asked. I'll tell you about my wild days sometime. I rode over ten thousand miles one summer, almost half of them unpaved." She pointed to the row of motorcycles. "And *I'll* take the Triumph."

James smiled. "Better listen to the lady."

Brice nodded. "I guess I'd better." He turned to the guys, who were in the process of fastening night-vision goggles over their foreheads. "Okay, gents. Gather around. Here's what I have in mind..."

———◆———

Jessie spent the next couple of hours thinking and watching the movements of Natalie's men in the prison yard below from the cell window. They were milling about and didn't seem to be in a hurry. Probably waiting for orders from the Queen Bee.

Steps in the hall again.

She went still and then moved over to the door.

Sackler was coming back down the hall. He was carrying two boxes in his left hand, and in his right hand he was holding a gun.

"Hello, Sackler," Jessie said. "A gun? Are you here to kill us?"

"No, I'm here to feed you, believe it or not."

"A last meal?" she asked.

He tried to squeeze the boxes through the narrow bars and then gave it up and started to unlock the cell door. "I don't know why...I honestly didn't think she would keep you around this long."

Sackler paused for a moment, obviously sizing up Jessie to see if his words frightened her.

Don't give him the satisfaction, she thought. "So this is what it's come to, Sackler. You're Natalie Durand's sandwich boy."

He tossed the food boxes on her bunk. "I'll be doing lots of things for Gauntlet. And making more money than I've ever made in my life."

"You're an escaped felon. How long do you think she's going to keep you around?"

"Gauntlet has offices all over the world."

"Quit fooling yourself. For the rest of your life, you're going to be Natalie Durand's bitch. From now on, you'll be doing her shit work that's too dangerous or too degrading for anyone else."

Sackler backed out of the cell, keeping his gun aimed at her. "You don't know what you're talking about."

Jessie stepped toward the open cell door and gripped the bars. "Here's what I *do* know: You can make a hell of a deal for yourself. You're a small fish, no one cares about you. It's Natalie Durand the cops want to bring down. You're in a position to do that for them."

He held up the gun. "Step back."

Jessie held up her hands and took two steps backward. "Think about it."

"I'm going to be a rich man."

"More likely a dead man." Jessie laughed. "Have you ever wondered why she recruited a small-timer like you, Sackler? It's because you're easy to control. You don't have other options. And you're disposable, like your buddy. If you'd gotten yourself killed along with him, she knew no one would ever connect you with her. That was your only value to Natalie Durand."

Sackler was clearly angered by her words. "You talk too much."

"So I've been told. Whatever arrangements you've made to reveal her plans in the event of your death or disappearance, I hope it doesn't involve you going online. Because it's a sure bet she's having all your activity monitored in here. One way or another, she's going to figure it out. Who's she going to choose to bring *your* last meal, Sackler?"

"Bitch." He slid the door closed, locked it, and whirled away.

Ferris waited to speak until the cellblock door clanged shut. "You sure like to live dangerously. He could have shot you, and nobody here really would have cared. If that was your idea of an escape attempt, it was a bad one."

"Not necessarily." She gripped the bars of the cell door and gave it a tug. It slid open.

Ferris made a low exclamation. Jessie let her breath out with relief. She reached down to the doorjamb and peeled off the adhesive-backed strip she'd torn from her boot sole insert.

She smiled. "Sackler was too busy being pissed at me to notice I was pressing this over the lock. This place is definitely far from finished. No way would I have been able to get away with that if the sensors had been installed." She cocked her head toward the open door. "This way."

CHAPTER

16

Jessie motioned for Ferris to follow her down the dark corridor that ran the length of the main cellblock.

"Do you know where we're going?"

"Hell, no. First, we have to find a working phone and call LAPD. After that, all I know is *out*. Hopefully in a direction where we won't be seen."

But they'd only traveled down two corridors when they were brought to an abrupt halt.

WA-WA-WA-WA-WA!

A high-pitched alarm blasted from speakers inside and outside the prison.

"They know we're gone," Ferris said frantically. "What now?"

"We don't panic." Jessie frowned. "I'm surprised. I haven't heard anybody in the cellblock since we got out of there." She cocked her head. "Hear that?"

"The alarm? I can hardly hear anything else."

"No." She ran to a window and looked out. "Hallelujah. I can't believe it."

He joined her as the sound of revving engines became more pronounced. "What is it?"

She pointed to eight headlights drawing closer on the dark desert floor. "It's the cavalry."

"For us?"

She smiled with relief. "Yes. It has to be Brice. Thank God, he must not have been hurt. No one but him would pull a stunt like this."

"Who is he?"

"You'll see."

The headlights abruptly turned off.

Jessie whirled away from the window. "But we have to do our part. I need to make sure Natalie Durand can't get away."

"I thought we were just trying to get the hell out of here."

"We are." She nodded toward a stairwell opening off the corridor. "But there's something I need to do first..."

———◆———

WA-WA-WA-WA-WA-WA!

The earsplitting alarms echoed in the prison corridors as Natalie punched the elevator button again. She finally gave up and took the stairway that would lead to the prison's command center. Jesus. Didn't anything in this place work yet?

She strode into the security command center, which she

thought was deliberately designed to look like a NASA mission control room, fronted by a dozen high-resolution big-screen monitors offering views in and around the prison complex.

"What in the hell is going on?" She looked back at the two white-shirted security officers seated at a massive console in the back of the room.

Dale Reece stood. He and his partner, Angelique Duff, were longtime Gauntlet employees who had proven their loyalty in ways that few in the company would ever know. Natalie had worked with them on several other sensitive operations.

"Perimeter breach," he said.

"You're crazy. That's impossible. I was down at the cell earlier. And Sackler just came back from there."

Angelique stared at her console. "You're right. It isn't a breakout. It's a break-*in*."

"What?"

With a few keystrokes, a digital graphic of the prison appeared on the largest of the control center screens. Six red dots flashed at various points around the complex.

Angelique pointed to the screen. "The fence has been cut at each of these places."

"All at once?"

"Within seconds of each other. It looks like a coordinated breach."

Natalie joined Angelique behind the console. "Where in the hell did they come from? I thought there were cameras and motion sensors on the road."

"There are. And they're fully operational. Whoever it is didn't come from the road. They came from the desert...or the sky."

"Shit. Show me the thermal sensors."

Angelique froze.

"What are you waiting for? Put it on the big screen."

Angelique displayed a page of grayed-out buttons on the massive front screen. "There aren't any. They haven't been installed yet."

"Dammit." Another fluke, but this one was more serious. "Keep watch on the cameras." She turned toward Reece. "Take Sackler with you and gather the team and get them out there. Stop them, whoever they are."

———◆———

Kendra, Brice, and Delilah's bodyguards ran from the several openings they'd cut in the prison's outer fencing as the wailing alarm pierced the night.

Floodlights lit up the yard, and the group froze. Brice pointed to George Keller, who pulled a long gun from beneath his overcoat.

"What's he doing?" Kendra asked.

"Watch."

Keller fired at the floodlights, whirling as he hit the targets with almost supernatural accuracy. He extinguished each one with one or two shots, leaving the group once again cloaked in darkness.

"Damn," Kendra whispered.

"Goggles on," Brice said to the group through their in-ear receivers. They slid the night-vision goggles over their eyes, providing a detailed, if monochromatic, view of the prison grounds.

"Company's coming," Kendra said. "Dead ahead."

Six armed guards had emerged from doorways on either side of the prison's main building and were quickly fanning out in front of them.

Brice nodded toward the building. "We have to find Jessie. I figure you and I can cut around through the rec yard and find an entrance on the far side."

"How are we going to get past those guys?"

"Our friends are going to clear a path for us."

"Not the same way Keller turned out the lights, I hope," she said warily.

Brice shook his head. "They're used to neutralizing threats with non-lethal force. Watch."

Brice had barely finished speaking when Bob Kosack leaped to his feet in front of two of the guards. Before they could react, he felled them with a series of chops to the neck and back. They dropped to the ground unconscious.

"The Brachial Stun," Kendra whispered. "I've never seen one in real life."

"You have now. He's the best."

On the other side of the yard, she saw that Zach had another agent in a choke hold. Yet another agent, sensing the threat, fired his weapon into the darkness. Kosack brought him down with a hammer-punch to the head.

"See?" Brice whispered. "They've got this."

349

"I believe you." She spoke into her transmitter. "Kosack, your guy has a key card clipped to his belt. Grab it and meet us at the fence."

Kosack turned and gave them the thumbs-up.

She and Brice stuck close to the fence line and made their way toward the building. Kosack approached and handed the key card to Kendra along with the automatic rifle he'd taken from the security guard. "Just in case." He grinned. "I gotta get back out there. Good luck."

"Thanks. You too." Kendra pocketed the card and motioned for Brice to follow as she crouched low and moved around the side of the main building. From there they ran across a concrete recreation yard toward a pair of double doors. Kendra held up the key card and leaned toward a wall-mounted panel. "Fingers crossed."

She waved the card over the panel, and the door mechanism unlocked with a loud click. Brice pulled on the door, and it swung open.

They were in!

They ran through the white-tiled kitchen, which was equipped with racks and shelving alongside large gaps for ovens and refrigeration equipment.

"Where do you think she'd be?" Brice said.

"If you want to hold somebody against their will and you have a few hundred prison cells at your disposal, I'm guessing you'd put her there."

Brice nodded. "But I somehow doubt that card is going to open up the cell doors."

"You're right." Kendra held up the automatic rifle Kosack

had given her. "But maybe we can persuade someone to unlock them for us."

Brice grinned. "I like the way you think."

"This isn't really my area of expertise. But Jessie's taught me a few things." Kendra leaned forward to see around the corner. "All clear. One long corridor that runs alongside a cellblock. About halfway down there's a security camera with a red activity light. Maybe we can—"

Before she could finish her sentence, Brice stepped around the corner and fired a single shot. Pieces of the destroyed camera rained down onto the concrete floor.

He stepped back next to her. "You were saying?"

"Well done." She nodded her approval. "You actually know how to use that thing."

"Besides my stint in Afghanistan, I've had some of the best marksmanship instructors in the world. I figured the best way to look like I know what I'm doing in my movies is to actually know what I'm doing."

"Good plan. Let's go."

They ran down the dim corridor, ducking from one shadow to the next. They saw no sign of anyone in the eerily deserted prison, and the still-droning alarms made it difficult to hear any activity in the adjacent cellblock.

They had traveled about three-quarters of the way down the long corridor when a shadow suddenly appeared in front of them. A man appeared from a recessed doorway and blocked their path. He was aiming a handgun at them.

Brice and Kendra stopped short.

"Patton?" Brice said.

Federal Marshal Elrond Patton stepped into a pool of light. He let out a relieved sigh and lowered his gun slightly. "You guys almost got yourself killed. I wasn't notified you were coming."

Kendra stared at him. "We didn't call you. When did you get here?"

"Just a few minutes ago. We helicoptered in. Jessie managed to get to a phone a little while ago and called for help."

"Where is she?" Brice asked.

"I was hoping you could tell us. I have my people combing over every square inch of this place." He cocked his head behind him. "She isn't back there. Let's go back the way you came."

"After you," Kendra said.

Patton looked between them for a long moment. "Look, I need you to put away your weapons. For your safety, as well as the safety of my agents. This is now a U.S Marshals Service operation. So if you wouldn't mind..."

Kendra looked at him for a moment longer. "You first."

Patton half smiled. "Are you kidding?"

"No."

"I'm afraid I have the authority here."

"You mean Natalie Durand has the authority," she said softly.

He gripped his gun harder and raised it. "What in the hell are you talking about?"

Kendra's eyes narrowed on him. "You're on her payroll."

He forced a laugh. "I really don't have time for this."

"If you came here on a helicopter, it was with her. Natalie. Because I didn't hear another one. I tend to notice things like that. And that earpiece you're sporting isn't government issue. I've never seen anything like it, except in the ears of every single one of Natalie's men. Which now obviously includes you."

Patton's smile faded. "Very clever. You live up to your reputation."

"That's not the half of it," Kendra said. "I also know you're the one who killed Jennifer Dayton."

If Patton was surprised, it didn't show on his face.

Kendra nodded. "I'm assuming you thought she knew something that she had spilled or was about to spill to Jessie. Something that may have included Natalie Durand's scheme and your involvement with it. You couldn't have that."

He shook his head. "No, I couldn't."

Kendra thought for a moment. "You poisoned her helmet for the same reason. You wanted her off this case."

Patton nodded. "Jessie was digging too deep, and in the wrong direction. It could have ruined everything. Natalie Durand may have been willing to take that chance, but I wasn't."

Brice stepped toward him. "Now where's Jessie?"

Patton's hand tightened on his gun. "I'd be more worried about yourselves."

Brice took another step toward him. "You're going to take us to her," he said with soft menace. "Right now."

"You're in no position to demand anything."

"Sure we are," Brice said. "Two guns to your one."

"Then you'd better shoot me now, because we won't be alone here for much longer. I can wait."

"Wait for what?" Kendra asked. "Natalie Durand's people? They're being rounded up outside by a group of extremely efficient men. And Natalie sure isn't coming to your rescue. Whatever you've done for her, it won't matter. She's going to save herself. Think about it, Patton."

Patton hesitated for a moment. "Here's my offer. Put down your guns, and I'll take you to the cell where Jessie is being held. You can wait in there with her. It'll buy me the time I need."

"Just like that," Kendra said.

"Take it or leave it."

"The only question is, will you shoot us on the way or wait until we get there?"

"If I wanted to shoot you, I could have done it already."

"Maybe one of us," Brice said. "But trust me, the other would drop you so fast."

Patton smiled and raised his gun. "Maybe we should see what kind of action hero you really are, Mr. Brice."

THWAPP!

Patton fell to the floor, unconscious.

Kendra and Brice barely had time to register their shock when Jessie stepped out of the shadows behind Patton. She was carrying a pair of cast-iron dumbbells. "I *really* don't like that guy."

Kendra smiled and rushed to pick up Patton's gun. "Way to make an entrance, Jessie."

"It's what I do."

Brice stepped forward, and his hands gripped her shoulders. "Are you okay?"

"Fine."

He looked down at the dumbbells, one of which had Patton's blood dripping from it. "Weight room?"

"One door back. It's fully equipped. Evidently Natalie likes her guards to keep in shape."

"Lucky for us," Kendra said.

Jessie called out behind her. "You can come out now, Ferris."

Ferris poked his head out from a doorway and then stepped toward them. He looked at Patton sprawled on the floor. "Just so you know, I could have kicked that guy's ass."

Brice smiled. "Sure you could've." He turned to Kendra. "How did you know he was the one that killed Jennifer Dayton and attacked Jessie?"

"The same way I did," Jessie said. She bent over and pulled Patton's shirtsleeve up over his wrist. She showed Kendra and Brice the jagged X cut into his lower arm.

"No way," Brice said.

Jessie let go of his wrist. "I scratched it there myself, just after he killed Jennifer Dayton at UCLA. It showed as soon as he raised his arm and aimed his gun at you."

"We need to find Natalie Durand," Kendra said. "Which way?"

"We were on our way when we saw Patton." Jessie jumped to her feet. "Follow me."

———◆———

It was a damn shit show.

Natalie Durand ran up the two flights of stairs that would

take her to the helipad where her copter was waiting. She'd lost contact with all her people, and even that twit in the control room wasn't responding to her messages.

She had to get the hell out of there.

She emerged next to the helipad and twirled her index finger in the air, her signal for the pilot to fire up the rotors.

Nothing.

She squinted toward the helicopter's front windows. The pilot wasn't there.

"Hank?" She looked around the helipad, which was lit only by the blue and white landing lights. A desert wind blew hot from the east, blasting sand over and around her. "Hank!" she yelled.

Jessie appeared in the stairwell door. "Your pilot's out of commission."

Natalie turned. Kendra, Brice, and Ferris appeared in the doorway behind Jessie, spreading out behind her.

"Jessie Mercado." Natalie's gaze flicked toward Kendra. "And Dr. Michaels. Finally we meet."

Jessie stepped toward her. "Going somewhere?"

"I seemed to have misplaced my pilot." Natalie was holding a thick sheaf of papers in one hand, her phone in the other.

Jessie pointed to a rolled-up black plastic tarp on the other end of the pad. It was secured to a railing with duct tape. "Right over there."

Natalie's eyes darted to the tarp. "Is he . . ."

"Dead?" Jessie said. "No, not my style. Though I'm not positive your rent-a-marshal is going to make it."

"Clever. You knew I needed my pilot to get away from here."

Jessie shrugged. "Just a few days ago, I disabled a yacht to keep a basketball star from getting away. I figured I could do the same thing to you by sidelining your pilot."

Natalie walked toward the tarp, which was now wriggling. "Help me get him out."

"I kind of like him where he is," Kendra said.

"I need him in that pilot's seat," Natalie said. "And you're going to help me."

Jessie looked at her in disbelief. "Why would we do that?"

"Because I'm about to make the four of you fabulously wealthy." She raised her phone. "And I'll do it before I even leave this helipad. I'll transfer the money into each of your bank accounts. All you have to do is get my pilot into that copter and turn your back."

Jessie stared at her as the desert winds blew even harder. "Is that the deal you made with Patton?"

"Never mind him. Do we have a deal?"

Jessie shook her head. "I've already turned down one woman who wanted to make me a millionaire. I don't mind doing it again, especially if it's you."

Brice smiled. "And you forget, I've already done quite well on my own."

Natalie stepped closer to them. "You're awfully quiet over there, Ferris. Do you really want to go to prison?"

Ferris shook his head. "It's over, Natalie."

"It doesn't have to be."

Jessie pointed toward the dark road that led to the prison's main entrance. Four SUVs were speeding toward them, red lights flashing. "They just texted me. That's Detective Dan

Wheeler and a few of his professional colleagues. You're about to know them *extremely* well."

Natalie watched impassively as the caravan drew closer. "No. It's my legal team who will get to know them. And by the time they're finished, your detective and his friends will wish they'd never heard of me."

"Keep telling yourself that," Jessie said. "But you're going to prison. Who knows? Maybe it'll even be this one." Jessie's words were punctuated by another gust of the hot Santa Ana winds roaring across the desert floor. "The only way you're getting out of here is in the back of one of those police cars."

"I really did want to be civilized about this." Natalie let the sheaf of papers fall from her hands, and the wind took them over and around her. Suddenly it was revealed that she was holding a Springfield .45 automatic handgun.

It was aimed at Jessie's chest.

"Stay very still," Natalie said.

Brice stepped forward. "Don't!"

"I don't want to shoot her, but I will."

Brice showed her his bare palms. "We'll work something out. Whatever you want."

"You know what I want." She nodded to the rolled-up tarp. "Release my pilot. Mr. Brice, you do the honors."

"Don't do it," Jessie said.

"Don't worry," Brice said as he moved toward the tarp. "We'll get her later."

Jessie shook her head, anger brimming up in her. "No. Now!"

She flew toward Natalie.

BLAM! BLAM!

At point-blank range, Natalie fired twice at her chest. Jessie's body twisted violently with each shot, but her trajectory never slowed as she grabbed Natalie's wrist and twisted the gun out of her grasp.

It fell to the ground.

Jessie grabbed Natalie and slammed her head against the helicopter once, twice, three times until she lost consciousness.

Jessie released her and stumbled backward.

Kendra rushed toward her. "Jessie!

"Hurts . . . like hell," Jessie rasped.

Brice grabbed her arms. "We'll get you help. Lie down."

Jessie held her sides. "No. I'm okay."

"Like hell you are," Kendra said.

"No, I mean . . . *I'm okay.*" Jessie managed a smile and then pulled back her leather jacket to reveal a Kevlar vest.

Brice gasped. "Where did you get that?"

"I took it off the helicopter pilot before I tied him up. I thought it might come in handy." She looked down at the vest. "Credit where it's due. Gauntlet makes some really good stuff."

Brice laughed and touched his forehead to hers. "Let's get out of here."

CHAPTER

17

Jessie watched as the police detectives put Sackler and Patton in their cars before Wheeler crossed to his own vehicle where he'd placed the handcuffed Natalie Durand. He was about to get in the car when he glanced over and saw her standing there watching. He hesitated and then crossed over to her.

"You okay?" Wheeler asked.

"Yeah. Just a couple nasty bruises."

"Good job," he said. "The U.S. Marshals Service will spend months trying to unwind everything Patton has done for Gauntlet. I have a feeling this is just the tip of the iceberg."

"No doubt. Watch out for Natalie Durand. She's smart, and she'll try anything she can."

"I'll watch her. She's not going to wriggle out of this." He smiled. "Take care of yourself, Jessie." He turned and headed back toward his vehicle.

Jessie headed across the prison yard to where Brice was surrounded by her dad and Dee's four security guards. She pushed through them until she confronted Brice. "That was quite a parade you were leading. But did you have to drag my dad and Kendra along?"

He smiled. "No choice. You have quite a fan club, and it was more a question as to whether they'd take me and the guys along." His smile faded. "How are you? Am I going to have to inflict dire and unusual punishment on any of Natalie's men? Though you appear to have done pretty well in that department yourself."

"No problem. Though I admit I was glad to have a little help. How did you—" She broke off, her gaze flying to his shirtfront. "You're bleeding! Shit. One of her men shot you?" She was quickly unbuttoning his shirt. "Why didn't you tell someone?"

"Because it didn't happen here." Kendra was coming toward her. "He was shot when they took you and Ferris. He got it stitched and came after you anyway."

"Why didn't someone tell me? Why didn't you stop him? He was bouncing all over those hills like an idiot teenager." She saw the blood on his T-shirt and yanked it up and saw the bloody bandage. "No, don't answer me. You couldn't stop him because he *is* an idiot. He broke open the stitches."

Brice tried to draw back. "Maybe a couple. But otherwise I'm fine. They'll just have to sew—"

"Be quiet." Jessie turned to her dad. "Will you get me a first-aid kit? I need to patch this so that he doesn't hurt himself any more than he already has. Then I have to find a way to get him to a hospital in a way that doesn't mean he's jarring that wound open with every mile."

James nodded. "I drove his rental up here. The Range Rover. I saw a first-aid kit in back. They wouldn't let me take a motorcycle. You can take the SUV. I'll just have to suffer through riding his glorious motorcycle back to the shop . . . after Kendra and I finish handling the police." His lips tightened. "Which I'll enjoy enormously. I haven't been able to boss anyone around since I retired."

"Liar," she said. "You boss around everyone in Cactusville." She turned to Dee's four security guys. "Get Brice into the Range Rover, will you?"

The four men hesitated and looked warily at Brice.

"Do what I say," Jessie said. "Dee gave you to me, not Brice. You were just on loan to him."

Brice was suddenly chuckling. "You heard the lady. But if you're going to take me to the SUV, I prefer not to be dragged. Lift me on your shoulders like a conquering hero."

The guys liked that idea. They were laughing as they lifted Brice on their shoulders, whooping and hollering as they ran toward the SUV.

"I don't believe I won that battle," Jessie told Kendra.

"Nonsense," Kendra said. "You got your way. He just made it fun for them. That's no small talent." She tilted her head. "Why are you so angry with him?"

"She's scared," James said. "And she doesn't know how to handle him."

"I'm just angry that he took such a chance," Jessie said. "I feel responsible."

"Maybe you feel a little of all three?" Kendra asked. "Well, you go get him fixed up and we'll take care of everything here. I'll call you if we run into difficulties with—"

"We won't," James said. "Get out of here, Jessie."

She nodded. "Yes, sir. Whatever you say, sir." Then she gave Kendra a hug. "See you later."

Then she was running after the guys triumphantly marching up the hill with Brice on their shoulders.

EPILOGUE

Brice nodded toward the unmarked wooden door. "I didn't even know this place was here. Is it a private club?"

"No," Jessie said. "It's a restaurant. The Little Door. Everyone's welcome. Good drinks, great food, nice people. I celebrate the end of a lot of my cases here."

Brice grabbed the iron handle and pulled open the door. Inside, the main dining room was actually a vine-bordered patio that opened up to the night sky. It was decorated with dark woods and Spanish tiles, and the soft yellow lighting bathed the restaurant in a warm glow.

Jessie's party stood at the bar on the left. Kendra was there, along with Wheeler, Peter, and Jessie's dad, who was hanging out with Dee and her security team. The bodyguards were downing a series of shots with, amazingly, no obvious effect on their sobriety. George Keller, the marksman of the group, was the only one not drinking.

Jessie grabbed his arm. "You're not joining in, George?"

"Nah, I agreed to stay on the clock tonight. Someone's gotta keep Dee safe and get the rest of these losers home in one piece."

Dee hugged Jessie. "Hopefully, I'm not included in the 'loser' category."

Jessie smiled. "Not as long as you keep signing his checks."

Dee drew back. "Hey, we leave for Hanoi tomorrow night. Want to come with us? We've got plenty of room in the jet. It's gonna be great."

"I'm sure it will be, but I have some things to tie up here. Maybe I'll meet you in Sydney."

"Aw, come on. My tour will be in fifteen awesome cities before we make it there." She suddenly called out, "Hanoi!"

The bodyguards started chanting "Hanoi! Hanoi! Hanoi!"— softly at first, but gradually louder until their chant began to disturb the restaurant patrons.

Then, as if communicating by some testosterone-charged telepathy, the men abruptly stopped chanting. They each downed a shot, roared with laughter, and then downed another.

Dee turned back to Jessie and smiled. "They're idiots, but they're *my* idiots."

Kendra grabbed Jessie from behind and hugged her. "Congrats."

"I couldn't have done it without you."

"Liar."

Jessie turned to face her. "I'm serious. Thanks, Kendra."

"Maybe it would have taken you an extra day, but you had

this from the start, Jessie. I knew what I was doing when I recommended you to Owen."

Jessie rolled her eyes. "Even if I helped destroy his firm."

"Don't be so hard on yourself. Mamertine's business has gone through the roof since the story broke."

"You're joking."

"Nope. When your clientele is entirely made up of criminals, it turns out they don't mind that your firm has engaged in some illegal behavior. They actually like it. Ferris will go down, but Owen was smart enough to keep his nose reasonably clean. He'll be able to keep Mamertine going, no problem."

Jessie shook her head. "I guess that's a good thing."

The group talked, drank, and laughed for another half hour before the hostess told them that their long dining room table was ready for seating.

Jessie pulled out her credit card, but the bartender waved it away. "Your tab's been paid."

"By whom?"

The server pointed to the last barstool, where an extremely tall African American man was sitting alone. He turned toward Jessie and gave her a slight wave.

It was basketball star Lamar Wood.

He was wearing jeans, a black leather jacket, and his trademark aviator sunglasses.

"I told him we'd be here," Brice said. "I hope it's okay."

"What if it isn't?"

"Oops."

"It's fine." She put away her credit card and walked over to Wood. "I like your yacht."

"Yeah? I just had some engine work done on it."

"I hear those things can be temperamental."

Wood broke out in the dazzling smile that launched a thousand magazine covers and sneaker ads. "I just wanted to say thanks."

"For what?"

"I came close to sailing into disaster. If I'd left the country with my kids, things could have been bad for me. I could have lost my contract, my endorsements...Just brutal."

"I hope things are okay for you now."

"Yeah. Shared custody isn't easy, but we're working it out. Anyway, thank you."

She nodded. "That's it? You just came by to say thanks?"

"Not exactly."

She looked at him.

He leaned close to her. "I have a case for you."

"Really?"

"Yeah. Something's come up, and I can use a good private investigator."

"Look, if this involves your ex-wife..."

"It has nothing to do with her. I need help, and I think it could be an interesting case for you. Can we talk about it?"

Jessie looked over at Brice and her friends taking their seats in the dining room. "How about if you come to my office at ten tomorrow morning?"

"Sure."

She reached into her jacket pocket and pulled out a business card. "It's in Santa Monica."

"I look forward to it." He took her card. "You should get back to your friends."

"Would you like to join us?"

"Thanks, but I think I'm going to see my kids before they go to bed." He nodded to the group at the long table. "It's good to have friends like that, people who love you. I've had an amazing career, but aside from my kids, nothing's made me happier than the good friends I've kept in my life. You're a lucky woman."

"You're right. I am."

He held up his drink. "Here's to good friends."

She clinked glasses with him.

"See you tomorrow, Jessie Mercado." Wood left the bar and walked out the restaurant's front door.

Jessie lingered for a moment longer, looking at her friends at the long table.

They *did* love her, and she loved them.

She finished her drink and placed the glass down hard on the bar. She turned and moved to join them at the long table.

A lucky woman indeed.

ACKNOWLEDGMENTS

Of course, I owe many thanks to my frequent collaborator (and mom!) Iris Johansen, with whom I created the characters of Kendra Michaels and Jessie Mercado. She was my biggest cheerleader when I told her I wanted to write a book that would bring Jessie to the forefront and allow me to further develop this character we love so much.

I also owe much to my editor, Alex Logan, who brings out the best in a story and characters while preserving what made them so special to me (and hopefully, the reader) in the first place.

I'm so fortunate to have such great agents, Andrea Cirillo and Rebecca Scherer, who not only navigate the business side of the publishing world for me, but also provide such insightful story advice.

I also owe a debt of gratitude to my dear friend Kimberly Gost, an attorney whose work with the Innocence Project has given me a tremendous new perspective on our penal system, not the least of which is the importance of a "prison bra."

And finally, I'm eternally grateful to the love of my life, Lisa Johansen, for her support and enthusiasm (not to mention her mad proofreading skills) during the crazy year I spent bringing this book across the finish line. Thank you, honey.

ABOUT THE AUTHOR

Roy Johansen began his professional writing career with his original screenplay for *Murder 101*, for which he won the national FOCUS award, sponsored by Steven Spielberg, George Lucas, and Martin Scorsese. The movie starred Pierce Brosnan and the script won the Edgar Allan Poe Award from the Mystery Writers of America in the Best Television Miniseries or Movie category.

Johansen has also collaborated with comic book legend Stan Lee in creating The Accuser superhero character and has written screenplays for Warner Bros., Universal Pictures, Disney, and MGM. His novels include *The Answer Man, Beyond Belief,* and *Deadly Visions,* in addition to nine works co-authored with Iris Johansen.

To find out more, visit:

RoyJohansen.com

Facebook.com/RoyJohansen.Author

Twitter @RoyJohansen